TAKE
THE SPIRIT OF
MURDER

MILLIE MACK

ISBN: 978-1-7346234-0-6
Library of Congress Control Number: 2020920568

Publisher: Dark and Stormy Night Mysteries
Darkandstormynightmysteries.com

Other Books
in the Faraday
Murder Series

Take a Dive for Murder

Take Stock in Murder

Take a Byte Out of Murder

DEDICATION

There are different types of spirits.

There are spirits like the ones in this book who materialize in the form of ghostly apparitions. They make a brief appearance and fade away.

I dedicate this book to my good friend Stacy, who represents a different class of spirit. She's the spirit that inspires my writing and the person who lifts my spirits when I'm down. She's always there for me and does not fade away.

Stacy represents the true spirit of friendship.

ACKNOWLEDGMENTS

Thank you to members of my critique group Eileen and Janis, with their unique abilities of both honesty and wisdom in helping to make the book a better tale of murder.

My grateful appreciation to Frances and Stacy for proofreading the original manuscripts. I rely on their eagle eyes to catch all the things I always miss.

A special thanks to my final readers Janet, Frances, and last but certainly not least, Mark. Great Job!

To Kimberly of Revision/Division for editing the book and focusing on those details that provide the reader with an equal opportunity of solving the crime.

A big thank you to Beth Martin Books who provided all the talented skill in formatting the book for publication.

1

While selecting books at the Tri-County Bookstore in their home village of Nottingham, Carrie thought about her marriage to Charles. This was the first marriage for both of them. When they took the leap, she was in her late forties and Charles was in his mid-fifties. They may have married late, but she couldn't be happier. Their life together was wonderful except for all the murders.

Carrie returned to Tri-County to investigate the murder of Jamie Faraday, Charles's brother. Carrie and Jamie dated in college, but she moved onto a career in photography while Jamie became a reporter for *World News* magazine which his brother published.

Initially, Charles was on Carrie's suspect list. But soon they joined forces and worked together gathering clues that revealed the real murderer After the successful conclusion of the case they found they shared more than friendship. Charles asked her to marry him and she accepted.

Marriage didn't stop the murders. Two more murder cases interrupted their marital bliss.

Now, with all the cases solved, Carrie knew it was time for them to have a real vacation without any murders. They would pay for their books and then decide where they wanted to go for some relaxation. Charles joined her near the front of the store.

"What did you find to read?" Carrie asked. She looked at the two-inch thick book her husband Charles held. "Looks like a mighty heavy book to drag along on vacation."

"It's the new best-selling thriller on secret societies. I would rather take one good exciting book to keep me entertained instead of several books that are mundane."

"Oh, really! I planned on keeping you entertained during our vacation, but if you would rather read a book," she said with a naughty smile.

"I'm putting this book back right now," Charles said and turned back towards the bookshelves.

Carrie tugged at Charles's shirt sleeve. "Now that I think about it, there may be a few moments when you'll have time to read. Perhaps you should buy it...just as a back-up plan."

Carrie leaned up as Charles lowered his six-foot two frame and kissed her on the forehead.

"And what did you find to occupy your few moments of free time? Those two books look mighty light compared to mine," Charles said.

Carrie laughed.

"What did I say that was so funny?" Charles asked innocently. "It's your use of the word light. I've a mystery about ghosts and a book on ghost hunting." She held up her book selections.

"Ghosts huh," he chuckled. "Let's say we float over to the cashier and get these purchases paid for before that line gets any longer. Otherwise, we'll be spending our vacation in the Tri-County bookstore."

"Hello, Maddy," Carrie said to Mrs. Madge Luther, one of the owners of the bookstore.

Mrs. Luther was the same age as Charles. Her sister, Marge Millford, the other owner, was closer to Carrie's age. Maddy always looked the same with her shiny gray hair neatly piled on top of her head. Attached to a beaded chain she wore around her neck were her glasses. Her sporty bright green polo shirt with a store logo and her neatly pressed khaki slacks offset her dated look.

"Hello, you two. What have we selected today?"

Carrie saw that Maddy's entire face lit up as she spoke to the couple. She knew they were two of the store's best customers, but they also shared a friendship with the sisters.

"We seem on opposite ends of the spectrum today," Charles said. "I've the latest best seller and Carrie has selected some light reading on spirits."

Carrie noticed that Maddy missed Charles's subtle play on words as she picked up the book Charles selected.

"Charles, you'll like this book. It's exceptionally good. I read it. In my opinion, it's better. Yes, better than the author's previous one."

Carrie knew that Maddy liked to talk in short, choppy sentences. Maybe it was because she shared only a few moments with each customer when they were in line.

Then as she picked up Carrie's books she exclaimed, "Ghosts! Carrie, do you believe? I mean in the supernatural?"

"I'm not sure I would quite call it a belief. More like an interest, especially with all the current television shows, movies and books on the subject," Carrie said.

"Oh, I thought. You know, because of your crime solving."

Carrie noticed Maddy checked to make sure other people in line weren't listening before she continued, "have you ever had a personal encounter with the paranormal?"

"Well, Maddy, Carrie and I have experienced some strange encounters with solving murders, but they've all been with the living," Charles said.

"Maddy, why do you ask?" Carrie was sensing a change in Maddy with the talk about ghosts. As excited as Maddy was when she first mentioned the topic, she now seemed deflated.

"Do you two have some extra time? I mean to join me for a cup of tea. I would like to discuss something with you."

Carrie knew they wanted to get home and finish planning their vacation but when she looked at Charles he nodded. "Sure, we have the afternoon free. Besides, I would love to have a cup of tea," Carrie said.

Carrie could see relief in Maddy's face when she agreed to the invitation.

"Dawn," Maddy called to one of her workers. "Could you handle the line for me?"

"Hello Dawn," Carrie said as she recognized the young clerk. Carrie and Charles met Dawn during their second case. Dawn dated the victim, Todd Barrington, and provided a clue about the murder gun that helped solve the case.

"Hello, Mr. and Mrs. Faraday. It's nice to see you again," Dawn said, stepping behind the counter.

"Have you seen Marge?" Maddy asked.

"I believe she went off to fix some tea," Dawn answered.

"Perfect, if you'll follow me," Maddy said. She lowered her voice as they passed several people, "I've a murder case you two might find interesting."

Carrie exchanged a glance with Charles but said nothing as they obediently followed Maddy.

2

The unusual thing about the Tri-County Bookstore was its size. It was not a small shop wedged in between other stores in a shopping center. The sisters housed the bookstore in their family's home. It was one of the largest and oldest Victorian homes on the main street known as Brighton Boulevard in the Village of Nottingham. It was a perfect location for a bookstore.

According to town gossip the settlement from Marge's divorce and the insurance money after Maddy's husband died provided the sisters with the cash to renovate the house and open the bookstore. The group was walking along the hallway that overlooked the newly remodeled children's section in what had been the basement of the original house. Carrie stopped the procession.

"Maddy, you and your sister must be very pleased with your latest remodeling effort that created this wonderful children's area."

"You know, when we were young girls growing up in the house, we thought the basement was a dark and scary place.

Neither Marge nor I ever wanted to go down there," Maddy said. "Even though in the summertime that's where the family stored the homemade root beer."

"Well, you've changed that feeling," Carrie added.

"Opening the back wall and adding the large windows to show off the gardens made a big difference. They let in so much light it's almost like being outdoors," Maddy said. "It's really a pleasant place for the children to spend time. No longer the dark and the scary place of my childhood."

"I like the large comfy floor cushions. Although I've the feeling if I got down on the floor, I might need help to get back up," Charles said.

"Believe me I understand, Charles. If I do the children's story hour, I sit on a grown-up chair. But there's no doubt the children love the floor and the pillows."

They moved beyond storage rooms, an employee break room and ended at a small elevator. Marge used a key allowing her to press the button for the third floor. Within seconds the doors of the elevator opened into an apartment the sisters shared. In contrast to the rest of the Victorian-styled building the apartment was modern in both design and furnishings.

Across the open floor plan Marge was busily preparing tea in the kitchen area. The table with its smoke blue and white abstract print tablecloth was in the back far left corner of the room. They positioned the table in front of the french doors that opened onto an oversized deck overlooking the gardens at the back of the house.

Without looking, Marge said, "I'm glad you came, I was just about to call down to let you know the tea was ready."

Carrie watched as Marge poured the hot water into the teapot. Marge looked nothing like her sister other than wearing the green polo shirt and khaki slacks. She was shorter and thinner. Her short brown hair reflected a stylish cut.

"Look who I brought with me," Maddy said.

"Carrie, Charles, how delightful. Let me get two more cups."

Carrie took their book purchases from Charles and set them on the end of the table. Then she seated herself in the chair Charles pulled out for her on one side of the table. Charles seated each of the sisters and then took the seat opposite Carrie. Maddy poured the tea while Marge passed a plate of homemade lemon bars and chocolate pecan cookies.

"Marge, I asked Charles and Carrie to join us for tea. I thought we could discuss the situation at Millford Manor. You know, get their opinions on solving crime."

"Oh, that's an excellent idea. With their background in murder, they're the perfect ones to tell us what to do," Marge said.

"Why are you looking for someone with a background in murder? Has something happened at this Millford Manor? Was there a murder?" Charles asked.

"Yes, there was a murder," Marge said. "Although that murder occurred almost sixty-five years ago."

"Sixty-five years!" Carrie exclaimed. She wondered what advice the sisters wanted concerning a murder that old.

"It's not exactly the murder we want to discuss," Maddy said. "Marge, you need to start at the beginning. You're better at explaining these things than I am."

"All right. I'll start, sister, but you jump in if I leave something out." Marge took a sip of tea and then set her cup back in the saucer and began. "Our family for years has owned and managed an inn in the town of Millford called Millford Manor. And yes, the town is also named after our family. The Manor and the town date back to the 1800s when our family owned one of the largest cattle and horse farms in the region."

"During the Civil War Millford was a staging area for the Union Army because of our location near a train line. The farm sold horses to the army and provided rooms for the officers," Maddy added.

"In the next century during the Depression the family again rented rooms to travelers to help make ends meet. Those were the beginnings of our hotel business. As the years passed, it also became known as a location for people wanting a place to stay for extended periods of time. It had clean rooms, good food and offered a quiet location and those characteristics continue to this day."

"Don't forget the government," Maddy said.

Carrie gave Charles a scowl as he reached for his second lemon bar to go with the two chocolate cookies he'd already devoured.

"Yes, thank you, Maddy, for the reminder. After the Civil War, the government built an army base and other buildings over in Hanley. We get long-term guests who are working on government projects."

"And more recently we've developed a wonderful reputation as a great conference center for the corporate world," Maddy added. "Carrie, you'll like this next feature since you're writing a mystery book. Marge, don't forget to tell them about our special project."

"Yes, I was leaving the best for last. Maddy and I developed a program where we have individual cottages on the property available as writers' retreats. Plus, the Manor offers discounts for writers' conferences," Marge said. "The Manor has always been at the center of the Millford economy and a major employer in the area. Our family, including the two of us, has made a fair profit from the place. Of course, the profits were based on having full bookings."

"Marge, has something changed that's affecting the hotel?" Charles asked.

"Yes, bookings are way down from previous years," Maddy jumped in.

"Now, sister, I'll get to that in just a moment. The money we've made from the Manor allowed us to do many of the renovations here and open a second bookstore in Millford. You see the Manor doing well is important, not only to our cousins, but to us."

"I never knew you had a second store," Carrie said. "How do you manage two stores in different locations?'

"Our young nephew, Tom, runs the store for us. He's our cousin, Lizzie's boy. He may be a relative, but he has a degree in library science and is very qualified. We feel extremely comfortable with him managing."

"Marge and I sit on the board of the Manor along with Beatrice's son Martin Barry. He's a lawyer here in Tri-City. We're the three board members, not involved with managing the Manor's everyday operation," Maddy said. "The board meets every month. We offer our suggestions to improve the Manor's operation. Just like when we suggested the writer's retreat."

"You said you're not involved in the daily operations. Who runs the Manor?" Carrie asked as she took a bite of a lemon bar. The bars were delicious. She needed to get this recipe.

"The day-to-day operation is in the hands of our cousins. There's Beatrice, Elizabeth or Lizzie, their brother, Albert and his son, Ryan," Marge said. "Now, mind you, they have plenty of other help. They have a complete staff including desk clerks, bell-hops, maids, and maintenance workers. Plus, there's another team that supports the meal preparation, restaurants and bars."

"After all these years, we manage a very efficient property," Marge added.

"And after all these years we're being bothered by ghosts," Maddy blurted out.

3

"There I said it. We have ghosts," Maddy declared. From the expression on his face, Carrie knew Charles thought they were about to hear a tall tale. Carrie was glad the sisters were so excited telling their story they missed Charles's facial gesture.

They really were genuinely nice, and Carrie was very fond of them. They were also part of a small group of people in the village who was supportive when Carrie was charged with the murder of Todd Barrington. If the sisters felt they needed help, the least she could do was offer a sympathetic ear.

Carrie said, "I would think an old property with so much history, would have a few ghost sightings long before now."

"Oh, yes, over the years there were reports of paranormal activity. Some people have seen soldiers dressed in Civil War uniforms. Others have seen a woman in dress from the nineteen-fifties," Marge said.

"She's often seen dancing down the hallways," Maddy added laughing.

"Let me think, what else. Oh yes, there were reports of unexplained footsteps, doors opening and closing, even sounds of faint music playing," Marge said.

"In fact, we list the possibility of seeing a ghost as a positive attraction in our advertising material. We've discovered there's a segment of the population that loves to stay at a place where there is a history of ghosts," Maddy said.

"Wait, I'll get you one of our brochures." Marge left the kitchen area and went to a teak desk on the other side of the room. She returned to the table and handed the brochure to Carrie.

"You'll find the reference to the spirits on the second inside panel," Marge said.

Carrie accepted the brochure. On the front was a pen and ink drawing of a roadhouse with a horse-drawn carriage in front. Carrie prepared brochures for businesses and thought this brochure had an outdated look.

She opened the brochure and scanned the copy for the section about ghosts. She read out loud. *While the Manor offers the quiet serenity for a restful stay, you may find yourself sharing your lodgings with some friendly spirits. For years there have been sightings of the occasional ghost wandering about the many hallways and outside walkways. Don't worry, the spirits are friendly. You might even capture an unexpected addition in your photos.* Carrie closed the folder and placed it on the table.

"Unlike the fanciful wording in the brochure we're now experiencing different types of spirits. Ones that are causing problems," Marge said.

"What types of problems?" Charles asked as he took another chocolate pecan cookie.

"With past sightings the spirits have never attempted to annoy the guests. They were just fleeting shadows in the distance or an occasional sound or voice," Marge said.

"Now the spirits are having direct contact with the guests. Guests are reporting items in their room being moved. They're hearing angry voices demanding they 'get out' of the Manor. They're being awakened in the middle of the night with banging and other sounds coming from rooms that aren't occupied," Maddy added.

"It's even affecting our staff. The kitchen crew arrived one morning to find several freezer doors opened. Vegetables and other frozen items were scattered across the floor. We had to throw the food away, which was a financial loss for the Manor," Marge said. "In the bar, glasses are mysteriously slipping off the racks during the night and breaking. Lights are going on and off, and there are many more sightings of apparitions."

"As my mother would say, something seems to be stirring the pot. What was once a light-hearted attraction for the Manor is becoming a distraction," Maddy added.

"You mentioned a murder from sixty-five years ago. How does that relate to these sightings?" Charles asked as he took one more lemon bar.

Maddy's eyes came alive. "The dancing lady, I mentioned earlier, who wears a fifties outfit. We believe she's Roxie Fenton. The girlfriend of our cousin, Bernie Millford."

"Is she the murder you mentioned?" Carrie asked.

"Yes. The authorities concluded Bernie murdered her. He was the general manager of the Manor during the fifties," Maddy said. "They were getting married, you know. They made a lovely couple. Then something happened. Roxie was murdered."

Marge interrupted her sister, "Maddy you're drifting away from the story."

"Sorry, where was I? Oh yes. When Bernie lived in Tri-City, he worked for the underworld. One story was he bought and sold guns. Another theory has him shipping bootlegged liquor into cities along the east coast." Maddy said the sentences so quickly she had to take a deep breath before continuing. "The authorities thought Roxie found out what he was doing. She was about to... what do they say, oh yes, 'squeal on him.' They think Bernie shot her to silence her. When he realized what he did, he disappeared. No one ever saw him again."

"That's when our side of the family took over the operation of the Manor. And as they say, 'the rest is history.' Our family has been running the business ever since," Marge said.

"We've always had sightings of Roxie dancing down a hallway or appearing as an apparition, but we've never seen Bernie. The staff thinks it's Bernie who has returned and is breaking things and telling the guests to get out," Maddy said.

"I've a question," Carrie said. "Is the Manor having any renovations done?" Carrie's question seemed to come out of the blue and she was aware everyone was looking at her wondering if she had listened to the sister's story.

"Interesting that you ask that. We just finished adding a theatre and a new restaurant. And we're about to start the construction of a new wing with more meeting and guest rooms," Marge said. "Is that important?"

Carrie saw Charles's questioning look directed at her.

"Not sure. According to some TV shows I've watched, renovations can stir up paranormal activity. Spirits don't like change and prefer to keep their location the way it was when they were there," Carrie said. "That's if paranormal activity is even a possibility as the cause of the problem you're experiencing."

"Hello up there."

A voice boomed into the room and Carrie and Charles jumped at the unexpected sound.

"Sorry to bother you, but we've got quite a crowd down here. I'm on the register but some folks need help finding books."

"Okay, Dawn. I'll head down," Marge said. "Sorry for the interruption, but we have the intercom on during work hours. That way we don't have to keep running up and down to the store to see what's going on. Maddy, you stay with our guests. I'll go help with the customers."

After Marge departed, Charles asked Maddy, "What would you like Carrie and me to do for you?"

"Well, I heard you two mention a vacation. You two should take your vacation at the Millford Manor. It's a lovely place. All expenses paid by us, of course," Maddy said. "Then you can use your investigative skills and find out what's going on. Who knows, you may even find out who killed Roxie and what happened to Bernie."

4.

Two days later, early in the morning, Charles and Carrie were ready to depart for Millford Manor. When the sisters made their offer, the couple hadn't decided on a vacation destination. Staying at Millford Manor would give them some well-deserved rest along with the diversion of checking out the problem the sisters discussed. They were intrigued by puzzles and enjoyed solving them together. It was more than a hobby. They were good at finding answers.

They reviewed a list of items with their house sitter. The list had little to do with watching over the house, but more to do with Baxter's routine. Baxter was the Faraday's orange and white Maine Coon cat.

They found it easier to hire a sitter for the house and avoid the trauma of boarding Baxter for extended periods of time. Since the sitter was the daughter of one of Charles's employees at Faraday Press, they felt comfortable having her stay in their home. After a few minutes of watching Baxter and the house sitter play, they felt satisfied he would survive their absence and left.

Since their vacation destination was a little under two hours away, they took travel mugs of coffee and thought they would have their breakfast when they reached Millford Manor. This way they could get acquainted right away with the facility and meet some of the staff.

"I wish we could have brought Baxter. I hate leaving him," Carrie said as she was reading the directions to the Manor Marge provided for them.

"I'm sure with everything going on at the Manor, the last thing they need is Baxter wandering around. Anyway, he'll be happier staying at home."

"True, but animals supposedly have a special ability for knowing when spirits are present. He could have helped us detect," Carrie said.

"Ah, you think we're dealing with ghosts?" Charles asked.

"No, I was just trying to justify bringing Baxter, because I'll miss him. Putting Baxter aside, any new thoughts about what Maddy and Marge shared with us?" Carrie asked.

She watched as Charles maneuvered their car through the traffic of downtown Tri-City and out onto the North bound expressway.

"Are you asking if I believe in ghosts or if I believe the story Maddy and Marge related about what's happening at the Manor?"

"Both," Carrie said.

"I believe people experience things they can't explain. Saying it was something supernatural gives them an excuse not to dig deeper into what they really saw. I think most ghost stories prove to be something else," Charles said. "For instance, finding freezer doors opened with food thrown on the floor suggests there are some real problems at ye old manor. I suspect the problem is something more human."

"Do you think there's any danger if we get involved?"

"I doubt there's any real danger. It seems more like high school pranks. I'm thinking it's a disgruntled employee or supplier."

"I feel like I want to help the sisters. They are so nice and provide a valuable service to our village. And we've had good success solving murders."

"But their murder is sixty-five years ago," Charles added.

"Yes, but I still would like to help out," Carrie said.

"Not to mention the sisters have promised to hold a book signing for you if you ever finish that mystery book you're writing." Charles paused for a moment and then gently added, "Even though we want to help the sisters and think the incidents are probably pranks, we should be vigilant and keep our eyes open while fully enjoying our vacation."

"Is that why you didn't want to accept a free vacation from the sisters and their cousins, because you're planning on enjoying yourself?" Carrie asked.

"More or less. First, there's no reason for them to give us a free vacation because we were going on vacation regardless of their offer. Second, I want us to take full advantage of whatever amenities this little hotel might offer. And I know how you think. When someone else is picking up the tab, you hold back."

"No, I don't. Do I?" Charles's comment surprised Carrie.

"Yes, you do. And finally, if there's a prankster within the Manor's staff I want everyone to think we're only regular guests.

If our expenses are on the house, someone sooner or later would find this out and blow our cover," Charles said.

"Okay, we're just a regular couple on vacation, except they've hired the wife to write a new marketing brochure. Don't you think the staff might be a little suspicious of that?" Carrie asked.

"No, not really. It's a good cover. You create promotional pieces all the time for companies. If anyone checks you out, it's not a lie," Charles said. "And it helps our investigation because it gives you access to locations the normal guest wouldn't visit. You can take photos, talk to the staff and gather information we need to hopefully solve this problem."

Carrie patted Charles arm. "I guess it was a good idea for us to use my work as our reason for being at the Manor. Besides, I don't mind taking photos and writing some new copy. The Manor could sure use a new promotional piece."

"Just don't work too hard. I want you to have some time to play with me," Charles said.

"I take it you'll be vacationing the entire time," Carrie said smiling at her husband.

"Well, I brought that large book to read. But as the vacationing husband I can chat with other guests and find out what they're experiencing. Rest assured, I'll be on the scene if you need someone to carry your camera."

* * *

After a couple of hours, Charles was motoring along a highway with little traffic. They drove in relative silence for most of the trip.

Then Carrie said, "Speaking of a different scene, have you noticed how gorgeous this countryside is? It's hard to believe we didn't have to drive that far out of the city to reach this pristine landscape."

She made this comment after they left the expressway and were traveling on the local roads towards the village of Millford. "That's what I love about our section of the east coast. We have the harbor in Tri-City, farmland to the south, the mountains to the west and this lovely countryside all within a short distance."

"Yes, it's a beautiful area and I believe we're nearing the Manor," Charles said.

"Instructions say bear left at the covered bridge. And here's the bridge coming up on our right," Carrie said reading from Maddy's directions. "I'm glad we're going left and not going over that bridge. It looks like it wouldn't hold a horse and a rider, let alone a car."

"Clearly, it's seen better days, but it adds a certain charm," Charles said.

"Charles, look out!"

Carrie no sooner gave the warning, when a speeding yellow jeep rumbled up and over the wooden bridge and passed awfully close to the couple's car. Charles had to brake hard and pull left to avoid a collision.

"What were you saying about the bridge not supporting a car?" Charles asked.

"I hope almost being hit by that crazy driver is not a premonition of what we will be experiencing at the Millford Manor," Carrie said.

The couple continued until they were driving through the main street of the village of Millford. It was a lovely street with lots of individual stores. Each store displayed a unique personality offering various items from clothing and crafts to eateries. Carrie decided the variety of shops on the street would provide a nice diversion one afternoon from their ghost-hunting vacation. When they reached the end of Main Street, Carrie spotted a sign for Millford Manor.

"There's the sign, Charles. Take the next right."

They started a steep climb up a winding road. They made one final turn and Millford Manor appeared on the hill in front of them.

"Holy Mackerel!" Carrie exclaimed. "I didn't expect this. Was it just me or did you think Maddy and Marge were talking about an old hotel with a few modern updates?"

"Yes. And based on the awful brochure the sisters showed us I assumed it was bigger than a bed-and-breakfast, but nothing this large," Charles said. "Although this helps our cover."

"How's that?"

"No one will doubt they hired you to update the Manor's brochure," Charles said. "This place reminds me of that hotel in the movie. The one with all the rooms and long hallways where the caretaker husband goes crazy with an axe."

"That's a comforting thought," Carrie said. "Speaking of the brochure, can you pull over? I might as well start my work by taking some pictures."

Charles pulled the car over to the shoulder of a perfectly landscaped drive. Carrie reached into the back seat and grabbed her digital camera.

"Do you need me to help carry your camera equipment?" Charles asked smiling.

"Thank you, Dear. I can handle this one camera."

Carrie got out of the car. She took a few minutes lining up different shots of the lawns and the entrance to the picturesque Manor. When she got back into the car she said, "Wow! All I can say is, wow."

The Manor was a massive U-shaped structure that was five stories high. The center structure was the largest part of the building with a stone facade and cocoa wood shingles on each side. Although modernized, the front section resembled the original look of the roadhouse drawing from the brochure.

Attached to the main building but set slightly back on the left and right sides were two matching additions. These side structures repeated the same cocoa shingles with burgundy shutters. At the far side of the left wing the couple could see a glass-enclosed veranda and on the far right a series of steps that led down the hillside. Carrie surmised the steps might lead to the gardens and the individual writers' cottages that Maddy and Marge mentioned.

"I guess we should check in and get our bearings," Carrie said.

"You know, I feel better about this vacation than I did this morning. I thought we would be in a small room with mediocre food choices and limited activities. This place shows great promise for an entertaining vacation," Charles said.

"I agree," Carrie said. Although she realized with a hotel this large it would be harder to discover who or what was causing the problems.

Charles maneuvered the car back onto the main lane and drove the remaining distance to the entrance. Charles no sooner pulled the car under the portico when two staff members jumped up from their seats and ran to meet the car. The first staff member opened Charles's car door.

"Sir, if you leave your keys with me you can proceed right to the registration desk. We'll bring your luggage in and take care of parking your car."

The second young man helped Carrie out of the car. Another bellman held open the large double beveled glass doors as the couple passed through. When they entered the lobby, Carrie stopped suddenly, and Charles plowed into her back.

"Hey, watch it buddy," Carrie said.

"Sorry Dear, I didn't see your brake lights," Charles said.

"My fault. I thought the outside was special, but this lobby is something else."

Carrie's eyes quickly scanned the massive lobby with its high beamed ceiling that resembled a western hunting lodge and was no doubt part of the original roadhouse. Next to the registration desk was a wide formal staircase that rose elegantly to the upper floors. To the right of the staircase was a sitting area with a variety of overstuffed chairs surrounding a large stone fire-place. Carrie moved forward and felt her feet sink into the thick deep plush burgundy carpet that highlighted the cherry wood furnishings.

The concierge interrupted Carrie's gaze around the lobby. He wore a crisp white shirt and black bow tie complementing his burgundy coat with tails and perfectly pressed black slacks.

"Right this way, folks, you can check in at the desk," he said.

"This place is something else. Really magnificent," Charles said.

"Ah, this must be your first time here. Your reaction is typical of our new guests. Once you've checked in, we'll bring your luggage to your room," he said. "My name is Joseph and I'm the day concierge. If there's anything you need during your stay, please be sure to contact either me or one of the other staff members."

Joseph guided them to the desk and went back to his duties at the door. A young woman with long blond hair in a ponytail and tied with a colorful ribbon gave them a big smile. She wore a burgundy blazer with the Manor logo on the pocket and a name tag that said Meagan.

"Welcome to Millford Manor," Meagan said.

"Hello, we're Mr. and Mrs. Charles Faraday," Charles said.

"Oh yes, the Faradays. We've been expecting you. I'll inform Mrs. Barry that you've arrived. In the meantime, Mr. Faraday, if I could have your credit card." Meagan picked up the phone and dialed a number. While waiting for Mrs. Barry to answer her call, she asked, "Are you a friend of the family?"

"We're friends of Mrs. Barry's cousins, Mrs. Luther and Ms. Millford," Charles said.

"Oh, yes the bookstore owners. They stop in all the time," Megan said.

Meagan spoke into the phone announcing the Faradays' arrival and then listened for a few moments before hanging up.

"Mr. Faraday, here is your credit card and two electronic room keys. Now, if you'll follow me. Mrs. Barry will meet you in the restaurant."

Meagan led them across the lobby. The brass sign on the wall of the hallway pointed to the Old Mill Restaurant. At the entrance to the restaurant, Meagan said, "I'll leave you with our hostess and Mrs. Barry will join you shortly."

6

"Hello, welcome to the Old Mill Restaurant," the hostess said.

She offered the couple a warm smile as she led them to their table. Carrie noticed the hostess was decked out in a white blouse, burgundy vest with the Manor logo and a black skirt. Apparently for each staff position, the Manor issued a specific uniform. She seated the couple at a window table on the far side of the room. The window looked out onto the veranda.

"I'll send Taffy, your waitress, right over."

Carrie looked around the room and saw only two other tables occupied. "I hope they're still serving breakfast."

"I hope so too. I would really prefer breakfast to lunch. But I'm hungry so I'll eat whatever is available." Charles said as their waitress approached.

"Hello, and welcome to the Old Mill. Are you here for light refreshments or an early lunch?" Taffy asked.

Taffy was young and probably one of the local high school students. She was thin with wispy blond hair that went with her very fair skin. Her company uniform of the burgundy polo shirt with black slacks had the addition of a black apron wrapped around her waist.

"I guess we missed breakfast if you folks are ready to serve lunch," Charles asked.

"It's true we're getting ready for the lunch crowd, but the Old Mill serves breakfast all day."

The waitress opened the oversized menu to the breakfast page before she handed it to Charles.

"Good. While we look at the menu, we'll start with two large orange juices and two coffees," Charles said.

While their waitress was getting their drinks, Carrie checked out the room. On the far side of the room was a replica of a water wheel gently turning and producing a mild swishing sound as water tumbled into a circular stone pool. Around the pool were dark blue tiles to protect the carpet from any water spills.

The rest of the room had a thick dark blue carpet with small gold coin images creating a rich pattern. The circles matched the color of the gold drapes that hung on several long windows that adorned two of the walls. All the windows gave the room a light and airy appearance.

When the waitress returned with juice and a thermal carafe of coffee, Carrie and Charles ordered Canadian bacon and swiss cheese omelets.

Carrie was taking her first sip of juice when she noticed a very tall, gray-haired woman in a straight dark green dress entering the restaurant. She stopped for a moment at the reception counter and then headed straight for their table. Charles stood and Carrie saw that the six-two frame of her husband was almost eye level with this woman.

"Hello, I'm Mrs. Barry," she said extending her hand.

Charles took her hand, "Nice to meet you, I'm Charles Faraday, and this is my wife, Carrie."

Charles held the chair for Mrs. Barry before taking his seat. Mrs. Barry barely settled into her chair before Taffy was immediately at her side.

"Mrs. Barry, did you want your usual coffee?" she asked.

"Yes, Taffy, and if there are any of our cheese pastries remaining, I'll have one of those. Have you taken the orders for our guests?"

"Yes, Mrs. Barry," Taffy said. "Their order is being prepared." Taffy turned and quickly headed to the kitchen.

"It's such a beautiful day. Did you have a pleasant drive to the Manor?" Mrs. Barry asked.

"I agree it is a beautiful day. And we were amazed how quickly we could get here from Tri-City," Charles said.

Carrie was debating whether to mention the jeep that nearly ran them off the road when Taffy returned with a small coffee pot and a stainless-steel pitcher of steamed milk. While Mrs. Barry poured the strong coffee and the steamed milk simultaneously, Carrie took the first sips of her coffee and saw Charles nodding approvingly after his first taste. Carrie always felt good coffee indicated the quality of a restaurant.

"Speaking of Tri-City, what did Marge and Maddy tell you about our recent events?" Mrs. Barry asked.

Carrie liked this woman with her no-nonsense approach. She went right to the heart of why they were at the Manor. Charles had just taken another mouthful of coffee so Carrie answered the question.

"The sisters said that while there were always stories of supernatural sightings or unexplained activity at the Manor, you now seem to be experiencing more activity than usual," Carrie said. Then added, "and the activity seems more menacing."

"Did they give you any specific examples?"

Before Carrie could answer, Taffy returned with the food. Carrie looked at the cheese pastry Mrs. Barry ordered and mentally made a note to try one of those during her stay. Carrie took a bite of her omelet before answering the question.

"Maddy and Marge said the sightings included the woman killed sixty-five years ago, supposedly by your cousin Bernie. Along with seeing her apparition, people are also hearing dance music from the fifties. They told us about the food from the kitchen freezers being tossed." Carrie said. "But their greatest concern is that some of this activity is frightening the guests away and some won't come back. Charles, did I leave anything out?" Carrie asked.

"No, that was a good summary. Then your cousins asked if we would spend our vacation here and see if we could discover what was happening," Charles said. "They knew we had solved cases in the past and hoped this experience would help us uncover what was happening here."

Carrie didn't mention what triggered the discussion with the sisters was her purchase of books on the supernatural. She was glad she hadn't revealed this fact based on Mrs. Barry's next comment.

"Let me state right from the start that I don't believe in spirits, ghosts or paranormal activity. I believe there's an explanation for everything and that explanation involves a living human. It's pure nonsense to assume these current events are related to a sixty-five-year-old murder," Mrs. Barry said. "That's why when my cousins mentioned that you two solved several actual police cases well…I thought you might have the skill, the experience to uncover the facts of our little mystery."

Mrs. Barry stopped speaking for a moment while she sampled her pastry, then she continued, "some staff members suggested I call in a paranormal team to prove there are ghosts. That was out of the question since I don't believe in that stuff."

"I'm in complete agreement with you," Charles said. "I feel there's a logical explanation for what you're seeing and experiencing. What would you like us to do for you?"

"I want you two to find the person or persons who are disrupting the routine of our Manor before it turns into something more than silly pranks. These incidents are affecting our staff but more importantly our customers are being impacted."

Carrie noticed that Mrs. Barry never raised her voice but emphasized certain words showing her frustration with the situation.

"Now that I've met you two, I'm sure you're the right choice. What else can I answer before you tour the Manor?"

"The natural assumption would be that you've a disgruntled employee. Have there been any recent changes?"

"The Manor is always going through changes. As we expand, we've added staff. We also employ many local youngsters. Some stay and become permanent employees. Others work part time between classes or during the summer and then go back to school," Mrs. Barry said. There's a constant rotation of employees, but most of these folks are members of the Millford community. I have faith in our staff, but I understand your need for a list of anyone recently hired."

"That list should also include employees who were let go," Charles added.

"That's not a problem. I don't think we've let anyone go in nearly two years. I'll ask my brother Albert to prepare the list and give it to you when you meet him for your tour of the property."

"The sisters mentioned you're doing some new construction," Charles said.

"That's correct, we've added a new theatre to show films for our guests but also for corporate presentations. The new theatre includes dressing rooms and storage areas for costumes and sets so we can put on live theatre and musical presentations," Mrs. Barry said proudly. "Along with the theatre we're about to open our new Island Grill café."

Carrie was hoping Charles wasn't about to share her thoughts about how new construction can enhance paranormal activity considering Mrs. Barry's disbelief in ghosts.

Mrs. Barry continued. "In another month, we'll start construction on a new wing of guest rooms and meeting facilities to increase our conference capabilities. This phase of our business has doubled over the last five years." She paused, "Why are you asking about our construction?"

"It means you've people on the grounds who aren't part of your regular staff but have access," Charles said.

"Yes, I see what you mean. I'll get you a list of those names from Toberson construction." There was a slight pause and then Mrs. Barry stated, "I need to get back to work. I'll leave you two to finish your breakfast in peace." She drained the last of her coffee. Then moved her chair away from the table. "There's one other item," she said lowering her voice although no one was nearby. "I want you to stick to your cover that we've hired Carrie to write a new marketing brochure for the Manor. I understand that you write commercial brochures for other companies and can make your cover seem realistic."

"It's true. If anyone checks they'll see I've helped many businesses with sales and marketing materials," Carrie said.

"Good. Since you're doing all the work as part of your cover, I would love to see a finished product. Our current brochure is… how should I describe it–outdated."

"Not a problem. I'll be happy to prepare something for you to see," Carrie said. "Have you told any of the staff why we're here?"

"My brother and I have told several people you were coming. Not the key people we rely on to run the place, but the people who we know will spread a rumor. Having told these people, by now the entire staff at the Manor knows who you are and that we're producing a new brochure," Mrs. Barry said.

With that comment Mrs. Barry rose to leave but paused, smiled, and said, "there's one more thing. I've placed you two in one of our supposedly haunted suites. It's the suite originally occupied by Roxie Fenton, the girlfriend who our cousin Bernie Millford supposedly shot." She turned and left the restaurant.

7

Charles would have preferred to take a nice nap after their big mid-day breakfast. But there was little time between finishing their meal and their scheduled meeting with Albert. Instead, he and Carrie used the remaining time to get settled in for what they hoped would be a pleasant stay at the Manor. Their suite occupied a corner on the fourth floor. Both the living room and the bedroom had French doors that opened onto a wrap-around balcony overlooking a magnificent series of gardens at the back of the Manor. Beyond the gardens, nestled near the edge of the woods, Charles could see individual white cottages.

"This suite is lovely. What's our view like?" Carrie asked as she entered the bedroom.

"We have a very nice view of the gardens." Charles put his arm on her shoulder and turned her slightly to the right, so she was facing the woods. "Those white cottages might be the writers' retreat Maddy and Marge mentioned."

"We'll have to ask Albert if there are any writers in residence," Carrie said.

Charles knew Carrie had been working for several years on her own mystery novel.

"It would be nice if you could meet some fellow writers while you're here," Charles suggested.

"I would enjoy that," Carrie said. "This suite is more like a small apartment."

"I like the fact we have a galley kitchen and our favorite appliance—a coffeemaker," Charles said.

"I hope one of the complimentary coffee packs is the brew we enjoyed with breakfast. It was delicious!" Carrie said.

Charles felt that everything about the Manor was designed to make the guests feel comfortable during their stay. The staff placed their luggage on a rack at the bottom of a king-size bed. He started unpacking and hanging his shirts and slacks in the closet.

The soft colors enhanced with a tiny floral pattern didn't make the room feel feminine, just relaxing. He wondered how much the room design changed since Roxie Fenton occupied the space.

"What was your impression of Mrs. Barry?" Charles asked Carrie as she came away from the window to help with the unpacking.

"She's straightforward, no nonsense. I like that because you know where you stand with her. It's also clear her concern with all these incidents is the effect it's having on the guests," Carrie said. "Otherwise, she probably wouldn't care if some people thought the Manor experienced paranormal activity."

"You like her even though she doesn't agree with your theory it could be paranormal?"

"A good paranormal investigator sets out to prove that something other than ghosts are causing the activity," Carrie answered as if she was reading from a prepared script.

"Are you a good paranormal investigator?" Charles asked.

"I doubt it, since I'm new at this," Carrie said. "I appreciate you covering for me when the Manor's recent construction came up in the conversation. I'm glad you didn't tell Mrs. Barry I read that construction can stir up paranormal activity."

"That's why I'm here, Darling, to watch your back and carry your camera equipment. Do you really believe that statement is true?"

"I've no idea, but the sisters said the activity increased since the construction started. Unless I find evidence to the contrary, I agree with both you and Mrs. Barry. It's probably something human," Carrie said.

"Forgetting the ghost aspect, we should still inspect the construction. It might provide some clues." Charles looked at his watch. "I guess we better go downstairs to meet Albert."

Charles watched as Carrie changed her shoes to ones more appropriate for walking and ran a comb through her brown curly hair.

"Do you think Albert will be as formidable as his sister?" Charles asked as they headed towards the elevator.

Ⅷ

When the elevator doors opened a small man stood in front of them. He was about five-foot nine, a little pudgy in the middle, balding with snow-white hair and wire-rimmed glasses.

"Hello, I'm Albert Millford. You must be Carrie and Charles?"

A large welcoming smile filled his round face as the couple got off the elevator.

After shaking hands, Albert said, "Shall we get started?"

Carrie pulled out a small notebook from her jacket pocket. "I'm ready, Mr. Millford."

Albert stopped in his tracks. "First, before I forget, here's the list Beatrice said you wanted of our employees and outside workers. Second, there's no need for formality. You both must call me Albert."

Charles took the papers and placed them in his pocket. At that moment, he realized Albert wasn't as formal as his sister.

"Sounds good, Albert. Where are we going first?" Charles asked.

"I thought I would start at the heart of our business," Albert said.

Albert led them to an area hidden from the public located directly behind the registration desk. They walked down a long hallway passing cubicles and offices where staff members were busy working.

"Our guests rarely see the engine that keeps the Manor running. These good people handle the business side for us. They make sure the right supplies get ordered, delivered and we pay our vendors on time. And the most important element of what they do, they make sure our staff gets paid."

Charles noticed that several of the workers looked up from their desks and smiled at Albert's comments. Albert stopped at an office where a young man with a full head of wavy red hair was intensely working on his computer.

"Mr. and Mrs. Faraday, I would like you to meet my son, Ryan. He manages our back-office accounting staff and helped to get all our records computerized. He also..."

"Enough Dad. I'm sure the Faradays want to get on with their tour and not hear more about me. Hello," Ryan said as he stood and shook hands with both Carrie and Charles.

Charles could see Ryan's resemblance to his father. He was taller, over six foot, and was lean but with the same great smile as his father. Charles couldn't help wondering if Albert was a red head prior to his hair turning snow white.

"Okay son. I'll take your advice this time and move the tour along. Right this way folks."

They walked to the end of the hallway and entered a room larger than most corporate boardrooms. Pushed together in a U-shape on one side of the room were three heavy dark wood desks. Over by the wall was a large rectangle table with seating for twelve and on the opposite side of the room was a casual seating area in front of a fireplace. It was a pleasant spring day, so there was no fire burning. But if the temperature changed there was a stack of wood ready to light.

"This is the office, Beatrice, Lizzie and I share. You may wonder why we share an office," Albert said. "Besides saving space, it makes it easy to discuss matters. We have only to lift our heads to talk with one another. Plus, we all believe our place is on the floor and not in an office."

"That makes perfect sense to me. My editors for Faraday Press magazines share one office," Charles said.

Albert nodded his head agreeing with Charles as he said, "Let's head to our restaurants next."

Albert opened a door on the far side revealing another hallway which led to the Old Mill Restaurant. Instead of entering the restaurant they went to the kitchen area behind it. The kitchen was massive. Staff members were busily preparing food at three distinct locations. Charles handed Carrie her digital camera and watched as she took several shots of the dishes being prepared.

Albert walked over to four chefs working intently at a fourth preparation area. "Benson, can we interrupt you and your team for a moment?"

Albert asked politely, but Charles couldn't imagine that his request would have been refused.

A tall man decked out in full chef's attire looked up from his preparations and smiled at Albert. "Mr. Albert, we always have time for you and your guests."

The other chefs wore checkered pants and white tops. Instead of the elaborate chef hat that Benson wore they were all wearing brimless caps to protect the food.

"Benson, this is Mr. and Mrs. Faraday who are staying with us for several weeks. We've hired Mrs. Faraday to write a new marketing brochure for the Manor. They have our full permission to wander around the premises to gather whatever research they might need."

"Benson is our executive chef in charge of our kitchens including all the catering for our conferences. Working with him are chefs Patrick, Harold and Kathy," Albert said. "Each of these individuals is an incredibly talented chef and responsible for the food preparation for one of our three restaurants. Once a quarter they switch restaurant assignments so we can keep both our chefs and the menu ideas fresh."

Albert turned back to Benson and asked, "What are you folks working on?"

"Tonight, we're featuring a salmon fillet with a special shrimp sauce for the Williamsburg Room. As you know Mr. Albert, when we serve something new, we prepare it for the four of us to taste first," Benson said. "This way we know if we need to make any changes."

Charles winked at Carrie who he knew loved salmon.

"I hope you don't mind if I take some photos of the four of you at work." Carrie didn't wait for an answer and began to snap some pictures.

Charles noticed that Harold moved slightly behind the other chefs. This hid his face from Carrie's camera. Charles made a mental note to tell Carrie about this in case she missed Harold's shift. He also hoped Carrie captured a picture of Harold when she first arrived in the kitchen.

"The interesting thing about the Manor kitchen is it's centrally located to all of our restaurants. We're hiring another chef and we will service our newest restaurant from this kitchen, too." Albert pointed to an opening in a wall. "By having only one kitchen we save a great deal of money. We can manage staffing issues easily and it also fosters the sharing of ideas which you just witnessed."

They left the kitchen and entered a magnificent dining room where the tables were set with linen cloths, fine china, and crystal stemware. The room had several Palladian windows that flooded the room with light and added an elegance.

"This is the Williamsburg Room, which offers sophisticated dining and is open only for dinner," Albert said.

"Oh my, this room is beautiful," Carrie said.

The room was a smoky blue color, with a cranberry carpet and drapes that picked up both the cranberry and blue motif.

"Yes, it's lovely. Lizzie, my sister, designed it. She trained as an interior designer and really has a flare for décor. She handles all our interior designs at the Manor," Albert said. "Unfortunately, she's away on a buying trip purchasing items for our new restaurant and conference guest rooms, but as soon as she returns, I'll make sure you get to meet her."

"We require our guests to wear proper attire when they eat here. Service is available from 4:00 p.m. with the last seating at

9:00 p.m. If you wish to eat here, you need to make a reservation a few days in advance. It's fully booked most nights," Albert said.

Charles saw the look on Carrie's face. "Yes, Dear I'll make a reservation when we get back to our room."

Albert led them to the Old Mill Restaurant. "I believe you ate here earlier today, so you had a chance to see the menu. It's open for breakfast, lunch and dinner and offers casual dining from 6:00 a.m. to 11:00 p.m.," he said. "And finally let's take a look at our Manor Pub."

The pub had a different feel from the other two restaurants with its long horizontal wooden bar anchoring each end of the room. Wide plank wooden flooring and heavy wood tables reminded Charles of the pubs he visited in the United Kingdom. Large stone fireplaces graced the right and left side of the room. Charles noticed the rack above the bar laden with glasses and wondered if these were the glasses the ghosts liked to rattle and break.

"The pub opens for lunch at 11:00 a.m. and stays open until 2:00 a.m. and serves casual food like sandwiches, burgers and pizza."

"Perfect. I can't wait to come here for a burger," Charles said.

"You will also want to try our newest restaurant, the Island Grill. We will open it during your stay, and it offers a selection of grilled items, fresh pasta and several vegetarian choices for both lunch and dinner in an outdoor casual dining experience. We can close the glass doors in case of inclement weather or during the winter months," Albert said. "One last thing about food at the Manor. It's always available to our guests since they can order room service 24 hours a day."

"Very impressive! I always hate staying in a place where you can't get anything to eat if you arrive late or get up early," Charles said.

After the restaurants, the couple took a tour through the laundry and the engineering section, then the indoor pool. They saw the outdoor pool, the new theatre complex, and the Island Grill. Just beyond the Island Grill was an area under construction.

"What's in the building that's not finished?" Carrie asked.

"That's our new utility complex. It will house newer and larger generators to keep the Manor running should we lose power," Albert said.

They re-entered the building and were taking the elevator to the floor with the meeting rooms. Charles noticed a "PH" on one of the elevator buttons.

"Does the Manor have a penthouse?" Charles asked.

"It does, but it's not available for guests. Beatrice lives there. She feels one of us should always be on the premises. When she's away, either Lizzie or I stay in one of our suites."

"It makes sense to have someone here and I bet it's comforting after a long day to retire to a pleasant suite," Carrie said.

"Yes, but don't let the word penthouse fool you. It's smaller than the condos Ryan and I have in Millford."

The elevator doors opened, and they were on the floor with the meeting rooms.

As they passed by the meeting rooms, Charles noticed most were empty. Only one group was gathered in one of the smaller rooms. Several servers were setting up a buffet table in the hallway for the meeting participants.

"Has there been any unusual activity with these meeting rooms?" Carrie asked.

"There's been reports of shadows and a lady dancing. But the biggest prank was during a wedding," Albert said.

Charles noticed that Albert used the word prank and not paranormal.

Albert continued, "We had champagne glasses set up in a pyramid formation at the back of the room waiting for the toasts to begin. There was no one near the table when suddenly the pyramid collapsed, and all the glasses fell with most of them breaking."

"Did it disturb the festivities for the bride and groom?" Carrie asked.

"Fortunately for us they were still taking pictures in the chapel. We had everything cleaned up by the time they arrived for the meal," Albert said. "You've seen most everything in the main complex, let's head outside."

On the opposite side of the rooms were windows that looked out on the parking lot. Charles nudged Carrie and nodded towards a yellow jeep parked on the lot. It looked like the same jeep that had nearly run them off the road that morning.

Carrie took the hint, "Oh Charles, look, there's one of those jeeps I've been thinking about buying."

"It looks sharp parked on the lot, but I still think it's more for a young person who wants to go on camping trips and drive through riverbeds. I bet it's an uncomfortable ride with lots of bouncing. What do you think, Albert?" Charles asked.

"I've been in that vehicle and I agree the ride is very bumpy," Albert said. "But I also know that vehicle isn't owned by a youngster. Our events manager, Ken Harvey, owns the jeep. He's in his late forties."

"See Charles, It's not just for kids."

"Just between you and me, he might be in the middle of a mid-life crisis. Besides the new jeep he bought a condo in one of the newest buildings in Millford," Albert said staring out the window at the jeep. "Carrie, I've set up an appointment for you to meet with Ken tomorrow afternoon, so you can ask him more about the vehicle at that time."

Charles enjoyed walking, but he was beginning to tire. However, guiding Carrie and Charles around the Manor seemed to invigorate Albert. It was obvious to Charles that Albert loved the Manor and took great pride in sharing his knowledge.

"And now Carrie I've saved the best for last," Albert said smiling.

9

Albert led them down a winding path with well-manicured gardens on each side. Every several hundred feet a smaller path broke away from the main walk and offered the guest another themed garden to explore.

Each breakaway section had a small wooden sign indicating the garden type such as English, Japanese, Azalea, and Water. Carrie took photos of the various entrances and made a mental note to come back later for more extensive shots of the gardens. Then she caught up with the men as they walked towards the six individual white bungalows she saw from the balcony of their suite.

"I assume these are the writers' cottages that Maddy and Marge mentioned," Carrie said.

"You're correct. My cousins are enormously proud that we offer this opportunity for writers," Albert said.

"They didn't say much about how the program works. Are the cottages reserved just for writers and how do you select the writers?" Carrie asked.

"Well, it depends. We do occasionally have requests from guests, mostly honeymooners who want the privacy afforded by the cottages. But with those few rare exceptions, the cottages are just for the writers," Albert said.

Carrie noticed there was a change in Albert's demeanor as he talked about the cottages. He seemed extremely excited to show them this latest addition to the Manor. She waited as he talked about the construction of the individual bungalows. She was about to ask again how they chose the writers when Albert remembered her question.

"You asked a second question about the selection process. Writers apply for either four or eight weeks. They outline their writing project and why we should consider them and whether they are applying for a free or reduced rate for the cottage.," Albert said. "We leave the selection to Marge, Maddy and Tom, that's Lizzie's son. Did the girls mention that Tom manages their second store in Millford?"

"Yes, they did. They also said Tom did a great job, and they didn't have to worry about spending time at the second store with him in charge," Carrie said.

"Tom is a great asset to our team and the writers' cottages are a great asset to the Manor."

They arrived at the path that crossed in front of the cottages and Albert unlocked the door of the second cottage.

"These were designed with the writer in mind. There's a small kitchen to prepare meals so they can write in relative seclusion unless they want to come up to one of the main buildings, to eat, use the gym, the pool, or take part in any of the other activities," Albert said.

Carrie looked at the other cottages but saw no signs of activity.

"Do you have any writers staying here now?" Carrie asked.

"Currently we have two writers checked in. We have Mrs. Kent in the first bungalow. She's on the reduced rate program while she finishes her current manuscript."

"Roxanne Kent?" Carrie asked excitedly.

"Yes, I believe her first name is Roxanne," Albert said. "Do you know her?"

"I don't know her personally, but I've read many of her books. She writes mysteries that take place in a bed-and-breakfast in a small town. Maybe she uses the town of Millford for inspiration."

"That's interesting. I really wasn't familiar with her work," Albert said.

"And the other writer?" Charles asked.

"We also have the delightful Ms. Millicent Ford in bungalow three. She's here for the full eight weeks. She's writing a history of the area, including a large section about the Manor. She says it's non-fiction, but she's including 'a touch of romance.' Delightful, yes, delightful woman. I mean, both ladies are lovely, and we're glad they're staying with us."

"Oh my, these are nice," Carrie said as she entered the front room.

Carrie loved the cozy feel of the cottage. The room had a bay window with a seat that looked out on the vast property. Next to the window was a writing desk with lots of space for working and a printer. On the other side of the room was a fireplace with a sofa and a reclining chair for reading.

She peaked into the kitchen and found it equipped with all the necessary appliances. There was a small round dining table that provided another writing space. She opened the only other door in the main room and saw a comfortably furnished bedroom.

"Charles, if I need a quiet spot to finish my mystery book, these cottages would be top of my list. Did your sister design these?"

"Yes, she did. Of course, I'm prejudiced but I think Lizzie did a fine job with the cottages. The writers who have taken part in the program have all given rave reviews," Albert said. "Don't know if you noticed, but there's no television. If a writer wants one, there's no problem hooking one up for them, but most prefer the quiet."

"Well, Darling, you can come anytime you want and hang out here in the cottage to finish your book. I'll be staying in the main building and taking advantage of all the Manor's great amenities," Charles said.

"That works for me," Carrie said smiling.

"Thank you for all your compliments about the Manor and the cottages." Albert paused for a moment and then said, "To maintain these cottages and everything we do at the Manor we need an occupancy rate of seventy to eighty percent. That's why it's important we find out what's happening with all these incidents. With the construction costs, finances are tight. We can't continue to lose business."

Carrie felt bad for Albert and the rest of the family. It was obvious Albert truly didn't understand why these incidents were occurring. She liked the family. They offered a good product and shared their success with others. She hoped that she and Charles could help them.

They started their walk back up the hill to the main buildings when Carrie saw Albert's eyes light up. Approaching them was a young woman that Carrie guessed was in her thirties and another woman nearer fifty. The younger woman was thin with a head of shiny Shirley Temple blonde curls that she wore shoulder length. The older woman was slightly plump with short gray hair in a mannish cut and sporting large red framed glasses.

"Oh, how fortunate. Here come our two resident writers now," Albert said.

"Albert, my dear, were you looking for me?" The younger woman oozed.

Carrie noticed that contrary to her little girl hairstyle, her voice was deep and sultry.

"Oh, well no, not really. I was showing one of our writers' cottages to Mr. and Mrs. Faraday. But it's delightful to see you.

Millicent, urr... Ms. Ford and Mrs. Kent," Albert said fumbling. "Let me introduce you both to Charles and Carrie Faraday. We hired Mrs. Faraday to write a new brochure for the Manor and I've been showing them around."

"How nice to meet you both," Millicent said. "Likewise," Roxanne Kent said.

Carrie noticed that while Mrs. Kent directed her welcome to both herself and Charles, Millicent stared only at Charles. It didn't bother Carrie because this often happened. Charles was a striking man with his thick silver hair and intense blue-gray eyes.

"Mrs. Kent, I've been a fan of yours for a long time. In fact, you've been an inspiration to me. I've been trying to write a mystery book for several years," Carrie said.

"Perhaps over tea one afternoon, you writers could get together and discuss your projects," Albert suggested.

Carrie jumped right on the suggestion. "I would love that. And, Ms. Ford, perhaps we could compare notes about the history of the Manor. I understand you're doing some research about the Manor and I want to make sure the historical facts I include in the brochure are accurate," Carrie said.

"That sounds like fun. I love talking about the Manor. In fact, I've a few additional questions for you, Albert, if you can spare some time." Millicent said.

Carrie could tell Albert was struggling as he looked from one group to the other trying to decide to whether to escort the Faradays back to the main building or stay with Millicent.

"Albert, we're fine finding our way back. Thank you for the tour. I can't wait to check my photos and get started on the brochure," Carrie said.

Carrie and Charles started back up the path when Charles stopped and called to Albert. Albert walked away from Millicent and joined Charles. Carrie saw Charles briefly say something to him before returning to where she was standing.

"What did you forget," Carrie asked.

"I just reminded Albert to maintain the secrecy around our real purpose for being at the Manor."

"You noticed it, too."

"Yes. It's obvious that Albert is partial to Millicent. Just wanted to make sure that whatever they're sharing with each other, it doesn't include our detecting."

10

"I can't believe after our long tour with Albert you're going for another walk," Carrie said.

"I'm not sure how much walking I'll do. I want to find a quiet spot to read my book and give you some time to organize all the things we heard and saw this morning," Charles said as he grabbed his book, kissed Carrie and left the suite.

Carrie appreciated the time Charles was giving her to work on the new brochure in the suite's quiet atmosphere. She wanted to get both her notes and photos organized. Then it would be easy to find information for solving the case or finding information to layout the brochure. She knew the project was only a cover for the real job of solving the Manor's problems, but the more realistic she made the project the easier it would be for her and Charles to move around the premises.

She also liked the cousins and wanted them to succeed. Why not create a marketing piece for the family to review as a replacement for what they were currently using?

She quickly finished typing her notes in her computer, since they were fresh in her mind. She then loaded the digital photos on her computer and sorted them by location. Carrie took a moment and isolated the photo of Chef Harold. Charles still had the employee list from Albert in his pocket. She would have to wait to do more research on Harold when she could find out his last name.

After several hours of working, she was ready for a break. She thought of going out on the grounds to see if she could find Charles. Then she remembered seeing an announcement about afternoon tea being served in the lounge off the main lobby. *Perfect*, she thought. *I'll have tea with Ms. Ford and Mrs. Kent on another day, but a cup of tea would taste good right now. And I'll still be working on the brochure by experiencing the tea and getting more photos.* She grabbed her camera, left Charles a note and headed for the lobby.

Carrie hoped the tea included small sandwiches and sweets. She could do with a little snack before dinner. The tearoom was about to open but there was a substantial line beginning to form. Carrie jumped the line and went up to the hostess.

"Hi, I'm Carrie Faraday and...."

Carrie didn't need to explain because the hostess said, "Oh yes, you're the lady who's doing some marketing for us. How can I help?"

"I was hoping to get some photos of the tea before the guests entered and disturbed the beautiful arrangement of food," Carrie said.

"No problem, we're still setting up. I'll keep our guests from entering until you give me a sign that you've finished your shots."

The hostess stood aside and gave Carrie access to the room. She went right to the food tables and began snapping pictures. The staff was filling one table with multi-layered silver trays with small sandwiches. There were the typical cucumber and watercress sandwiches, but also egg, ham and chicken salad and thinly sliced turkey on a cranberry nut bread.

The next table contained the sweets. The pastries were all miniature and included a red velvet cake, vanilla and chocolate cakes, éclairs, cream puffs, Neapolitans and a large selection of cookies, blondies, and brownie squares.

Mmm, this is my kind of tea, Carrie thought as she moved into position to snap a picture of the last table. This table offered fresh sliced fruits and berries, a selection of scones and mini muffins and two large bowls of clotted cream and fresh whipped cream for toppings.

The servers for the afternoon tea weren't wearing the traditional Manor burgundy vest. Instead, the tea ladies were wearing long black dresses with a white bib apron and a burgundy trimmed lace cap. The lone male server wore black knee pants, black stockings, white shirt, and burgundy apron.

Carrie quickly positioned two servers around the tables and got several more pictures. Then Carrie signaled the hostess, and the guests flooded into the room. She took a few more snaps of the area where the teas were being prepared.

She then looked for a spot to sit to enjoy her tea. She would have preferred one of the lounge chairs near the fireplace, but they were all taken as were the smaller tables for two. She settled for a table for four in the corner near the dessert table. She couldn't ask for a better position to satisfy her sweet tooth.

She was no sooner seated when a tea lady appeared and took her order for Darjeeling tea. Carrie didn't wait for her tea to arrive but went immediately to the food tables. She selected one of the sliced turkey sandwiches and then turned to the dessert table. So many items were her favorites, but she limited herself to a miniature éclair, two petit fours and a blondie. She would save the fruit and scones for her second trip.

By the time she returned to her table her server was back with a two cup Brown Betty teapot along with a fine china cup that featured scenes from the Manor. *Nice*, she thought. *Tea served in an authentic English teapot and with a fine china cup was perfect.*

Before Carrie poured her tea, she positioned her cup next to her plate of treats and snapped a picture then another picture after she poured her tea. She set her camera aside. Now for the real reason she was there. She sat back, closed her eyes, and took her first bite of éclair.

/ /

The éclair was even better than she thought it would be. Carrie was savoring the explosion of sweet cream filling her mouth when she realized a couple was standing next to her table and about to interrupt her moment of bliss.

They were both of medium height, a bit overweight, in their late forties. Both had reddish-brown hair but where the woman sported an unattractive chopped cut, the man's hair looked professionally styled. Carrie thought they might be brother and sister until they introduced themselves.

"Hello, we're wondering if we could share your table? I'm Bill Toberson and this is my wife Leslie."

They both seemed pleasant as Bill smiled at Carrie through bright white, slightly crooked front teeth.

"I hope you don't mind the intrusion. We saw that you were sitting alone, and we don't see another available table," Leslie said.

"Not at all, please join me," Carrie said pointing to the open chairs. "I ended up at this table because the single lounge chairs were all taken."

The tea lady appeared and took Bill's request for coffee and Leslie's herbal tea order.

"Are you staying at the Manor alone?" Leslie asked.

"No, my husband is with me. He went off for a walk with the latest best-seller under his arm. I'm sure he's found a nice spot on the grounds where he's reading his book," Carrie said smiling. "I finished my work and thought I would treat myself to afternoon tea."

The server was back immediately with their order. While Bill was fixing his coffee, Leslie went to the food tables. Carrie finished her éclair and bit into one of the petit fours. The cake was silky smooth with just the right balance of cake, jam, and icing.

"We saw you taking some photographs and at first weren't sure if you were part of the staff or a tourist," Bill asked.

"A little of both," Carrie said, patting the corner of her mouth with a napkin. "Management hired me to create a new marketing brochure. Since my husband and I were also looking for a vacation spot, we combined both activities and here we are."

Leslie was back from the food tables with two plates. Carrie gazed at Leslie's plates that seemed to include every selection from both the sandwich, dessert, and fruit tables. Carrie wished she had selected more items as she realized she was down to her last treat. Carrie focused back on her two guests, "And what brings you two to the Manor?"

"We have a similar situation," Leslie said as she lined the plates up on the table. "A little work and a little vacation. Bill's company is offering a seminar here at the Manor and I tagged along because I enjoy staying at the Manor. I love all their amenities, like this afternoon tea."

"Now you know Leslie, you're not really on vacation. Running a seminar takes lots of coordination. Leslie is the brains behind the scenes keeping everything running smoothly," Bill said smiling at his wife. "She may not be up front doing the actual teaching, but my trainers rely on her completely."

"What type of seminar are you offering?" Carrie asked.

"Bill's company is Toberson Construction and Security," Leslie said proudly.

"Then you're doing a sales seminar for potential customers?" Carrie asked.

"No, this one is an informational security seminar about what a company needs to have to protect themselves," Leslie said. "We discuss today's security from a technology perspective. We look at door locks, computer safeguards for employee equipment, security cameras on the premises, human guards and anything else to ensure a business has proper security."

"Even though it's informational we always hope we make some sales after the presentation," Bill said.

"Is it mostly government employees who attend?" Carrie asked. "I understand we're very close to several government installations."

"I do a lot of my business with the government, but my systems are equally valuable to any business. We usually have a mix of attendees from both the government and the private sector," Bill said as his took a big gulp of coffee to help wash down his second sandwich.

"These teas are delicious," Leslie said.

"Obviously, you're in marketing since you're writing a new Manor brochure. Is your husband in the same field?" Bill asked.

Carrie enjoyed the final bite of her last treat before answering, "No, he's in the printing business and publishes several magazines, including the *Tri-County Monthly*."

"I'm familiar with that magazine. I've taken ads in it. Every time I've run an ad, I get several new leads. I would think a magazine of that quality would need top computer security to protect their writers' work. Do you know what type of computer security your husband has installed?" Bill asked.

"I don't know, but you can ask him." Carrie said as she looked over at the door and waved at Charles. "I see he's finished his reading for the afternoon."

Charles nodded and headed for the table. After brief introductions, Charles placed his order for coffee.

"Darling, Bill was just asking me what types of security systems you have at your business? I was about to go into detail when you arrived."

"Please don't let me interrupt your discussion," Charles said.

"Hilarious, you know I don't have a clue what systems you have," Carrie said. "But I'm sure you want something to nibble before dinner. You folks can discuss security and I'll be back momentarily."

This time, Carrie followed Leslie's lead and filled one plate with sandwiches and piled the second plate with dessert items and fruit. When she returned to the table, the men were still discussing security. Carrie placed the food selection on the table between her and Charles.

"These look good. I was getting hungry," Charles said picking up one of the mini ham salad sandwiches and disposing of it in two bites. "Bill, what you're saying makes sense. Why don't you prepare a proposal and send it to me at the office and I'll look at it after we return from vacation?"

"That's great Charles, and it will be nice dealing with someone open to recognizing how important security is to his business," Bill said. Then as an afterthought he added, "I wish the folks here at the Manor were more open to improving security. It was quite a challenge to convince them to install the latest security systems in their new buildings."

"Is the Manor security in need of upgrades?" Carrie asked innocently.

"Any updated security would be helpful," Leslie answered sarcastically. "It would probably frighten most guests to know what little security they have. They still rely on alarm bars for their outlying doors and guards walking a beat."

"I mean we're already on the premises installing systems in the new buildings, now would be a great opportunity to upgrade the older areas of the Manor," Bill said. "I don't want to gossip about a client, but maybe you're aware they've had some incidents."

"I heard there was some mischief," Carrie said trying to be vague about any specific knowledge.

"I don't know if I would classify it as mischief," Leslie said. "This mischief is becoming more frequent and costlier to the bottom line. And when I say costs, I don't just mean damaged food in the kitchen and minor property damage. Guests are cancelling and businesses are deciding not to book company events here."

"I felt obligated to book my seminars here as a courtesy even though Tri-City would have been more convenient for this latest seminar. But the Manor folks are good construction customers of mine," Bill said. "If you weren't aware, my company built the new theatre and restaurant and we're about to start the new conference wing."

Bill looked around and then leaned forward and spoke in a low voice. "I'm only mentioning these incidents because you're a potential new client. I want you to know what good security can prevent."

"Well, we appreciate your confidence in sharing this with us. You've made me realize I need to review my company's security," Charles said.

Leslie looked at her watch. "Oh, good grief, where has the time gone? Bill and I need to get ready for the seminar's opening cocktail party," Leslie said.

"I'm afraid we must run. It was a pleasure to meet you and I'll call you once your back in Tri-City to go over my proposal for your company's security," Bill said.

Bill and Leslie left the table. Carrie waited until Bill and Leslie were out of the room before asking Charles. "What do you think?"

"Aside from Bill being a terrific salesman, I find it interesting they knew about the kitchen and other incidents affecting the Manor's business. I thought the family wanted to keep things quiet," Charles said.

"Could someone selling security systems create some issues to make management think about purchasing more equipment?" Carrie asked.

"You've a suspicious mind, Darling. They could have learned about the problems from someone working here or even management since they are dealing with them about construction and security issues."

"It's interesting what Bill said about the lack of security. No wonder stuff happens, and nobody sees anything. Unfortunately, the family is old-fashioned and believes in the goodness of their workers and their guests," Carrie said.

"But what about the goodness of ghosts and other disgruntled spirits?" Charles asked as he reached for another treat.

12

Between the drive to the Manor, the large breakfast, the long tour and the afternoon tea, Carrie thought she might take a nap before dinner. Charles stretched out on the sofa and was reading his book but within minutes Carrie noticed he was asleep.

Carrie picked up one of her books and curled up on the chair opposite Charles. Instead of dozing off, she found she was enjoying not only the paranormal techniques discussed in the book but eyewitness accounts of the different encounters. She didn't realize how much time passed and that Charles was now awake. She jumped when he spoke.

"Sorry, Dear, didn't mean to startle you. You must be reading a good book. Oh wait, you're reading about ghosts. Maybe it wasn't me but the gh-oo-sts who scared you," Charles said in his best Halloween voice.

"I was, and no, I didn't jump because of any ghosts. It was so quiet in here and I thought you were still asleep."

"Okay, I'll let you off the hook this time. What do you want to do about dinner?" Charles asked. He closed his book and placed it on the coffee table next to him. "I hope this isn't the night you want to dress up and go to the Williamsburg Room for fine dining?"

"First, I seriously doubt we could get a reservation this late in the day and you already made a reservation for later in the week. Second, I was thinking more like a pizza from room service," Carrie said. "Although, I would consider visiting the pub for a drink and a burger. That is if the right guy came along and asked me."

"I know the right guy and he would very much like to share a burger and a drink with you. But we have some time if my wife would like to take a nap with me in the other room."

"She would, but a nap isn't what I had in mind," Carrie said leading the way to their bedroom.

* * *

The Manor Pub looked different in the evening than it did during their daytime tour. The overhead lights were off, and the tables were lit by lantern candles. The lanterns along with the gas fire in the large stone fireplaces gave the room a cozy feeling. In daylight, the different alcoves were obvious but now in the low light each section offered a more secluded spot for meeting and eating.

"I hope we can get a table. It's a lot busier than I thought it would be," Charles said. "You don't get the impression the Manor has this many people staying here."

"It's the way they designed it. There are many places through-out the property for meetings and activities. Until the guests get hungry and show up for dinner you don't have a true sense of how many people are here," Carrie said.

"The good news is it means there are people staying here generating dollars for the Manor. The bad news is it looks like everyone staying here wants to eat in the Manor Pub tonight," Charles said as they approached the reception desk.

"Hello, my name is Tim. Welcome to the Manor Pub. Are you joining us for drinks or dinner?"

"Both," Carrie answered.

"As you can see, we're a little busy at the moment. Could I start you two at the bar for your drinks and then as soon as a table is available, I'll seat you?" Tim asked for their names. "Oh yes, you're here doing some work for the Manor."

Charles exchanged a glance with Carrie, as Tim led them to the bar.

"Is everyone eating in the pub tonight?" Carrie asked Tim.

"At this hour, a large crowd is normal. The local folks from Millford come in for the Happy Hour specials we've added to attract business. Our only seminar group has a free night scheduled for the participants. This means there's no planned dinner and many of those folks are in here," Tim said. "Plus, the Williamsburg Room is completely booked. It has a private party tonight which limited the number of regular reservations. We're getting their overflow."

"That's good news for the Manor to be this busy," Carrie said.

"It's a nice change from the lack of customers we've been experiencing lately," Tim said as he escorted them to the bar. "Paul, can you take care of the Faradays until I've a table available for them?"

"Absolutely, my pleasure. Pull up a stool folks. What can I get you to drink?"

"The lady will have a gin and diet tonic with lime, and I'll have the lite beer. The one featured on this coaster," Charles said pointing to the advertising card on the bar.

"Coming right up!"

Over half an hour later Charles and Carrie were still waiting for a table.

"I'm glad we had all those snacks at the afternoon tea, but I'm getting hungry," Carrie said.

"My motto—always take advantage of snacks. How about another round of drinks?"

Charles signaled to Paul, who was at the opposite end of the bar, that they wanted another round. While they waited, Charles noticed Carrie suddenly gave a shudder.

"Wow, even with the heat from the fireplace I feel a chill. When I was growing up, and this happened to a member of the family, my grandmother used to say, 'someone stepped on your grave.' As a child, that was a scary thought."

"Putting your grandmother's saying aside, do you think you're coming down with a cold?" Charles asked.

"No, I'm fine. It lasted for a moment and was only on one side. Here, touch my left hand."

Charles took her hand. "This hand is ice cold. Give me your other hand," Charles said. "There's a definite difference in temperature between your two hands. That's strange."

Charles was still holding Carrie's hand when they heard rattling and clicking. Above their heads was a rack holding various sizes of glasses for serving wines and liqueurs. They both looked up and then at each other. Before Charles could say anything, Paul returned with their drinks.

"Sorry the drinks took so long, I had to grab more diet tonic from the storeroom."

Neither Carrie nor Charles responded. Paul continued, "Are you two all right? Did something happen?"

"Before you got here, we had an unusual experience," Carrie said.

"Ah, did our resident bar ghost make an appearance?" Paul said as he exchanged the new drinks for the empties. "I bet the glasses above your head started to rattle."

"That they did, but first, my wife experienced a slight chill," Charles said.

"Yup, that's how it works. You feel a cold spot on some part of your body and within a few seconds, the glasses rattle."

"That's exactly what happened. Does your ghost have a name?" Carrie asked.

"Some people think it might be Roxie Fenton. Most people believe it's Bernie Millford. He was the Manor's general manger during the fifties."

"Didn't I hear that there was a murder associated with Bernie and Roxie?" Charles asked.

"Yup, they found Roxie murdered in their suite and before they could question Bernie, he disappeared. Many folks believe because of the crime he committed he cannot rest and roams the Manor," Paul said. "Supposedly, Bernie used to sit in this very spot waiting for Roxie to come down from their suite."

"In this spot where I'm sitting?" Carrie asked.

"That's what they claim. Anyway, one night she was late coming down to meet him and Bernie went up to check on her. He saw a bellboy leaving their suite who was adjusting his clothing. Bernie jumped to a conclusion. The bellboy returned to his station with a bloody nose and a black eye."

Charles almost laughed at the suspenseful way Paul was relating the story. Just as he was building the story, he pulled a cloth out from under the bar and wiped away a wet spot for a dramatic pause.

"Was Bernie known to have a temper?" Carrie prodded.

"Apparently not before this incident. Anyway, a few minutes later, guests complained of screams coming from their room," Paul said. "The night manager went to the suite. As he approached the room, he heard gunshots. When they broke the door down Roxie was dead. The door to the balcony was open and there was no sign of Bernie. Vanished!"

"Sounds like everyone assumed Bernie did it with little more than circumstantial evidence," Charles said as he took a sip of his beer.

"That's true. They had only the bellboy's word that Bernie punched him. Other people think someone else killed both Bernie and Roxie. Then they hid Bernie's body to put the blame on him. Or was Bernie the real killer, and he got away with murder," Paul said lowering his voice. "But Bernie never resurfaced, and the case remains open and a mystery to this day. We may never know who did the murders."

"Interesting! How often does your pub ghost appear?" Charles asked.

"In the past, only a few times each year. Lately our ghost seems to appear at least once a week. You both should feel honored because you're now members of an elite group who experienced this." When neither Carrie nor Charles said anything Paul added, "I hope you two aren't the type who frighten easily. A few folks checked out and vowed never to come back after having this experience."

"Paul, I'll share a little secret with you. The Manor's management hired me to write a new marketing brochure. We won't be leaving until my work is complete, ghosts or no ghosts," Carrie said. "In fact, many view these ghostly visits as adding charm to the history of the Manor. It makes the piece I'm writing more interesting, don't you agree?"

Paul simply smiled and then wandered off to make more drinks.

13

Shortly after the ghost incident, a table was ready for Carrie and Charles. The dinner crowd was thinning, and it was still too early for the folks wanting a nightcap to wander in.

The couple was seated at a corner booth with a screen divider that offered them privacy from the next section. Charles placed orders for the day's special pub burger made with fresh ground beef, aged cheddar cheese and grilled onions on a rye roll with pub fries.

"Are you sure you should have told Paul management hired you? It might make it harder for us to do undercover work," Charles said.

"I don't think it matters. Some staff may not know what we look like, but believe me, they know we're here. Look how Tim recognized our name and when I arrived for tea this afternoon, the hostess knew who I was," Carrie said as she took another sip of her drink. "I doubt there's anyone who doesn't know we're on the premises and doing something for management."

"Are you implying some staff may think we're doing something other than marketing?"

"I think at this point they're not sure," Carrie said. "But if we stick to our cover about wanting information for a new brochure, we'll pick up little bits of information. Look how much we learned about Bernie from Paul."

"As always, you make perfect sense." Charles raised his glass in a toast to his wife. "Should I assume the employee will only share information that doesn't involve him or her in the incidents?"

"Either that or they may tell us something to misdirect us," Carrie said. "I'm more concerned about what just happened at the bar. What do you think caused the glasses to rattle like that?" Carrie asked.

"The obvious answer is some sort of a vibration," Charles said.

"Wouldn't we have felt a vibration? All I felt was a chill."

"Not if it was something on the floor above, or something directly connected to the beam that holds the rack or even something generated by the bartender."

"I see what you mean. Perhaps tomorrow we should investigate what's above the pub," Carrie suggested.

The burgers arrived, and Charles put aside their ghost talk to dig into their platters. He spent the next half hour enjoying the food and discussing what they might do for recreation over the next several days when they weren't looking into ghostly problems. When their plates were clean, Charles sat back and patted his tummy. "What a good burger. That has to be one of the best burgers I've eaten."

"I agree. I bet they have those rye rolls specially made by a bakery," Carrie said.

"Considering the business, the Manor provides to the area, I'm sure they can have special items made whenever they request them. You want dessert?" Charles asked.

"After that meal? No thank you, but I would like some coffee."

Charles ordered coffees, and they were quietly sipping their drinks in what was now an empty section of the pub. Other parts of the pub were buzzing with activity as most of the new patrons arriving were gathering at the bar. Charles was watching the bar crowd when he heard voices on the other side of the divider screen.

"I finished work a while ago, but I wanted to touch base with you before I left. That's why I asked you to meet me here."

The voice was deep and scratchy as if the person had a cold or suffered with allergies. The speakers were on the other side of the screen and a few tables down from where Carrie and Charles sat.

"We may need to be careful over the next few days or even weeks."

"Do you want to pull back on the operation?" the second voice asked.

This voice was a much higher pitch, but Charles was sure it was a man.

"No, not yet. I just want everyone to keep an eye out for this couple. They're supposedly writing a new brochure."

Charles looked at Carrie but said nothing.

"Do you think they're here for some other purpose?" high pitched voice asked.

"I've no reason to think they're doing anything other than what Mrs. Barry says they're doing. I'm more concerned with their access. The old dame gave them the run of the entire Manor and brother Albert gave them the official tour today. It means they know the layout of the Manor with lots of time to explore which the family doesn't have."

"True, but this is a big place. That doesn't mean they'll come across what we're doing. I'll alert the others so we can set up a network to track their movements," the high pitch voice said.

"Sounds good. Are you in tomorrow?"

"Yes, but to be safe, let's avoid any contact between us unless it's absolutely necessary," the high pitch voice said.

Charles and Carrie were straining their ears to capture every part of the conversation. It was several seconds before Charles realized the conversation stopped. He sprung from his seat and hurried down the length of their section and around the corner to the other side. He scouted the area and then returned to the table from the opposite direction.

"Anything?" Carrie asked upon his return.

"No. By the time I got to the other side all the tables were empty. They could have left the Pub or blended in with the bar crowd. I noticed Tim isn't at the greeter's station," Charles said. "I guess at this hour they let people seat themselves."

Charles looked across the room. "Paul is at the bar mixing drinks, so it couldn't have been him. What do you think about what we heard?"

"It's good and bad news," Carrie said. "The good news is what we heard supports the theory that the events at the Manor aren't supernatural."

"And the bad news?" Charles asked.

"The bad news is it sounds like there's definitely some mischief afoot and that mischief could present problems for the person writing the new brochure." Carrie said.

"I've changed my mind. I'll be an active part of helping you prepare this brochure. I don't want you wandering around this place alone."

"I'm always glad for your company, Darling." Carrie paused and then added. "You realize that they've already failed with one thing they're trying to do."

"What's that?" Charles asked.

"They didn't do a very good job of keeping track of us tonight."

14

It was late when they returned to their room from the pub. Carrie thought after a long day and with a full tummy she would go right to sleep. Instead, once she was in bed, she tossed and turned. She glanced over at Charles, but he was sound asleep.

Carrie's mind kept thinking about everything she saw and heard during the day. The Manor was massive, and they had already met many of the staff. Did she meet the person or persons creating the problems? Why did Chef Harold avoid having his picture taken?

And what about the two writers? There was no mistaking that Millicent stared at Charles as if she knew him, but Charles didn't seem to recognize her. Was a famous writer like Roxanne Kent really staying at the cottages to overcome writer's block or did she have some other motive? Was it just a coincidence her first name was Roxanne, or could she be a relative of Bernie's girlfriend?

The family members they met seemed open, honest, and genuinely concerned about their business. What about the family members they hadn't met? *Enough, enough* she told herself. She needed to get some sleep, otherwise she would be too tired to find more answers tomorrow.

Reading usually helped her fall asleep, but she didn't want to wake Charles by turning on the bedside light. She was debating whether to slip out of their bed and go to the living room and watch television. Old black and white movies sometimes helped her to fall asleep.

Before she could decide, Carrie was aware the room had turned dark. There was no light coming through the French doors from the outside. *There must be clouds overhead covering the moon.*

The atmosphere in the room changed again when a large clap of thunder rattled the French doors. An explosion of lightning followed the rumble filling the room for a split second with light. The day which was so beautiful turned into a dark and stormy night. She looked at Charles, but the noise from the thunder and illumination from the lightning had no effect on him as he continued to sleep.

She could feel goosebumps on her arms and then felt a chill like she experienced in the pub. Carrie instinctively pulled the covers up around her neck, but this didn't keep her from smelling what she thought was a faint whiff of perfume. It wasn't a heavy scent but a light passing fragrance. Maybe the rain caused smells from the garden flowers to seep into the room.

Then she saw it. Across the room, an image was forming. Carrie closed her eyes, shook her head, but when she opened her eyes, it was still there. Although it was transparent, Carrie could see the outline of a young woman sitting cross-legged on top of the bureau.

Carrie couldn't move. When she worked as a photographer, she traveled throughout the world and many times found herself in dangerous situations. She always called on an inner strength that got her safely through the danger. This time she felt helpless.

Carrie couldn't take her eyes off the image. The young woman's dress was made of a blue silky material and was a design popular in the fifties. The woman slid down off the bureau and Carrie noticed her stockings had seams running down the back of her leg.

Carrie thought she might know who this woman was. She summoned her courage and quietly called her name, "Roxie, Roxie Fenton is that you?" The sound that came from Carrie's throat was more like a dry whisper than her normal voice.

The figure now turned and looked at Carrie. Roxie smiled at Carrie and Carrie saw how pretty she was. "Roxie, is this your room?"

Roxie nodded her head.

"Are you causing the problems around the Manor?" Carrie asked.

Roxie vehemently shook her head no. Carrie could feel Charles stirring next to her. Roxie saw Charles moving, and she started to fade.

"No wait," Carrie pleaded. "I want you to meet my husband."

It was too late. There was another flash of lightning, revealing that Roxie was gone.

"Who do you want me to meet?" Charles asked.

"Charles, did you see her?"

"See who?" He mumbled.

"Charles, wake up."

"I'm awake," he said through a yawn. "I thought I heard you talking to someone."

"Charles, I just saw a ghost."

"That's nice, dear."

Charles tried to roll over, but Carrie grabbed his arm and shook him. "Charles, did you hear what I said? I saw a ghost."

"You what?" Charles was now fully awake as he sat up in bed. "Did you say you saw a ghost? Where?"

"Right there," Carrie said pointing. "She was sitting on the bureau."

With Charles awake, Carrie mustered additional courage. She turned on the light and left the bed. She approached the bureau area and carefully looked for any evidence of Roxie.

"You need to tell me exactly what you saw," Charles said.

Carrie spent the next couple of minutes telling Charles what she witnessed.

"Wow, that's some story. Carrie, I don't want you to get upset by my next question. Are you sure you weren't waking up from a dream?" Charles took her hand. "There's a nasty storm overhead, and you heard all the talk about ghosts in the pub. Perhaps the storm stirred you and you weren't aware you were still dreaming?"

"It wasn't a dream, Charles," she stated. "I wasn't dreaming because I wasn't asleep. Because I couldn't sleep, I was about to go watch television in the living room. You've got to believe me."

"It's all right, I believe you. But I doubt Roxie will come back again tonight," Charles said. "I suggest we get some sleep and tomorrow with fresh eyes we'll re-examine this problem."

"How do you plan on 're-examining' the problem?" Carrie asked, thinking Charles still didn't believe her.

"We'll go buy some ghost-detecting equipment."

15

Early the next morning Carrie awakened to find that Charles was not in bed. She wasn't concerned because he was an early riser. If they were at home, he might be in his study doing paperwork or in the kitchen working on a special breakfast for her. But they weren't at home.

Maybe he was making coffee in the suite's kitchen. Carrie got up and went out to the front rooms. No aroma of brewing coffee greeted her. She soon realized Charles wasn't in the suite. *Where is he?*

Carrie finished dressing and returned to the living room in time to hear a gentle knock at the door. Since Charles wasn't there, she was careful about opening the door.

"Yes, who is it?" she asked.

"Oh good, I'm glad you're up. It's Charles. Let me in, please," Charles said.

"Charles who? You can't be my husband. He's very responsible and would have taken his room card."

"Good morning," Charles said to a couple passing him in the hall and waited until they were in the elevator before he continued.

"Hilarious, but if you let me in, I'll tell you what I discovered. Plus, I bring coffee."

"Mmm, just what I need," Carrie said. She quickly unlocked the door.

"Great! So, a potential intruder needs only to bring coffee and you'll let him in," Charles said.

"That's probably true," said Carrie smiling.

Carrie took the carry tray loaded with four cups of coffee and all the fixings and placed it on the dining room table. Carrie said nothing until she took her first sip.

"What have you been up to at this early hour, aside from buying coffee? Oh, and thank you for this," she said holding up her cup.

"Since you were still sleeping, I thought I would check out what might have caused the glasses to rattle in the pub last night."

"And did you find the cause?"

"Maybe. On the second floor, above the pub, are several meeting rooms and the ballroom," Charles said. "Remember when Paul told us last night that the one conference staying here had a free night? I assumed there were no other bookings in the other meeting rooms."

"Me too. In fact, he added the Manor wasn't terribly busy," Carrie added.

"But I checked the schedule board and a company from Hanley held a sales recognition dinner. Over one hundred people were in the ballroom. But there's more," Charles said. "Right above the bar area where the glass rack is hanging are the restrooms. I'll bet you with that many people in the ballroom there was activity all at once in the restrooms. The heavy traffic could have caused the vibration that rattled the glasses."

"Well done, Sherlock. Mrs. Barry would be proud that you proved it wasn't a ghost. But you've missed one aspect of the rattling glasses."

"And what might that be?" Charles asked.

"Paul said the glasses rattling is increasing. You explained why it may have happened last night but if bookings are down, you would think Bernie's ghost would be less active."

"I guess we need to do more research. If Paul can remember the last couple of incidents, we could check this against the bookings for the rooms upstairs."

Before Carrie could discuss anything additional about the research they needed to do, the phone rang.

"Hello. Good morning, Albert. No, we're up," Charles said. "Yes, we can come right down. We'll see you in a few minutes."

"What's new with Albert?" Carrie asked. "Please tell me there isn't a second part to yesterday's tour?"

"No, not a new tour. It seems after we left the pub last night there was another incident of mischief. Albert thought we might like to see it."

16

When Charles and Carrie got off the elevator, Albert was waiting for them.

"Thank you for coming so quickly. Let's not discuss anything until we reach the pub area," Albert said quietly.

They followed Albert through the lobby and down the hallway leading to the Manor Pub. Charles was eager to see the level of damage in the room. When Albert opened the pub door, and they entered the room Charles saw no change from the previous night. Everything seemed in order. Chairs were upside down on the tables but that was to help facilitate the cleaning process. In the far corner where they ate the night before, a worker was running the vacuum while another staff member was wiping down the booths.

Albert led them past the bar and Charles instinctively looked up at the rack. But the glasses were quietly nestled in their slots. They went through the swinging doors behind the bar. To the left was a pass-through window from the kitchen for food service.

Straight ahead was another long hallway that ended at a heavy steel door.

Albert unlocked the door, and they entered a massive room with floor to ceiling steel shelves containing box after box of liquors, beers, and wines. At the back, was a refrigerated room with wine racks that housed the more expensive bottles. As they walked down the aisles, Charles saw opened cartons with bottles scattered on the floor.

"Okay folks, we can talk here," Albert said. "This morning, Ryan discovered someone broke into this storage room that houses all the liquor for the Manor. As you can see, they have thrown multiple cases on the floor."

"Since the Manor Pub doesn't open until the afternoon, what brought folks in this morning?" Carrie asked.

"A member of Ryan's team does an inventory each morning. They verify what's missing from stock matches what's in the computer as being removed or sold. Today it was Ryan's turn to do the check. He arrived around 6:30."

"Let's put together a timeline. If I remember correctly, the pub closes at 2 a.m." Carrie said.

"That's right. Based on how busy they are during the evening closing down can last from thirty minutes to an hour," Albert said.

"Carrie and I ate in the pub last night. We left around midnight and there was a nice crowd around the bar. For the sake of argument let's assume it took forty-five-minutes to finish the clean-up. The last person would have left at 2:45," Charles suggested as he stepped over several broken boxes at his feet.

"Then the window of opportunity was under four hours," Carrie suggested.

"Actually, less time. The cleaning crew you saw when we passed through the pub comes in at 5:30," Albert said.

While Albert and Carrie were talking through the timeline, Charles looked around the storage room. He saw something near the door of the glass enclosed refrigerated room for the wines. He picked it up and returned to where Albert and Carrie were in discussion.

"How do you think they got in?" Charles asked.

"We assume they entered the same way we did through this door. There was no damage to the door which means they had a key," Albert said. "We'll have the locks changed and I've called Toberson security to install cameras over this door and the out-side back doors. Our fault. We should have had this area more secure when the first incidents started."

Charles remembered Toberson's conversation from the previous day about the lack of security around the Manor.

"Not a lot of broken bottles. It looks like they took boxes off the shelf and placed them on the floor," Charles said.

"That's what happened with the other incidents. No real destruction, just mischief," Ryan said as he joined the group. "Good morning, Mr. And Mrs. Faraday."

"What have you found, son?" Albert asked.

Ryan tapped a few commands into the tablet he was carrying. "I didn't mean to interrupt, but I heard you mention no destruction. I believe they dumped these liquor boxes to misdirect our attention away from something else."

"What do you mean, Ryan?" Carrie asked.

"I don't know. I just get the feeling we're missing something," Ryan said. "There's more to all this mischief than a few broken bottles of booze and food thrown around the kitchen."

"You may be right," Charles said. "What's your theory?"

"I'll show you," Ryan said.

The group followed Ryan to the last aisle near the refrigerated room.

"We fill the shelves in this area with cases of different brands of alcohol. As you can see, they threw two cases of Jack Daniels on the floor and all the bottles broke," Ryan said. "But when I counted the bottle tops, there are only ten. Meaning they took two bottles. It's the same with these cases of Russian vodka. Lots of broken bottles but definitely three bottles missing."

"Maybe someone removed the bottles earlier in the evening to restock one of the Manor's bars?" Carrie asked.

"We don't manage the inventory that way. When we open a case and remove bottles, we move the open case to a shelf in the front rows. That way we don't have multiple cases opened at the same time. Both these brands have open cases up front," Ryan said.

"I've never heard of a ghost stealing bottles of Jack Daniels and Russian vodka, have you?" Charles asked.

"This stunt of stealing booze definitely shows we have a human problem," Albert said.

"Ryan, you said you thought this destruction was to divert our attention. What did you mean by that?" Carrie asked.

"One of the first areas I checked was the wine room. This is where we store our more expensive wines. If this were a pure and simple robbery, you would assume those bottles would be the target."

"Was anything taken?" Charles asked.

"According to the inventory everything matches. Nothing missing. But someone disturbed the bottles." Ryan said. "We keep the wine bottles in the rack with their labels facing up. It makes it easier for the morning count. This morning there were twenty-seven bottles with the labels turned around."

The group was quiet, taking in what Ryan said. Then Charles asked, "Do you open any of those wines back here before serving?"

Albert jumped in, "Heavens no. We always present the wine to the guest for approval and the wine steward opens the bottle at the table. Why do you ask?"

"I found this cork at the entrance to the wine room." Charles opened his hand and revealed the cork. He handed the cork to Ryan who looked at it and then handed it to his father. Charles waited while Albert examined it.

"This is a new cork. I guess it could have been loose in a case, but that's unlikely. Most wineries do the bottling and the packing in separate areas. It's a good quality cork but there are no markings showing the winery," Albert said.

"Dad, I'd like to hang onto that. Do some research and see if I can find who is using this brand of cork," Ryan said.

"Ryan, your father gave us a list of employees who have left the company in the last several months. Is there anyone you remember who left your employment with access to this room?" Carrie asked.

"Mrs. Faraday, I don't believe the problem is with anyone who has left. I believe our problem is with current workers."

Charles noticed Ryan used the word workers and not employees. He wondered if he had someone in mind.

"Think about it. You need to know the schedule for the Manor's activities. Things like when cleaning crews come in, when deliveries arrive, when we take inventories and when security checks occur," Ryan said. "The timing for most of these events is constantly changing. You also need keys. Only a current worker would have access to all these things. I believe current staff would spot and report former employees or an outsider if they were in any non-public areas."

Charles jumped in before Ryan could continue. "Ryan, do you have any ideas who the culprit might be?"

"Not yet, but I'm creating a computer program that scientifically evaluates a list of people working certain shifts."

Charles along with the others stared at Ryan. No one made a comment because no one knew exactly what Ryan was creating.

"That probably sounds strange. Let me explain. I'm creating a program that tracks the people who were working and had access to an area where there was a problem," Ryan said. "And no, I don't have any results yet. At this stage of the program I've a huge amount of data with all the names, schedules, and deliveries to enter. But I'll gradually narrow it down to just a few prime suspects."

"Ryan that's a terrific idea," Charles said. "Are you willing to share? I would love to see the programming."

"Sure, that would be great if you looked at what I'm doing because I'm sort of building it as I go. But keep in mind, while my program might reveal potential suspects, there's one question it won't answer."

Charles looked at Ryan waiting for his response.

"It won't tell us the motive for what they're doing."

17

"Ryan seems to be a bright kid," Carrie said when they were back in their suite. She put their room key card on the credenza near the door. "He must be really computer savvy to create a scheduling program like he described. I assume it would be near impossible to do this task manually."

"Yes, it would," Charles said. "That's why his computer program is a good idea, but I'm not sure he should ignore former employees and outsiders."

"Why do you say that?" Carrie asked, plunking herself in a chair and draping her leg over the arm.

"When I was wandering around in the storage room, I saw they receive deliveries at two bay doors and there's an entrance door next to them. I think the thieves could have just as easily entered from the back."

Carrie thought for a moment about Charles's theory and then said, "If they came in that way how does that support your theory it's a former employee?"

"You heard Albert say they were lax about changing the locks," Charles said. "An ex-employee could have made copies of the keys. And if it were an outside worker, it would be better to enter through the back door and avoid the main part of the hotel where they might be seen."

"Weren't they still taking a chance being spotted by someone else? I mean Mrs. Barry lives on the premises."

"If I remember the layout of the Manor, those doors are on the opposite side from most of the rooms including Mrs. Barry's penthouse," Charles said.

"Okay it's a possibility that it's someone from the outside."

"I hear a but...," Charles said.

"I think Ryan's opinion that the person knew the schedule for the Manor is correct. Would an outsider or a former employee have access to the latest schedule?" Carrie asked. "And one more observation. I find it interesting the incident occurs on the morning Ryan is scheduled to do the count."

"Are you suggesting Ryan really knows what's going on?" Charles asked.

"No, he's too loyal to the Manor. But someone might have picked his scheduled day to annoy or provoke him. Maybe there's another family member who's not as dedicated to the business," Carrie offered. "I need a cup of coffee. You want one?" Carrie headed to the kitchen in their suite.

"You know I do," Charles said. "Unfortunately, these are all assumptions. We still have no clues to identify the person or persons involved."

Carrie selected the coffee marked *Manor Blend* hoping it was the same coffee they had in the Old Mill Restaurant. "We have one small clue," Carrie said from the kitchen. "We have the conversation we overheard in the pub. One speaker was an employee who mentioned he finished work. The other person could have been an employee or an outsider."

"Don't get me wrong, I'm not eliminating a current employee. I'm just saying there could also be some outside help."

Carrie returned with two cups of coffee and sat next to Charles on the sofa. "Hopefully, Ryan's program will give us some names," Carrie said.

"Today's incident proved one thing. It wasn't a paranormal entity that did the damage. Taking bottles of vodka and whiskey makes it a human act," Charles said.

"You're right," Carrie said, although she couldn't help thinking about her recent encounter with Roxie. What part was paranormal activity playing? She changed the subject. "While we ponder these questions, we have some free time. I don't have to be back until three to meet with the event manager, Ken Harvey. But until then I'm all yours," Carrie said,

"In that case, Mrs. Faraday, what would you like to do before your meeting?"

"I've two suggestions. We could wander around the Manor and the grounds. I could take pictures and gather more information for the brochure or... we could ride down to Main Street and inspect the village of Millford," Carrie suggested.

"I vote for checking out the town. After all, I promised you last night that we would pick up some ghost detecting equipment," Charles said.

"I thought we just eliminated the paranormal from these incidents."

"We did from the storage room incident. We haven't eliminated what you saw last night and what the guests are seeing and hearing. Having some professional equipment could come in handy."

Carrie liked Charles's suggestion. "I would also like to check out the bookstore. Maybe we can meet Lizzie's son, Tom, and get his perspective on events," Carrie said.

"Good idea. While Ryan checks out the employees with his computer program, we can check out another family member at the bookstore."

18

Charles and Carrie set off for an exploratory trip to the Village of Millford, using the Manor shuttle which ran every hour to the town. Aside from transporting guests it also provided a means of transportation for employees of the Manor to get to and from their jobs.

Carrie briefly saw the village from their car when she arrived. Now, strolling along the main street, she noticed how lovely the village was. The shopkeepers remodeled their buildings to resemble a colonial town with brick fronts and long window shutters in different colors.

A variety of stores offered visitors lots of shopping opportunities. Everything from homemade candles, candy, and craft retailers, an ice cream parlor, a bakery, a tea and coffee shop, several antiques stores, various clothing boutiques, several restaurant choices, and the Millford Bookstore. The town also included stores not typical of a tourist village. Like an electronic store, a computer repair shop, and a large hardware store. Behind Main

Street was a free parking lot along with a sign pointing the way to several larger chain stores.

"Who would have thought this tiny village would have an electronic store?" Carrie observed.

"Perhaps there's a need for electronics to capture paranormal activity in this haunted village," Charles said.

"Very funny. With a large hardware store and several chain stores, there must be lots of housing nearby to support them."

"Remember, the sisters said they get business from government offices over in Hanley. All those workers need to live and shop somewhere," Charles said.

They walked across the street and entered the electronic store. It wasn't a huge store, but it seemed to have a wide selection of the major brands and the latest gadgets.

"Hello, folks," said a middle-aged man who was fixing a floor display. His dress was casual with dark blue slacks and a light blue, long-sleeved shirt with the name of the store stitched across the pocket. "My name is Greg. What can I help you with today?"

"We're looking to purchase a digital tape recorder," Charles said.

"A small one, but powerful with good battery life," Carrie added.

"I have what you're looking for right over here."

Greg led them to the other side of the store and selected two boxes from behind the counter. "Both these models are powerful with long battery life."

He opened the two boxes and laid the recorders on the counter. Carrie picked up one recorder and handed Charles the other one.

"What's the difference between the two?" Charles asked.

"Both, when fully charged, provide about twenty-four hours of battery life. I believe that is what you meant by powerful?"

Carrie nodded in agreement.

"This one costs more because of its smaller size and it's a little more sensitive to sounds that trigger the automatic record feature," Greg said.

"Even though it costs more, I like the one that's smaller," Carrie said. "I can put it in my pocket."

"You said you were going to use this recorder in your work?" Greg asked.

"Yes, I'm a writer," Carrie said. "I'm working on a new marketing piece for the Manor, and this device will help me record my thoughts after I conduct my interviews."

"I didn't mean to pry, but I asked this question for a reason." Greg said. "I like to remind folks that there's a state law about recording conversations without the other person's permission. The person you're recording needs to be told the conversation is being taped."

"Believe me, this recorder is to help my memory not to record others without their knowledge." For just a moment Carrie wondered if Roxie would give permission to record any conversations they might share. Then she focused back on what Greg was saying.

"Excellent! Like I said, I feel obligated to mention the law. What else can I show you folks?"

"I also need a small digital camera with a tripod," Carrie said. "One that automatically turns on with any motion in the room."

"I have several that will perform that function. The cameras are on the other side if you'll follow me."

Carrie looked at several cameras Greg selected as meeting her requirements.

"This one will make a nice addition to my other cameras. It's small, but I like the wide-angle lens," Carrie said. Carrie added a small folding tripod that could sit on a table or bureau. Secretly, she was hoping to capture a photo of Roxie.

While Greg was ringing up the order, he asked Carrie, "You said you were writing something for the Manor. Are you writing something about the paranormal?"

"Why do you ask?" Carrie said surprised by the question.

"I've heard some reports of recent paranormal activity at the Manor. And other Manor guests have recently bought equipment hoping to capture a record of events they've experienced."

"Really, do you remember their names?" Carrie quickly added, "I mean, I would like to interview them for the piece I'm writing."

"The first was a couple who kept hearing voices. They wanted a recorder so they could capture what they heard to give to management. But that was several weeks ago. I'm sure they've left by now."

"Anyone who made a recent purchase?" Charles asked.

"Yes, there was a woman who bought a recorder just last week. You know, she said she was a writer, too."

Carrie exchanged a look with Charles. "Did she give you her name?" Carrie asked.

"She paid cash, but I got her name for my sales slip just in case there was any problems. Give me a minute and it will come to me," Greg said.

"You know we met two writers staying at the Manor. One was an older woman in her fifties with short gray hair and the other was younger in her thirties woman with blond hair."

"Definitely, the older woman," Greg said. "As I remember her name was a bit different."

"Could it be Roxanne?" Carrie asked.

"Yes, that's it! Don't you agree that's not a name you often hear these days."

Carrie would have suspected Millicent might have wanted a recorder to use in her research. She was surprised when she heard it was Roxanne.

"Haven't there always been ghost sightings at the Manor?" Charles asked.

"Yup, that's part of the charm of the place. Have you two seen a ghost or heard something unusual?" Greg asked.

"No, the two of us haven't had any experiences," Charles said.

Carrie was glad Charles phrased his answer that way because she didn't want to discuss her experience with Greg.

Carrie jumped in, "I've been doing interviews and some people have mentioned stories about the paranormal. I'm thinking about including a little bit about the ghosts in the new brochure."

"I'm glad to hear you're creating something new. I've seen the Manor's current brochure and it definitely needs an update. All of us business owners here in Millford want the Manor to do well because they drive business for the rest of us."

"That's what I'm hoping to do is give them a new piece that reflects all the additions and improvements they've made over the years," Carrie said.

"Adding the new is good, but don't forget to mention those lovely old ghosts. Maybe something like 'with the right equipment you might even capture a ghost voice.' Ghosts are good for the Manor's business and mine," Greg said.

Even though Carrie was planning on mentioning ghosts, she thought Greg's approach was a little too commercial and benefitted only his business.

While Charles was signing the credit card receipt, he asked, "You've quite a selection of electronics. All this variety is somewhat surprising since Millford is a small village."

"Believe me, if I had to rely on the sales from the village of Millford, I would have been out of business a long time ago. No, most of my business comes from the government installation about eight miles off Route 28 and the other companies that support the government. I also do all the electronic installations for the Manor and Toberson Construction."

"Sounds like this is a village where everyone helps one another," Charles said.

"As I said, the Manor has been good to me and the other merchants in Millford. With the size of that place they could buy from anyone or produce things themselves, but they make a point of helping the merchants here in town," Greg said. "Besides my products and services, they use the local hardware store for materials and landscaping. They buy ice cream from the local parlor and rolls and cakes from the bakery. With all the ovens up at the Manor, they could easily bake anything they wanted. Instead, they share the wealth."

"We had a delicious sandwich in the Manor Pub with a unique roll," Carrie said.

"I bet it came from our Millford bakery. Sometimes the Manor chef will create the recipe with the understanding the bakery only sells it to the Manor until otherwise notified. The bakery agrees to the arrangement because there's no way they would ever sell enough of a single product in their store compared to what the Manor needs. It's a win, win for everyone," Greg said.

"I'll definitely work the local merchant angle into the new marketing materials," Carrie said.

"Thanks for the information and thanks for your help with the electronics." Charles said as he picked up their purchases.

Once outside the store Carrie turned to Charles. "Those Manor folks are just full of surprises."

"It's nice they support the town merchants. I'm sure they could make a lot more money handling business differently, but money doesn't seem to be the motivation of this family."

"Interesting, because money is often the reason for criminal activity," Carrie said.

"What do you want to do now?" Charles asked.

"I was thinking we should try some of that ice cream the Manor thinks is so good."

"I was hoping you would suggest that. A nice black raspberry cone would be a perfect treat," Charles said.

They purchased their cones and were enjoying them while sitting on the bench outside the ice cream shop. They heard a car peeling out from the light. Carrie looked up to see the jeep that nearly ran them off the road on the day they arrived at the Manor. "I assume that's Mr. Harvey, the event manager," Carrie said.

"You know the problem with people who own those vehicles?" Charles didn't wait for Carrie to answer. "They drive like they're invincible. I don't want anyone I know and care about to own a vehicle like that."

When Carrie didn't respond, Charles added, "Especially someone I love and don't want to get hurt." Still there was no response. He finally asked, "What are you thinking?"

"I'm thinking if I owned that vehicle I would never drive fast because it would worry the person who cares about me."

Carrie accepted a kiss from Charles and then said, "Ken's vehicle went by so fast. Did you recognize the passenger?"

"I thought it looked like Millicent Ford," Charles said. "If it was her, what she's doing with the events manager?"

"That may not be so unusual. He may have been showing her around the area for her historical research. If you've finished your ice cream, let's head over to the bookstore."

19

Charles and Carrie walked to the bookstore at the opposite end of the street from the electronics store. Unlike Maddy and Marge's Nottingham bookstore, the Millford store was in a stand-alone facility surrounded by a large parking lot.

"This differs from the Victorian home that houses the sister's store in Nottingham," Charles said. "This one has a more modern design especially with all those glass windows."

"True their family home was a Victorian building but remember the sister's upstairs apartment was very modern in design. Let's see what they've done with the inside," Carrie said.

When they entered the store, Carrie felt the same warm comfortable feeling they experienced at the sister's other store. The designers strategically placed bookshelves to create individual reading nooks with lots of comfortable chairs and light from the windows. She wondered if Lizzie helped with the design.

"Charles, look at the children's section. It looks like a Hansel and Gretel Gingerbread cottage. What fun."

"With all the categories of books on the same floor I bet they also designed it for noise reduction. Once the kids are in the gingerbread house, other visitors won't hear their little voices. I see meeting rooms at the back, and they look soundproof too," Charles said. "This store is much larger than it appears from the outside and really well-planned."

"While you look around, I'll see if Tom is working today," Carrie said.

Carrie spotted a clerk who was unpacking cartons and placing books on a display. "Excuse me. Is Tom Larkin working today?"

The petite blonde turned and stared at her. Carrie had the distinct feeling that had the girl not approved of her, she wouldn't have received the answer to her question. Carrie wondered if she was protective of the unmarried manager because of her feelings for him. Carrie must have passed her test because she responded.

"Tom is over at the reference counter," she said pointing to a spot on the far side. "But you might want to give him a minute. He's talking with his father, Doug."

"Thank you. I'll wait until they've finished." Carrie said.

Carrie moved half-way between the clerk and where Tom was talking with his father. The only way Carrie could describe Tom was 'drop dead gorgeous.' No doubt this phrase would date her with the younger set, but they were the only words that came to mind. *No wonder the clerk was protective of him.*

He was lean, but solid with Mrs. Barry's height which made him taller than his father. His angular face was similar to his father and was off-set with stylish glasses. He had a mop of light brown wavy hair that that seemed to have a mind of its own in contrast to his father's graying hair that was neat and trim.

Carrie was concentrating on the two men and the conversation between them that seemed tense. She didn't realize they spotted her staring at them. The next thing she knew she was being waved over by Tom's father.

"Hello, are you waiting to see me or my son?" Doug asked.

"Your son. But I didn't want to interrupt your conversation. I'm Carrie Faraday and I'm good friends with Maddy and Marge. I just wanted to stop by and introduce myself."

"I'm Doug Larkin and this is my son, Tom. Faraday, Faraday. Oh yes, you're the lady who's writing a new brochure for the Manor. They could sure use one," he said as he picked up one of the Manor brochures from a display and then flipped it back on the counter without opening it. "This old piece they pass around is really an embarrassment. The cousins mentioned you were here with your husband. Is he helping with the brochure? I understand he's in printing."

"No, my husband is here on a much-needed vacation and enjoying all the amenities the Manor has to offer," Carrie said. "He's not really a printer. He's the publisher of the Tri-County Monthly and several other magazines."

"I'm familiar with Tri-County Monthly," Tom said. "We sell completely out every month. Be sure to tell your husband how much we like the publication."

"You can tell him yourself. Here's Charles now."

After introductions and more praise for the magazine, Doug turned to Tom, "Son, I want you to think about my offer. I'm getting older and I would like for you to join me in the business. It will be a comfort for me to know I'm passing it on to my son."

"I'll think about it, Dad, but I'm really not interested in the liquor business. I love what I'm doing here," Tom said.

"Alright, but I'll keep asking, Tom. Mr. and Mrs. Faraday, it was nice to meet you," Doug said and then left the store.

"My two aunts, Marge and Maddy, think the world of both of you," Tom said. "Let's move over to one of the reading areas. No one will hear us since the books act as soundproofing, and we can see anyone approaching."

Carrie wondered why Tom felt the need for security to protect their conversation.

Once seated Tom continued, "I know you're doing undercover work investigating the incidents at the Manor while telling others you're designing a new brochure," Tom said. "I want to assure you aside from my Mom, Aunt Beatrice, Uncle Albert, my two bookstore aunts, Ryan and myself no one else knows why you're really here."

"And your father?" Charles asked.

"He and my mother are divorced, and the Manor is part of her family. Dad has the liquor contract for the Manor and is always on the premises, but he's not on the Manor's board. There's no reason for him not to believe your cover."

"That's good to know. What do you think is going on at the Manor?" Carrie asked.

"At first, I thought it might be an employee prank that went wrong. And to keep from getting caught they blamed it on paranormal activity," Tom said. "Then stuff kept happening and got more destructive. Now I believe someone has a calculated plan to drive the guests away."

"Any idea what the plan is?" Charles asked.

"They might be trying to create financial problems for the Manor. We have some heavy expenses right now because of the new construction. Not that we're financially strapped or at least not yet." Tom said. "But we're at a standstill right now."

"I noticed when I was walking around the property, there wasn't much construction activity," Charles said.

"That's because we're looking at a proposal to move the new conference building in a different direction. It might be a good idea but will delay the completion and tighten the finances even more."

"What do you think about the construction change?" Carrie asked. She liked Tom's open style and felt they might learn some additional details the cousins hadn't mentioned.

"Toberson, the construction guy, says we would save money in the long run. If we build on the steep hill at the back of the property, as planned, he feels we'll need to do extra ground reinforcement and retainer walls," Tom said.

"We met the Toberson's yesterday at the Manor's afternoon tea. He mentioned he was in construction, but we spent most of the time talking about security systems," Charles said.

"Yes, we're using the construction division of his company for the current building projects. Anyway, he's proposing we build in the opposite direction from the current plans to avoid these problems," Tom said. "And if we enlarge the access road it would provide the conference attendees with a separate entrance and help with traffic management. While a good idea, fixing the road will also cost additional dollars."

"And the downside..." Charles asked.

"One word—delay. The longer the new construction isn't progressing, the longer we're carrying the loan with no income being generated. If we continue to lose conference business and guests because of these incidents, then money will be a factor," Tom said. "That's why I believe it's more than a disgruntled employee. There's something else involved."

"That's quite a theory, but it makes sense. Causing a financial impact could explain a lot," Carrie said.

"Believe me, there are many people including several huge conglomerates who would be ready to make a buyout offer if we ran into financial problems," Tom said. "Or at the very least purchase enough of our loans to secure a position on the board and influence the way we run the business."

They sat for a moment thinking about what Tom said. Carrie could tell Charles was about to say something when the petite blonde she talked to earlier approached them.

"Tom, I'm sorry to interrupt, but the Millford Ladies' Guild is here for their appointment with you."

"Thank you, I'll be right there." After she walked away, Tom said, "I'm not sure I can add much more. I don't know who is behind this or if my theory has any merit. But I wanted to mention it to you in case you spot anything that supports it."

"Tom, thank you for sharing your thoughts with us," Carrie said.

"Here's my card and I've put my cell number on the back," Tom said. "Call me anytime day or night. I've a feeling we haven't seen the last incident."

After the bookstore visit, Charles and Carrie had limited time to explore additional shops. However, the universal view from the shopkeepers they visited was overwhelmingly the same. They appreciated the family, and all they provided to the village.

By the time they caught the shuttle back to the Manor, Carrie barely had enough time to keep her appointment with Ken Harvey, the driver of the yellow jeep.

20

"Do you want me to come with you?" Charles asked. "You can sit this one out. Besides, you're dying to relax on our balcony and read your book."

"You know me well. But I'm concerned about you," Charles said.

"Charles, I'm interviewing Ken in his office. There are plenty of people around in the area. If I go anywhere else, I'll text you. Don't worry, I won't be in any danger."

"I wasn't thinking of the Manor's problems. I was thinking about leaving you on your own with a man that owns the jeep you like."

"Very funny, but I promise I'll only talk about the Manor. No conversations about jeeps or any side trips to a car dealership."

Carrie left Charles reading his book. She took her notebook and camera and headed downstairs. She entered the office area behind the lobby and walked down the hallway and then stopped.

She realized she didn't know which way to go. Carrie heard her name being called and turned to see Ryan in his office.

"Hi Carrie. What are you doing down here?"

"I have a meeting with Ken Harvey but realized I don't know which office is his."

"I'll show you," Ryan said and started to leave his office when the phone rang. He saw the caller ID, and it was obvious he needed to take the call.

"It's all right, Ryan, I can find it. Just point me in the right direction," Carrie said.

"His office is in the first hallway off this one. Go towards the owners' den, turn left at the hallway and his office is the third one on the right."

"Got it. Thanks," Carrie said. She smiled when she heard Ryan call the cousin's offices the 'owners' den.'

Carrie easily found the correct hallway and the nameplate on the wall confirmed she was in the right spot. She held back from knocking on Ken's door, because of the loud voices she heard coming from within. It sounded like a disagreement was in progress between two people. Carrie couldn't quite hear what they were saying. They weren't yelling but she could tell they were expressing opposing viewpoints. One man had a high-pitched voice that sounded like the one she and Charles heard in the pub. She needed to see who was speaking. She knocked and then opened the door.

"Hi, Mr. Harvey, is this a good time?" Carrie called out as she poked her head into the office.

Ken Harvey at first looked surprised at the interruption, but then regained his composure and said, "You must be Mrs. Faraday."

As Carrie entered the office Doug Larkin was standing next to Ken by the credenza. "Doug, this is Carrie Faraday. Management hired her to produce an updated brochure. She's here to talk about our events."

Carrie couldn't help but wonder if Ken was one of the select employees Mrs. Barry told about the new brochure to spread the news around the Manor.

"I had the pleasure of meeting Mrs. Faraday earlier today at the bookstore. I'm delighted she's preparing a replacement for that hideous brochure you people use."

Ken was a small man. He was about five-foot eight, thin and not very tan for someone who rode around in an open jeep.

"Hello, nice to meet you," Ken said. He didn't extend his hand and his greeting was less than enthusiastic.

"I've been looking forward to meeting you. I'm excited to learn about the Manor's events. Though I'd another reason for wanting to meet you," Carrie said.

"Really. And what reason is that?" Ken asked as he raised an eyebrow and gave her a questioning look.

"I understand from Albert you own the yellow jeep I saw on the parking lot. I've been bugging my husband to buy a jeep like yours so we can explore country roads on weekends."

Carrie felt a little guilty after promising Charles to keep her conversation limited to the Manor, but she was glad she mentioned the jeep. What a difference one sentence can make in an interview. Suddenly Ken's entire attitude changed.

"I love my vehicle. Most of the countryside around here is rural. That vehicle lets me go anywhere, while still providing good transportation for the civilized roads," Ken answered enthusiastically.

"That's exactly what I tell my husband. Apparently, I haven't been particularly good at my explanations. He's still not convinced."

"I'm happy to give you both a test ride whenever you have the time," Ken said.

Doug interrupted, "Look, I'll leave you two to talk about events and... jeeps. I better get to work on those liquor orders you wanted, Ken. Nice to see you again, Mrs. Faraday."

As Doug left, Carrie wondered about his access to the Manor and staff members. Why was he discussing liquor purchases with the event manager? She thought all purchases went through the group Ryan managed. Were they discussing more than liquor purchases? Had she really heard a high-pitched voice? Not all men have deep voices. Maybe they weren't really arguing. They seemed friendly with each other when she entered the room.

"Shall we get started? Do you prefer Mrs. Faraday, or may I call you Carrie?" Ken asked.

"Definitely Carrie."

"Good, and I'm Ken. Albert said I should be open, honest and share any information you want about events. Where would you like to begin?"

"Can you tell me how many events on average you book each month?" Carrie asked.

"During our best months, between forty and fifty. These events can include small meetings to large conventions and weddings. But sales are extremely low at the moment."

"And why is that?" Carrie asked.

"Partly because of the season. We do fewer bookings in the winter months. Now with the warmer weather we should pick up reservations and we're not."

"I see. What types of events do you normally book at this time of year? By that I mean meetings, seminars, conventions or individual parties and do most events require rooms?"

"Events that carry room bookings are better for the Manor because it's added business. But it's all about customer service and repeat business. For instance, we do a lot of business with the companies that support the government installation over in Hanley. If they need a meeting room for one day with no overnight rooms, we'll still accommodate in the hopes of getting a bigger booking later."

"You must rely on more than just meetings," Carrie said.

"Yes, this is the season when we should sign up lots of social events. You know weddings, anniversaries, retirements, school dances and other special occasions," Ken said.

He leaned back in his chair. Carrie felt like an employee about to get a lecture from the boss.

"We always get the school proms and with the new theatre we were hoping for some graduation ceremonies, but so far, they haven't booked. Wedding bookings are also down. As a result, we're way behind last year's numbers."

"Are there other competitors stealing business?" Carrie offered this explanation knowing it wasn't the reason.

"The Manor really has no local competitors. No, I believe it's because of the mischief that's been happening around the Manor," Ken said. "These stories are getting out to the public and they are hesitant to book. They want nothing to happen that might spoil their event. You've heard about our incidents?"

"I heard about some damage in a storage room, but what other things have happened?" Carrie asked playing dumb.

"Unfortunately, there are many more incidents," Ken said. "One morning we had a report of a mouse in an upstairs hallway."

"A mouse. That's a problem," Carrie said. "Was it only one?"

"Only one and that one might not be unusual. It was in the building nearest the new construction," Ken said. "When we broke ground for the new construction, we might have disturbed a nest. Management caught the creature and no other intruders with whiskers and tails appeared, but an exaggerated rumor about mice infestation was out in the public."

"What else?" Carrie asked. She hadn't heard about the stray mouse from any of the family. She drifted away for a moment and thought of Baxter. If he was with them, the Manor wouldn't have to worry about a mouse. Baxter kept their farmhouse free from those pests.

Ken continued, "One night we had several people call the front desk asking why a band was playing at three in the morning. There was no band. And there are reports of other sounds."

"What kinds of sounds?" Carrie asked.

"Guests have heard voices, music, thumping, and squeaking. Even a low humming sound."

"Low humming. You mean like a motor or a machine running. Is there some machine on the premises that could cause this sound?" Carrie asked.

"No, no, of course there isn't. That's only one sound. One sound isn't important," Ken snapped.

Carrie realized Ken wanted to move on from his statement about machinery. She was trying to think what kind of machinery would run at an early hour and loud enough to disturb the guests? She made a mental note to discuss this with Charles. She also noticed that Ken's voice seemed a little higher in pitch when he responded to her question about machine noises.

"Here's another example. Just two weeks ago, we had a large dinner meeting in the ballroom," Ken continued. "At the back of the room were trays filled with wine glasses waiting for the guests to arrive. Suddenly the trays started to shake and within seconds many of the glasses fell and shatter."

"Albert mentioned a similar incident with glasses at a wedding party," Carrie said. "and we learned last night, while having dinner in the pub about the glasses rattling on the rack above the bar."

"You were in the pub last night?" He hesitated and then said, "I mean I hope you enjoyed your meal. I think they have really good food," Ken said.

Carrie thought Ken's reaction to her mention of the pub was revealing, but he recovered.

"One more incident occurred last weekend. A member of a wedding party reported a man in the ladies' room. She described him as wearing attire from the fifties."

"Bernie?" Carrie suggested.

"Oh, you've heard about Bernie. That's what the staff members think, but who knows. When I make phone calls to solicit bookings, instead of commitments, I'm getting questions about these occurrences," Ken said.

"What do you think is causing this increase in incidents?" Carrie asked.

"I think it's the new construction."

"You mean because of the mouse incident?" Carrie asked. Or did Ken believe that new construction was creating paranormal activity?

"Yes, that incident but also the construction could account for some of the sounds people are hearing. It might explain glasses rattling and falling from racks. You know vibrations from the digging and heavy equipment being used."

Carrie wondered if Ken mentioned construction sounds to cover his earlier comment about machinery. "Hasn't the construction stopped for the moment?" Carrie asked.

"It has temporarily. Several of us senior staff members suggested moving the new conference building to the north side of the Manor instead of the east. This would avoid a steep drop on the property," Ken said.

"I thought the plans for the new construction were complete. Isn't it late and costly to make a change?" Carrie asked. She wanted to get Ken's opinion on what she heard from Tom.

"The theatre is complete, and the new Island Grill is about ready to open. We haven't started construction on the main building that will provide additional conference and guest rooms. Fortunately, the cousins have listened to us and are pretty close to changing the plans to the north."

"What was the reason for the original site?"

"The new guest rooms would have a wonderful view of the gardens which Mrs. Barry liked. But we pointed out that people attending conventions would probably prefer to be closer to the bars, restaurants, and other amenities instead of a garden view," Ken said.

"What happens now?"

"Mr. Toberson, the president of the construction company we hired, is meeting with the cousins and me tonight. We should have an answer shortly on the direction for the new building."

"The cousins and their board seem very good at making the right decisions so I'm sure it will work out fine for the Manor's future," Carrie said.

Carrie noticed Ken stole a glance at his watch. No doubt he was hoping this interview would end. "Before I leave, do you have any information on the number and size of the various meeting rooms that I could include in the brochure?"

"Yes, I do. I created some sheets with that information." Before Ken could provide Carrie with the handouts, the phone rang.

"Excuse me just a moment," Ken said. "Hello, Event Department. This is Ken Harvey. Oh, hello, nice to hear from you. Yes, let me look."

Carrie turned away trying to give the impression she wasn't listening to the call. She glanced around the room. While Ken's desk was neat, stacks of papers including what Carrie thought looked like maps filled the credenza. Maybe they were maps of the proposed construction area. Her eyes returned to Ken as he pulled out a large calendar book.

He opened to a date page. "I'm sorry, it looks like that day isn't available. Perhaps another date. Yes, I understand your visitors are only here for that day. Sorry we couldn't help you this time. You too, goodbye."

Carrie watched as Ken closed the book. She was sure the calendar page he checked was blank.

"Wouldn't you know the one day he wants isn't available.

"Where were we?" Ken asked.

"You were getting some pricing sheets for me."

Ken opened a desk drawer and pulled out some sheets of paper. "Here you go. You'll see all the different rooms, their capacity and configuration. This sheet shows all the audio/visual equipment available from microphones, projectors, computers, etc."

"Thank you, Ken, this is perfect. I appreciate you taking the time to chat with me. I can see how busy you are."

"Well, don't hesitate to call with questions as you go through the materials. And maybe at our next meeting we can take a ride in my jeep."

Carrie left the office with several things to go over with Charles. She was sure Charles would have some follow-up questions for Ken.

21

Charles and Carrie followed protocol and made a reservation for the Williamsburg Room the morning they arrived.

They were able to easily secure a reservation showing the restaurant was not as busy as in the past. Happily, tonight was the couple's opportunity to enjoy the fine food they had heard so much about.

They were seated at a table where they could see the lighted water fountains in the garden courtyard. On each table there were three candles nestled in a gold-colored hurricane globe that provided soft lighting for the room.

Perhaps it was the candlelight, but Carrie felt nothing but warmth as she looked across the table at the man she loved. She savored the moment because soon the conversation moved to her interview with Ken earlier in the day.

"Charles, when I first came down the hallway to Ken's office, I thought I heard the same high-pitched voice from the pub." Carrie said.

"And was it Ken's voice?" Charles asked.

"I don't know," Carrie said as she took another bite of her duck. She debated whether to order the salmon dish they saw the chefs testing in the kitchen. Instead, she decided on the crispy orange duck. She loved duck, and the Manor's preparation was perfect. The duck was slow cooked to eliminate the grease then crisped in a hot oven before adding a delicate orange sauce.

"Like I was saying, after I started talking with Ken his voice seemed normal. Only once did his pitch rise, but it wasn't exactly at the same level as the voice we overheard," Carrie said.

"It could still be him. Remember when we were in the pub there was music playing and lots of conversation from the patrons. He may have raised his voice to a higher pitch so the other person could hear him," Charles said. "Also, we sat on the other side of a divider and several tables away from the speakers which could have distorted his voice."

"You're right. How's your end-cut prime rib?" Carrie asked. Carrie knew that Charles tried to limit red meat in his diet, but tonight he splurged.

"Perfect. The flavors are unbelievable. It's obvious it was slow cooked, but it's still moist. Not to mention it's so tender I could cut it with my fork," Charles said. "Back to what you were saying, I definitely wouldn't eliminate the event manager from our list of suspects."

"You think my first instinct is correct that he's the guy from the pub?" Carrie asked.

"I always think your instincts are right. Remember the man with the scratchy voice said he finished work," Charles said. "If he was a staff member, he probably would have said I finished my shift."

"That's a good catch and here's something else. Ken took a phone call from a client wanting to book an event," Carrie said. "He told the client there was nothing available on a particular date. But from where I sat the calendar page looked blank."

"Now, I'll return the compliment because that's also a good catch," Charles said. "One way to reduce bookings is to say the Manor is full."

"What's his game in disrupting service at the Manor? I assume, if Ken receives a bonus or even his next raise, management will base it on him increasing the number of bookings and sales," Carrie said.

"The obvious answer is that the payout from creating the disruptions is greater than what the Manor is paying him, but that's just a guess. It's like Ryan said this morning. He might find the people who were working on the premises during the incidents, but it doesn't give him the reasons for why they're causing problems," Charles said. "Speaking of Ryan. Tom, Doug and Ryan are seated at a table behind you."

Carrie turned around and waved to the group. "In some ways that seems like an odd group. I can see Ryan and Tom eating together as cousins. And I can see Tom and his father eating together, but not the three of them."

"Actually, it was just the two cousins then Doug walked in. He looked around and saw the boys and joined them," Charles said.

"That makes more sense. Back to what we were discussing. What do you think about Ken's comment or lack of comment about the machinery sound some guests heard?" Carrie asked.

"Machinery could explain the supposed paranormal activity," Charles said as he took a sip of his wine and savored it. "What do you think of this scenario? A machine running near their rooms wakes the guest. They're not sure what disturbed their sleep. Then they hear mumbling and unintelligent voices of the people who are running the machine."

"That makes perfect sense They've heard paranormal stories and immediately think ghosts," Carrie said as she soaked her last bite of duck in the orange sauce. Carrie was glad they ate at the Williamsburg Room early in their stay because she was definitely planning on coming back. "What else?" Carrie asked.

"You said after Ken mentioned the machinery sound, he immediately changed the subject. It's almost like he realized he slipped up and was trying to cover up his mistake," Charles said.

Before they could continue the discussion, their waiter, Luke, approached.

"I was about to ask if you were enjoying your dinner. But I can tell by your empty plates, I need not ask the question," Luke said.

"Our meals were superb. Perfectly prepared, great taste, just delicious," Charles said.

"That's what I like to hear," Luke said.

Carrie noticed that Luke, like most of the wait staff, made his comments personal.

"Now, what can I get you folks for dessert? Wait, I can tell by your faces you're about to say no. Before you do, let me just mention one thing," Luke said. "We're known far and wide for our bread pudding. And while we may be famous for this wonderful dessert, we don't serve it every night. But today our chefs made an extra-large batch. They must have known you were eating here tonight."

Carrie couldn't help but giggle at Luke's salesmanship. "Charles, bread pudding. One of your favorites. I believe we could splurge tonight."

"Let me add, while many restaurants serve this dish only with whipped cream. We serve it with a warm vanilla sauce and then we finish it with a dollop of fresh whipped cream," Luke said.

"We'll take two dishes of bread pudding along with two cups of coffee," Charles said.

Once they made their decision Carrie noticed how quickly Luke left to get their desserts as if he was afraid they might change their minds. While they were waiting for dessert, Carrie took time to glance around the room. The restaurant was definitely not at capacity.

"Looks like most of the family is eating here tonight," Charles said. "Eating at the table over by the window is Albert and Millicent. Looks like Ryan and Tom are joining them. Doug left."

Carrie turned and caught the eye of Albert and gave a little wave. "I think our assumption was correct. Albert seems smitten with Millicent."

"Smitten? Now that's an old-fashioned word, but it seems to fit," Charles said.

"Maybe we're being unfair and it's a planned discussion about hotel history. With Ryan and Albert's knowledge of the Manor and Tom's capability as a librarian, I imagine they all could help Millicent with her research," Carrie said.

"Here's a question for you. Over at a table by the door is Roxanne Kent sitting with a gentleman. Do you think he's her husband or a boyfriend stopping by for a visit?" Charles asked.

"I read that she's a widow, and I don't think he's a boyfriend," Carrie said sneaking a look at the table. "It looks to me more like a business meeting rather than a romantic dinner. If I were a betting woman, I would say her agent is checking on her writing progress."

Carrie saw Doug re-enter the room, carrying a drink. He stood at the entrance to the restaurant. She watched as he waved the hostess away and proceeded to Albert's table. He grabbed a chair from a nearby table and maneuvered between Millicent and Albert.

"Looks like Doug is back. What information could Doug provide about Manor history?" Carrie said sarcastically.

"Not only is he crashing but looks like he's commandeering the table. I want to watch these dynamics," Charles said.

Carrie didn't have to wait long to see what would happen. Albert stood up and helped Millicent from her chair.

"And there they go." Carrie said. "Oops, looks like Tom and Ryan are finished, too." She watched Doug sitting at the table all alone sipping his drink.

"You're right about everyone being here tonight. I see the Tobersons were just seated at a table on the opposite side of the room and here comes Ken Harvey," Carrie said.

22

Ken headed right to Carrie's table. "Hello, Carrie. I see you're taking advantage of the Manor's fine dining tonight. And this must be Charles. Hi, I'm Ken Harvey, the Event Manager," he said extending his hand.

"If I was enjoying fine dining with such a handsome man, and he wasn't my husband, I would be in big trouble," Carrie said.

"Don't pay any attention to my wife's humor. I'm Charles," he said while shaking Ken's hand. "It's nice to meet you. Would you like to join us?" Charles asked as he pointed to one of empty chairs at their table.

"I've a meeting with the Tobersons and management about our latest construction project. I'm part of the team helping to make these important decisions for the Manor," said Ken.

While Ken directed his comments to Charles, Carrie gently shook her head so Charles could see her disagreement. She seriously doubted Ken was helping to make important decisions about the Manor, but that made her wonder why management included him in the meeting.

Ken continued, "But it looks like I've a few minutes since Mrs. Barry hasn't arrived."

"We won't keep you. Carrie and I were just discussing her meeting with you this afternoon. I must admit I'm fascinated by all the paranormal talk."

Carrie sat back as she watched Charles use the direct approach with Ken.

"Please don't misunderstand. I'm not a believer in the paranormal. I was simply repeating to your wife the reports we've heard from our guests," Ken said.

"I'm glad to hear you're a non-believer, because I may have an explanation for all the ghost stories," Charles said.

"Really. I would be interested in hearing that," Ken said fiddling with the tablecloth.

"I was especially interested in the guests who heard the sounds of machinery along with voices."

Carrie listened while Charles repeated his theory that the machinery aroused the guests and the people running the machines explained the voices they heard. Carrie noticed Ken shifting uncomfortably in his seat, but he didn't respond to Charles's explanation.

"Did the Manor have machinery on the premises during the time of the reported incidents? Maybe something related to the construction?" Charles asked. When he received no response from Ken he added, "I guess we'll ask management."

Before Charles could continue, Ken jumped up, "Look, as I told your wife, the machinery sound wasn't important. The guests probably didn't know what they heard. The important information is they checked out before finishing their stay and asked for a full refund."

Carrie looked at Charles. As Ken was talking, his voice rose several levels. She knew Charles noticed it, too.

"Charles, we should check out the location of those rooms," Carrie said.

"There are no specific rooms. You'll find we've had guests all over the Manor leave because of ghost stories," Ken snapped.

"Carrie and I don't believe ghosts are scaring the patrons away. We believe someone created these incidents to sabotage the Manor." Before Ken could interrupt Charles continued, "You know, you and I almost met once before."

"We did," Ken mumbled.

Carrie could tell Ken was looking around the room for a way to escape.

"Carrie and I were eating in the pub last night. We overhead a conversation between two men discussing a project," Charles said. "What project were you discussing, Ken? How to create more disruptions at the Manor?"

Ken said nothing for several seconds. Then he said, "I don't know what you're talking about. I'm sorry to end this delightful conversation of fantasy. I see the Tobersons are here for the meeting. I need to join them."

Carrie watched Ken dash to the Toberson's table. Ken sat down and leaned over and said something to Bill Toberson. Then Doug who had finished his drink stopped by the Toberson's table. Doug didn't sit down but spent a few minutes chatting with them before leaving the restaurant.

"Don't say it! You think I shouldn't have confronted Ken and tipped our hand," Charles said.

"No, that's not what I think. I agree with you. It's time we stir things up." Before Carrie could add additional comments about Ken she said, "Ah, the last member of the family appears."

Charles turned to see Mrs. Barry enter the restaurant and head for their table. As she approached, Charles was about to stand, but she waved for him to remain seated.

"Good evening, you two. Are you waiting to order?" She asked as she looked around for a waiter.

"No, we've finished a most delicious dinner and are waiting for our dessert," Carrie said.

"I hope you've ordered the bread pudding. It's a house specialty and I must admit one of my favorites," she said.

"We did, based on the excellent recommendation from our most helpful waiter, Luke," Carrie said.

"Good, I'm glad you ordered the pudding and I'm glad you're receiving good service from Luke. He's one of our best."

Carrie could tell Mrs. Barry was pleased with the compliment about Luke.

"I couldn't help but notice Ken appeared upset when he left your table," Mrs. Barry said.

"I interviewed Ken this afternoon. He mentioned machinery sounds and ghostly voices causing some guests to check out," Carrie said.

"Tonight, when I tried to find out more information about these sounds, he panicked as if he told Carrie too much," Charles said.

"Now that's interesting. I've recently had reasons to doubt Ken's loyalty. We might need to have some further conversations with Ken," Mrs. Barry said. Then added, "remember when I mentioned we told certain people about your arrival to spread some gossip. Ken was in that group."

"Considering what you just said, why did you include Ken in the decision making about the direction of the construction?" Carrie said.

"Is that what he said?" Mrs. Barry asked.

Carrie nodded her head.

"We included him in tonight's meeting because we wanted his thoughts about the conferences we book and what type of facility they might like. But the Manor board, as always, will make the final decision."

"If you've time, we could share some things we've discovered including more things Ken said and a conversation we overheard."

"Yes, we need that discussion, but here's Albert. As Ken mentioned we have a meeting with the Tobersons to review the conference wing construction issues," Mrs. Barry said. "Tomorrow let's find some time to meet."

The couple's bread pudding arrived, and it was superb. They returned to their suite feeling satisfied with having enjoyed a wonderful meal and looking forward to a ghost-free restful sleep.

23

Carrie was half asleep when she heard a light tapping. At first, she thought she was about to have another paranormal experience. Except tonight there was a full moon, and it flooded the bedroom with light. And she wasn't experiencing the chill she felt the first time Roxie's apparition appeared. She looked at the clock and it was nearly 2:00 a.m. Then she heard the tapping again.

"What's that tapping sound?" Charles asked as he stirred in bed.

"I don't know. It woke me up, too," Carrie responded.

"I think someone's at the door," Charles said.

Before she could answer, Charles was up and out of bed, slipping into his shoes and grabbing his robe before heading for the door. Carrie put thoughts of ghosts out of her head and followed his lead. Before opening the door, Charles checked the peephole.

"Who is it?" Carrie whispered.

"Mrs. Barry."

"Mrs. Barry!" Carrie said slightly raising her voice.

When Charles opened the door, Carrie saw the very formidable Beatrice Barry standing before them in striped pajamas covered by a rather worn chenille bath robe. She was without makeup and her hair was in a braid on the side of her face. Carrie thought the only thing missing from this outfit was a candle in a holder.

"Mrs. Barry, is there a problem?" Charles asked.

"Charles, let Mrs. Barry in," Carrie said.

"I'm sorry. Come in." Charles said as he fully opened the door.

"I'm sorry to bother you both so early in the morning," she said. Mrs. Barry looked left and right to see if anyone else was in the hallway and slipped into their room.

"Please sit down," Carrie said.

"Thank you, no. I don't want to stay," she said remaining near the door. "I want you two to come with me. I want you to see the murder scene and the body before the police get here."

"Murder! What murder scene? Whose body? Mrs. Barry who's dead?" Carrie asked.

"Ken Harvey," she responded. "But we have to hurry. We can't wait much longer before we call the police."

"Ken Harvey is dead?" Carrie asked.

"We'll come right away," Charles said.

Carrie would have preferred to take a moment and throw on some street clothes, but pajamas, slippers and robes were the fashion statement of the moment. Before leaving the room, she grabbed the new small camera she purchased and handed the room key to Charles. They followed Mrs. Barry down the hallway to the elevators.

Instead of going down to the first floor, Mrs. Barry pushed the button for an upper floor. Then they took a different elevator down. This allowed them to enter the corporate offices from the back and kept the pajama-clad trio from walking through the main lobby. When they arrived at Ken Harvey's office, Ryan was standing a few feet from the door with his back to the room.

"I sent Lenny, our security guard, out to wait in the lobby for the police. Aunt Beatrice, I better make the call, or he'll wonder why it's taking so long for the police to arrive," Ryan said.

"I'll go with Ryan while he makes the phone call to the police. You two look around," Mrs. Barry said as she and Ryan walked down the hall towards the owners' den.

Charles started into the office, but Carrie held back. "I'll wait here," she said.

"I understand. Give me your camera," Charles said.

Carrie waited at the door as Charles entered the room. From where she was standing, she could see Ken Harvey leaning back in his office chair. His eyes were open and there was no missing the bullet hole located in the center of his forehead.

She watched as Charles snapped multiple pictures of the room from different angles including the furniture, the floor area, and the body. Carrie shuddered as Charles carefully lifted Ken's wrist and held it for a minute before carefully placing it back in the same position on the desk. Charles returned to Carrie.

"Were you checking to see if Ken was still alive?" Carrie asked.

"Not with that bullet hole in his head. I wanted to feel his body temperature. His body is still warm, and no rigor has started," Charles said. "I'm sure his murder was very recent."

Ryan and Mrs. Barry returned. "The police are on their way," Ryan said.

"Mrs. Barry, who discovered the body?" Charles asked.

"I did," Ryan said.

"Ryan, tell us as quickly as you can everything you saw. Your first observations are important, and we only have a few minutes before the police arrive," Charles said.

"I was working late on my computer. I've been using my spare time to develop the scheduling program I mentioned the morning of the liquor room break-in," Ryan said.

Carrie was sure Ryan mentioned he worked on the program in his spare time for his aunt's benefit.

"A little after midnight I realized I was getting both sleepy and hungry. I went to the pub for a sandwich before they closed."

"Was Ken working late too?" Carrie asked.

"No. I was the only one here when I left to get something to eat. I shut my computer down and turned my lights off thinking I might not come back."

"How long were you gone?" Carrie asked.

"Probably an hour. The pub was busy, and it took a while before they served my food. Between my food and several cups of coffee, I felt renewed and came back to work," Ryan said. "I'm close to having the program finished for tracking the employee schedules. Charles, I would like to show it to you and see what you think."

"Ryan, get back to the murder scene. You can tell Mr. Faraday about the program later," Mrs. Barry said.

"Not much more to tell, Aunt Beatrice. When I walked into the office area, I saw Ken's office lights were on. I went to Ken's door and said, 'What brings you back' when I... well... saw him in the chair."

Ryan stopped and Carrie thought he was trying to avoid thinking about finding Ken. "I know it's hard to think about, but you're doing fine," Carrie said.

"No, it's not that. I just remembered that the lights and the computer in my office were on when I called my aunt and told her what happened."

"That's interesting. It sounds like someone was searching for something in your office," Charles said.

"That's what I'm thinking. Anyway, Aunt Beatrice came down, took one look and told me to get security while she got you folks."

"Did you check your office out, while you were waiting for your aunt to get us?" Charles asked.

"No time. I went to the lobby and got Lenny, the security guard on duty. He verified Ken was dead and there was nothing we could do for him. He checked the office area to make sure no one else was around," Ryan said. "Then I told Lenny I would call the police and sent him back to the lobby to wait for them. He just left when all of you arrived."

Carrie heard the sirens approaching in the distance. She quickly asked, "Did you go to the pub by the lobby or the back hallway?"

"The back hallway. It's quicker."

"One last question. Going to or coming back from the pub did you see anyone around the office area that shouldn't have been here? Even a guest?" Charles asked.

"No one. I saw no one until I arrived at the pub," Ryan said. "Coming back the same thing. The hallway was empty."

The sounds of the sirens stopped, and Carrie knew the police reached the front door.

"Charles, we better go."

"Can you two find your way back to your rooms without me? I better stay with Ryan," Mrs. Barry said.

"Yes, we'll be fine. Ryan, I'll touch base with you later. Once I've digested the scene, I may have more questions," Charles said. "Also, I want to see your computer program,"

"Charles, we need to go," Carrie said as she took his hand.

They quickly departed using the back hallway and were almost back to their room, when Carrie said, "Look, look there at the end of the hallway."

"What, what's the matter?" Charles asked.

But Carrie was off running towards the end of the hallway. When she reached the corner, she stopped. Within a few seconds, Charles was by her side.

"What did you see?"

"I'm sure I saw a woman walking down the hallway. But no one is here," Carrie said looking the length of the hallway. "Did you see her?"

"I didn't, but maybe she went into a room."

"No, Charles, no doors opened or closed. Charles, it was the same lady I saw in our room the other night. I saw Roxie for a second time."

Carrie felt Charles put his arm around her. "You know I would like to meet this lady, but for now let's get to our room and discuss the murder."

24

Once the couple was back in their suite Carrie asked, "Should I make some coffee?"

"As much as I would like a cup of coffee, it's probably not a good idea. That is if we have any hopes of getting any additional sleep," Charles said. "Although I want something to drink, my throat is dry. Maybe some ice water." Charles looked at Carrie, "and yes, I'll get you a glass too."

Charles returned to the living room with two glasses of iced cold water and his leather notebook. "Before we turn in, I want to do two more things. Let's look at the photos I took of the murder scene and I want to get our first observations and Ryan's initial thoughts written down."

"Where do you want to start? Photos or observations?" Carrie asked.

"Let's do observations first so we're not influenced by anything we see in the photos. You start," Charles said.

"Looks like Ken was sitting at his desk when someone shot him."

"This is important because..." Charles prodded.

"Either Ken didn't have time to react or more likely he knew the person who entered his office and had no fear of the person who ultimately killed him."

"Exactly," Charles said. "He knew his murderer."

"Jumping ahead, I'm not sure Ken was the one who turned on Ryan's lights and computer," Carrie said.

"I agree. There are two possibilities. Ken and his killer arrived together. Ken went to his office while the killer was in Ryan's office searching for something."

"And the second possibility?" Carrie asked.

"Ken came to the office to meet someone. This person arrives. Kills Ken and then goes to Ryan's office to look for something," Charles said. "Anything else?" Charles asked as he took a long drink of water.

"The second possibility makes more sense." She paused. "Wait, a minute. Since Ryan's lights and computer were on, I think our killer didn't leave."

"Right. If he left before Ryan returned, he would have turned off the computer and turned out the lights," Charles said. "He probably heard Ryan returning from the pub and hid somewhere in the office area."

"Then the logical scenario is the shooter leaves by the back hall when Ryan went to the lobby to find Lenny. You know Ryan and Mrs. Barry are lucky they didn't run into the killer."

"You're right. Someone who just killed is unpredictable." Charles finished making a note and put his pen down on the table. "Fortunately for them, the shooter leaves and probably slips into the pub and blends in with the crowd or leaves from that side of the Manor with no one the wiser of what he did."

Charles watched as Carrie leaned her head back on the sofa and stretched her legs out on the coffee table.

"You look tired. Do you want to go to bed?" Charles asked.

"Not yet. We need to finish while the scene is fresh in our minds."

Charles sat next to Carrie on the sofa and displayed the photos on her digital camera. He quickly scanned through the photos of Ken, but Carrie stopped him.

"I appreciate you not wanting to linger on the shots of Ken's body, knowing I'm on the squeamish side. However, we need to look at these pictures to see what they reveal," Carrie said.

"You're right. I'll start again so we can look at every shot."

After viewing a few more shots Carrie said, "Look, Ken has a pen in his hand. He wouldn't be writing if a stranger walked in. He would have stood to confront the person."

"This photo proves Ken knew his killer," Charles said.

"It shows more than that," Carrie said. "Even with someone he knew Ken had no time to react to what was about to happen. Whoever it was, walked in and shot him."

"The question is why whoever he was working with felt this was the time to eliminate him." Charles continued clicking slowly through the rest of the photos.

"Wait, stop there," Carrie said. "Do you have more shots of Ken's credenza?"

"A couple more," Charles responded as he displayed additional shots. "What are you looking for?"

"When I was in his office, Ken had several layers of maps on his credenza," Carrie said.

"Maps like blueprints of the construction. Maybe he was studying them for his meeting last night with the Tobersons and the family."

"No, they weren't blueprints. More like area maps."

"There are no maps in the shots I took. The credenza is clear," Charles said. "He talked about off roading in his jeep. Maybe he was planning his next weekend get-away and then put the maps away."

"Maybe, but these maps, at least from where I was sitting, looked old," Carrie said. "I guess he could have straightened his office."

"Well, I don't think it would hurt to ask the family if there are old maps of the Manor available," Charles added. "We've done enough for one night or I should say one morning."

"There's one thing the murder has made clear to me."

"What's that?" Charles asked.

"When we started this case, I thought we would discover a disgruntled employee. In the meantime, I would help the folks here develop a new brochure, and we would enjoy a much-needed vacation."

"And now..."

"We need to help this family. They're nice people who need our expertise since we're good at solving murders."

Charles took their water glasses to the kitchen. When he returned to the living room, Carrie had stretched out on the sofa and was sound asleep. He didn't wake her but grabbed a blanket from the bedroom and gently tucked her in for the night.

25

arrie and Charles slept late. After a room service breakfast of bagels and coffee, they were discussing how they
should proceed.

"It would be nice if we could find out more about Ken," Carrie said.

"The police will do a thorough search of his residence, his family and his friends," Charles said. "Although we might learn from the cousins some additional information about him."

"Good, because we know the police aren't likely to share what they find with the family and they certainly won't talk to two amateur detectives," Carrie said. "We need to work on other things, while the police concentrate on Ken."

"What did you have in mind, my fellow sleuth?"

"When I was interviewing Ken, he mentioned Bernie. And the bartender said everyone thinks it's Bernie causing problems in the bar," Carrie said. "Maybe it's time we learn more about Bernie Millford."

"Good idea. I'll call Mrs. Barry. Hopefully, she can update me on the police investigation and share some family history while I tell her what we've learned. Do you want to come?" Charles asked.

"No, I'll stay here and review the information and the interviews I've gathered so far. Maybe there's a clue we've missed."

Carrie went to the table and started to spread out her materials as Charles dialed Mrs. Barry's number.

"Mrs. Barry, this is Charles Faraday. How are you doing this morning?"

"We're managing. The police finally left. They sealed off Ken's office, but they're allowing us to continue to operate in the rest of the office area," Mrs. Barry said. "It's difficult for folks to focus on the daily operations. Ryan moved his accounting team to a suite upstairs to get them away from the area and we're being liberal about people working from home."

"After all that's happened maybe I shouldn't ask, but I was hoping you might have few minutes to meet with me. There are things we should discuss."

"I'm so glad you called Mr. Faraday. I have time. You're right, I would like to share information and see what we know. Hold on a moment," she said.

Charles could tell Mrs. Barry placed her hand over the phone and spoke to someone. There was a moment's pause as if she was waiting for the person to leave.

Then Mrs. Barry said, "I can meet you now but not here in the corporate offices. Let's meet in the lobby near the large fireplace. It's usually quiet at this time of day," she said.

"Perfect, I'm on my way," Charles responded.

* * *

After Charles left their suite, Carrie downloaded all the photos from her camera onto her computer so she could view a larger image of her shots. She also included the photos from the murder scene. At some point they might be needed although she was sure the police captured the same shots.

While she was working, her mind was thinking of what other options they could explore to help solve the Manor's problems. Problems. It was more than a problem. It was murder!

Charles was hoping to gather more information about Bernie and the proposed construction from Mrs. Barry. What could she do? Maybe she should take Albert's suggestion and talk with Millicent. According to Albert, Millicent was doing a marvelous job researching the history of the Manor.

Carrie's knowledge about the Manor came from information gathered from family members and workers. It would be good to see if the factual historical data supported what the family said. She was about to give Millicent a call when the phone rang.

"Hello Carrie?" The voice on the line asked.

"Yes, this is Carrie."

"Hi, this Roxanne Kent."

"Oh, Mrs. Kent. How nice to hear from you."

"Millicent and I are meeting for afternoon tea and we thought perhaps you would like to join us."

"I would love to, Mrs. Kent," Carrie responded.

"There's one requirement for joining us. Stop calling me Mrs. Kent. When I was a little girl, my parents called me Roxie. As an adult and published author, I prefer Roxanne."

Carrie muffled a gasp with her hand. Then said, "Okay, err... Roxanne."

Her mind was racing as she heard the nickname Roxie. Carrie was having trouble believing it was just a coincidence that Mrs. Kent's first name was the same as Bernie's girlfriend.

"Good, we'll see you in a few minutes for tea," Roxanne said.

Carrie checked her appearance, grabbed the key card, and took the elevator to meet her fellow writers. Before the elevator reached the lobby, it stopped at the second floor. When the door opened, Carrie was face to face with Roxanne.

"Oh, hello Mrs. Kent... I mean Roxanne. What brings you to the second floor?" Carrie blurted the words out before she realized. "I'm sorry, I mean... that was a dumb question. It's just I didn't expect to see you in the main building on the second floor."

"I understand," she said laughing. "Just between you and me, there are days when I don't feel like wandering the grounds for inspiration. I come inside and walk around the floors," she said as she joined Carrie on the elevator. "Don't tell management but sometimes I sit near the conference rooms. I listen to what participants are saying and make notes about their conversations, record the phrases they use and also their physical characteristics."

"What a great idea. Do these notes help your writing process?" Carrie asked.

"Absolutely. When I'm developing my characters and creating dialogue for my book, I find my observations helpful," Roxanne said.

"That's fascinating." Carrie said out loud, but in her mind, she was wondering if there was another explanation. Many of the reports about paranormal activity occurred on the second floor and she knew Roxanne mentioned her digital recorder.

"Have you ever heard unexplained voices or seen an apparition while on this floor?" Carrie asked. She was hoping the direct question would get an honest answer.

"Ah, I see you've heard all the rumors about ghostly activity. Unfortunately, I've had no experiences, but I wouldn't mind if I did. I've thought for some time about including a little paranormal activity in one of my plots."

"Speaking of plots, I'm a fan of your mysteries. They take place in a small village. Was the village of Millford the inspiration for your stories?" Carrie asked.

"Actually, the village in my fiction is a compilation of various places I've visited. Although Millford is one of my favorite spots. I love it and I continue to return here for inspiration," Roxanne said.

Carrie didn't have time to ask Roxanne more questions. They reached the lobby and made their way over to the tearoom. As with the first time Carrie enjoyed afternoon tea, there was quite a crowd. They stood at the door for a moment looking for Millicent.

"There she is," said Roxanne. "And it looks like it will be more than just us ladies."

Carrie spotted the table with Millicent, and she saw what Roxanne meant. Albert was sitting with her. Carrie gave them a wave as they approached the table.

"Hello ladies. I hope you don't mind that I stopped by. I know you want to talk about writing, so I'll only stay a moment," Albert said.

Roxanne took the chair next to Millicent while Albert held the chair next to him for Carrie and kept his seat next to Millicent.

Albert raised his hand to call their server to the table. She took their tea orders and then Albert made a request.

"Since the ladies are here for a meeting, Marcy, would you mind bringing them a nice assortment of sandwiches and sweets? That way the ladies won't lose time in the line."

"I'll be happy to do that, Mr. Albert," Marcy replied.

Millicent turned to Carrie. "Albert was telling me about the new marketing brochure you're writing for the Manor. Roxanne heard you were working on a mystery book. I'm sure I've seen your name attached to photos and articles in several magazines. Do you have multiple identities?"

"Guilty as charged. All the above," Carrie said laughing. "Before marrying Charles, I was a professional photojournalist. After our marriage, I didn't want all the travel associated with photo shoots. I concentrated on marketing pieces for businesses or articles for magazines."

"And the mystery book?" asked Roxanne.

"The mystery book is a special project. But who knows? Maybe someday I'll finish it?" Carrie said.

"The family is very excited about the new brochure Carrie is developing," Albert added.

Carrie was glad that Albert was maintaining her cover with the ladies.

"Based on my research of the Manor the current brochure doesn't do justice to its rich history. I would be happy to discuss my findings with you," Millicent said.

"And I would love to discuss your progress on your mystery," Roxanne said.

The server returned with their tea selections and two abundantly filled plates of sandwiches and pastries.

"Thank you, Marcy, nicely done," Albert said. Marcy smiled at Albert's compliment and moved away.

"Well ladies, I'll leave you to your writing discussions. Enjoy your tea." Albert nodded to Carrie and Roxanne and smiled generously at Millicent as he left the table.

Carrie could see why Albert found Millicent attractive. She had beautiful fair skin enhanced by intense dark eyes that could hold you in their gaze. The only thing Carrie didn't like was her bright blonde hair. It was a little too bottled for her.

Roxanne waited until Albert was out of range to hear her comment. "I believe Albert is interested in you, Millicent."

"Albert? No. Don't be silly. I'm only a couple years older than his son, Ryan. We enjoy discussing Manor history together. That's all," Millicent said.

Carrie wondered if it was possible Millicent was missing all the signals Albert was sending.

"All right, if you say so." Roxanne turned to Carrie and winked. "Tell us about your mystery book, Carrie."

"My book is nearing completion. I've the plot, the murder, the victim, and the conflicts. I wrote the rough draft straight through without stopping to edit. Now I need to do major editing and fill in any gaps in the story," Carrie said.

"I use the same method. I like to get the story down as I do my research. Otherwise, I could spend all my time on research and never complete a piece," Millicent said.

"It's a mistake to keep rewriting the same sections over and over until it's perfect," Roxanne said. "I've learned the hard way that what I thought was a perfect piece gets chopped by the editor. Now I'm learning to let the plot and the characters take over and I'm producing much more."

Carrie wondered if she had discovered the cause of Roxanne's writer's block. Maybe trying to write the perfect piece kept her from finishing her latest book on schedule.

"Speaking of mysteries, I ran into Albert earlier and he was telling me about the suicide of the event manager, Ken Harvey," Roxanne said.

"Suicide!" Carrie couldn't hide her shock.

"That's what everyone is saying, or did you hear something else?" Roxanne asked.

Carrie quickly recovered and said, "Charles ran into Mrs. Barry earlier. She led him to believe the circumstances of Ken's death were unclear and still being investigated."

She didn't want to reveal to the ladies that Charles ran into Mrs. Barry when she took them to the scene of the murder.

"I don't buy the suicide theory. Ken was showing me around the town yesterday before dropping me off at the Millford Historical Society," Millicent said. "He told me he was taking his jeep for a run before his afternoon appointment. He loved driving his new jeep. That doesn't sound like a man on the verge of suicide."

"Does that mean we're talking about murder?" Roxanne asked.

"Sounds like it's a real possibility," Millicent said. "I bet the family wants to limit the gossip and not alarm the guests. Perhaps that's why they're telling everyone Ken took his own life."

"Millicent, maybe you and I should think about moving up to the main building."

"Oh, that's unnecessary. Since Ken's death occurred in his office, it sounds like he was the specific target," Millicent said. "But if you're worried, I'm sure Albert would give you a room in the main building. The Manor isn't fully booked."

"I might call him and see if he can do that. I don't like being isolated in the cottages. There isn't anyone around if we needed help."

Carrie listened but said nothing. Roxanne reacted the way most people would. She was concerned about her own safety with a murderer on the property. Millicent, on the other hand, seemed calm about what happened, and she knew there were rooms available in the main building.

Mostly for Roxanne's peace of mind, Carrie changed the subject. They spent the rest of the time discussing their current writing projects, agents, and publishing. Carrie was thoroughly enjoying the conversation. She was also enjoying a miniature version of the cheese pastry Mrs. Barry ordered when they first met her. It was delicious.

"Well ladies, this has been most enjoyable but if you'll excuse me—back to my desk I go. I need to finish editing the pages I wrote this morning," Roxanne said. "And I need to think about calling Albert to change my room. Millicent, if I move, you should think about doing the same. You would be alone in the cottage area."

"That's what I love about the cottages. A great place to work and to be honest I don't think we're in any danger."

Carrie waited until Roxanne left the room and then asked, "Millicent, I hope you can stay a few more minutes. I wanted to talk with you about the Manor's history."

26

"We'll need more than a few minutes to discuss the history of this place, but we can start the discussion. Do you have questions about a particular area of your research?"

"In a marketing brochure space is limited. As a result, I'm concentrating on two things. A short summary of events that helped the Manor develop from a roadhouse to this incredible resort. Second, I want to highlight any facts that make the Manor more interesting to potential guests. Maybe even add a romantic element or spirit sightings for a little intrigue."

"Ah, the paranormal rears its ugly head. Albert mentioned there have been some recent incidents that folks want to blame on the paranormal," Millicent said sounding annoyed. "I hope you're not sensationalizing these stories."

"No, I'm not. But for some people a friendly ghost being spotted is an added attraction for booking a stay." Carrie wanted to hear more of Millicent insights into recent events, so she added,

"If the ghostly activity turns negative and becomes destructive, then that's a whole different ballgame. Especially if it turns out not to be paranormal, but humans creating the mischief."

"Do you think someone is behind what's happening?" Millicent asked. "I mean especially with Ken's murder."

Carrie noticed Millicent readily accepted Ken's death as murder. Maybe Albert told her the truth. She also seemed interested that a human was causing the current problems.

"I've nothing pointing to any individual, but I found it unusual that after all these years and many previous sightings of friendly ghosts the activity suddenly turned negative," Carrie said.

"I agree, but the question is why."

"When we find the answer to that question, we'll have solved the problem. In the meantime, what are your thoughts about what I should include in the brochure?" Carrie asked.

"Let me offer two comments. The historical information in the original brochure, while a little dry, is accurate," Millicent said. "I'm sure with your marketing background you can —how do they say, 'punch it up.' And when you're ready, I would be happy to read a draft of your copy."

"It's good to know I can use the information," Carrie said. "Is there anything you've discovered in your research you feel is missing from the history?"

"Yes, they've left Bernie Millford out," Millicent said. "He was the manager during the biggest development period for the Manor."

"Really, I didn't know," Carrie said to Millicent, but she was thinking, yet another reference to Bernie.

"You pointed out the transition the Manor made from the roadhouse years. It was Bernie's vision to develop the Manor as a destination resort long before the concept was popular," Millicent said.

"Do you think he's overlooked because of his connections with the mob? Or perhaps it's the mystery surrounding his girlfriend's murder and his disappearance."

"You've done your research," Millicent said intensely staring at Carrie.

Carrie wasn't sure if Millicent's comment was a compliment or held some hidden meaning. Millicent seemed tense when she mentioned Bernie. "I can't say what I've learned about Bernie is based on pure research. More like a story the bartender told us," Carrie said and laughed to lighten the mood.

Millicent also laughed, and it broke the tension. "I bet it was Paul, the pub's bartender. He seems to relish in telling stories about Bernie's ghost. Did he also tell you about the glasses that rattle?"

"He did," Carrie said not wanting to share her personal experience.

"Here's the actual story. My research shows when Bernie took over management of the Manor from his father, he severed all ties with his mob connections," Millicent said. "This was his chance for a fresh start. He worked hard and developed a plan to help the Manor grow."

"You're right, no one mentioned this part of the story," Carrie said.

"He modernized the guest rooms and added bathrooms. He built the first ballroom and brought in entertainment on the weekends which attracted both locals and out-of-town guests. These changes helped the Manor expand from a roadhouse to a true hotel."

No wonder Albert enjoyed talking with Millicent. She was as passionate about the Manor's history as he was. "And Bernie's girlfriend, Roxie?" Carrie asked.

"Roxie was a singer and showed up one weekend with a band hired to entertain. When the band left Roxie stayed and helped Bernie manage the place. By all accounts they were very much in love. Her murder occurred the weekend before they were to marry."

"Paul also told us the police found out there was a lover's fight over a bellhop. Because of this incident, Bernie shot Roxie and his only choice was to run," Carrie said.

"That story is pure fiction. Bernie didn't murder Roxie!" Millicent's strong defense of Bernie struck Carrie as passionate. Then Millicent quickly recovered.

"I mean my research produced nothing that would show Bernie was the killer. I believe whoever killed Roxie, killed Bernie. It's just that the authorities never found his body," Millicent said. "With his disappearance the ownership of the hotel changed forever."

"Why was that?" Carrie asked. She remembered that Maddy and Marge mentioned Bernie's disappearance caused the management of the Manor to shift to their side of the family, but she wanted more details.

"Before his disappearance Bernie made his cousin, Edward, a full partner. When Bernie disappeared, Edward continued the day-to-day management waiting for Bernie to return which never happened," Millicent said.

"Did Bernie have any other family?" Carrie asked.

"He had a sister, but I'm still researching that part. I'll let you know what I find," Millicent said. "The important thing was that Edward followed Bernie's plans for making the Manor a premier resort."

"That's good information. I'll include Bernie and his contributions in my piece," Carrie said.

"Glad to help."

Carrie thought Millicent seemed pleased that she would include information about Bernie in the updated marketing piece. But why was Bernie important to her?

"I have one more question. It's not about the history but the current situation. I know your research takes you all around the Manor," Carrie said. "Have you seen anything suspicious or unusual that could explain all these incidents, including all the Bernie stories?"

"I can't help but ask the reason for your question. How does this relate to the new brochure?"

Carrie thought fast and then responded, "perhaps the reason the family decided they need a new brochure after all these years is because of the business I hear they're losing. I really like the family and the wonderful hotel they've built following Bernie's inspiration. I would hate to see them in financial distress."

Carrie waited while Millicent weighed her response.

"I see what you mean, and I've noticed a few things which raised questions in my mind," Millicent said. "Albert told me the family was thinking about making a change in the placement of the new conference wing. I question why a small construction firm like Toberson would be suggesting major changes to the plans this late in the game. The delay hurts the Millford family financially and keeps his men from working."

"That is an interesting observation. What else?" Carrie asked.

"This is probably nothing, but I constantly see Larkin liquor trucks on the premises and on the roads surrounding the property. If business is down why would the Manor be buying so much liquor?"

"That's another good question." Carrie was thinking that Doug was a perfect candidate for the liquor room break in.

"And last, but certainly not least, I'm fascinated that Bernie's ghost seems to be the focus of so much of the activity," Millicent took the last sip of her tea, and then said, "Well, I've got to go. I always try to get two hours of writing in before dinner."

Carrie sat for a moment as she watched Millicent leave the room. She and Charles thought the same thing as Millicent concerning Doug and the Tobersons. She thought again of Millicent's enthusiasm for defending the long-lost Millford relative. But Carrie also knew a good historian is passionate about her research and verifying the accuracy of her information.

Then she remembered there was something else she wanted to ask Millicent. She wanted to know if Millicent previously met Charles. Oh well, she would do her own research to find out more about Millicent Ford.

27

When Charles arrived in the lobby he saw Mrs. Barry entering from the office area. She wore a navy-blue dress with her hair perfectly styled. A stark contrast from the woman he and Carrie accompanied to the murder scene the previous night. As Charles headed towards her, he spotted Joseph, the concierge, also moving towards Mrs. Barry. Charles reached her first.

"Mrs. Barry, could you spare me a moment?" Charles asked as he nodded slightly towards the approaching Joseph. Mrs. Barry picked up on his hint.

"Mr. Faraday, are you and your wife enjoying your stay? I hope Mrs. Faraday isn't spending all her time working on our new brochure."

"Carrie is working hard, but she's also taking time to enjoy the Manor," Charles said. "Staying here is such a treat for us, it gave me an idea. I'd like to do an article in the Tri-County Monthly magazine about the Manor." Charles said this last statement loud enough to be sure Joseph heard it. "I was hoping you could take a moment to discuss some ideas with me."

"Perfect timing. I've a few minutes available. I'd love having an article in your publication," she said. "It's such a great magazine. Shall we sit by the fire?"

Joseph arrived. "Mrs. Barry, please excuse the interruption but one of our guests is asking if the movie being shown tonight is only for the participants attending the in-house conference or can anyone attend?"

"The conference leader reserved fifty seats for the first showing, but the rest of the theatre is available for guests," she said. "And the second show is open with no seats reserved. Why don't you get a stack of tickets from the theatre for both shows and keep them at your desk for anyone who asks?"

"Are we charging a fee for people not staying at the Manor who want to attend the show?"

"No Joseph, at this time the movie is available to anyone who wants to come at no charge," Mrs. Barry said.

Charles thought this was another smart move from management to attract outsiders to the Manor during a time when sales were down. Once Charles was sure Joseph was out of hearing range, he said, "As mentioned last night, I wanted to update you on our progress and ask some additional questions."

"Are you making any progress considering we are now dealing with a murder?"

"The problems here at the Manor are like our previous cases. It's a large jigsaw puzzle. We gather many pieces that seem unrelated and then gradually the pieces fit together."

"I take it you're still in the gathering stage since you've questions for me."

"Yes, I need to ask you about Bernie Millford."

"Bernie Millford?" Charles realized Mrs. Barry was not expecting this question, but she quickly regained her composure and said, "What do you want to know?"

"Tell me about Bernie Millford's disappearance."

"I hope this doesn't mean you're pursuing a paranormal line of inquiry," she said.

Charles thought quickly of how to best justify his question. "No, we don't believe what's happening here is paranormal," Charles said. "But many of the supposed sightings relate to either Bernie or his girlfriend Roxie."

"I hadn't thought about that, but you're right. Everyone's blaming Bernie and Roxie for the activity," Mrs. Barry said. "Over the years when we heard about a certain description of an apparition, we thought it sounded like Roxie. But the sightings lasted only for a few seconds and were harmless."

Charles decided not to mention Carrie's experience with Roxie, because to be honest he couldn't explain what she saw. Instead he said, "I think it shows the people behind these activities know about Bernie and Roxie," he said. "The question is why are they being resurrected now? I thought if I learned more about them it might provide some information about the culprits."

"Dear Bernie. What would you like to know?" Mrs. Barry asked.

"Anything about the events before and after his disappearance, including Roxie's death," Charles said.

"I'm afraid there are more innuendos and rumors than facts surrounding them," Mrs. Barry said and then paused for a moment to gather her thoughts. "I guess any conversation I have about Bernie would start with this statement. If it wasn't for the disappearance of Bernie, my family wouldn't be running the Manor."

"I don't understand. Hasn't the Millford family always owned the Manor?"

"Yes, but not my side of the family. Bernie was my father's cousin. Had Bernie married Roxie and had children, the Manor would have continued to be managed by their family," she sighed.

Charles realized this was a difficult topic for her. Perhaps a break would help.

"How about a cup of coffee?" Charles asked noticing the staff replenished the coffee bar near them.

"That would be nice. Just a little cream, please," she said. Charles returned with the coffee and noticed after a few sips Mrs. Barry relaxed.

"My father, Edward, was much younger than Bernie," Mrs. Barry said. "Bernie took my father under his wing and was teaching him how to manage the hotel. Then suddenly my father was in charge." She stopped and took another long sip of coffee.

"At first, it was difficult for my parents. Under different circumstances they might have sold the hotel."

"Why didn't they?" Charles asked.

"Because Bernie didn't die. He disappeared. My father was the caretaker for the property, not the owner. Fortunately, Bernie prepared paperwork giving my father the necessary signing authority for all business transactions in case he was not available." Mrs. Barry ran her hands over her lap smoothing non-existent wrinkles from her dress.

"That's a tough situation," Charles said.

"Yes, especially for our mother. Lizzie was a baby and Albert and I were toddlers, but my father needed my mother's help to keep the place running. They always felt guilty about not spending more time with us."

"Did you feel neglected as children?" Charles asked. His question was designed to keep Mrs. Barry talking and providing more details about the Manor even if not related to the current murder.

"Hardly. It was the complete opposite. Albert and I thought the Manor was one huge playhouse. We knew every nook and corner of this place and played all kinds of games," Mrs. Barry said smiling as she remembered her past. "We discovered locations my parents didn't even know existed. Growing up here was great fun."

"The challenge must have suited your parents. Based on what I've read it was under their management that the Manor went from a roadhouse to the beautiful hotel it is today."

"They worked hard with many long days carrying out the plans that Bernie created for expansion. Eventually, they began to not only embrace but enjoy the work they were doing," Mrs. Barry said. "After seven years, the courts declared Bernie was dead. His will left the Manor to Roxie and my father as equal partners with a provision for Bernie's sister. Roxie was no longer in the picture, so my parents were now the legal owners."

"Did your parents ever hear from Bernie or discover any information about his disappearance? I'm assuming there were lots of news stories, especially since you were dealing with the murder of Roxie."

"As children, we were unaware of the news and tabloid stories. It really wasn't until my parents retired from active management, they discussed more details about Bernie and Roxie with the three of us."

"Why discuss it at all?" Charles asked.

"They wanted us to know the past in case someone made any future claims."

"A claim. Really? It concerned them someone might come forward?" Charles asked.

Before Mrs. Barry could answer, Joseph was back. Besides packets of tickets he was carrying a small tray.

"On my way back from the theatre, I stopped by the kitchen," Joseph said. "When I mentioned you were sitting in the lobby with Mr. Faraday, Benson sent some pastries for you to enjoy."

"That's nice. Thank you, Joseph," Mrs. Barry said taking the tray from Joseph as he returned to his desk.

Both Charles and Mrs. Barry took a cheese Danish from the tray. After his first bite, Charles thought the pastry was the best he ever tasted. No wonder they were a favorite of the owner.

"Let me think, where was I? Oh, yes, when Bernie lived in Tri-City he worked for a local mobster, Joey Molanaro. Joey owned a nightclub which was a front for his bootlegging operation."

"Wasn't this after prohibition?"

"Yes, but that doesn't mean the bootlegging stopped. The mobsters made their own liquor at a lower cost, sold it at high prices and avoided taxes," Mrs. Barry said. "Joey required bars and clubs in his territory to buy their liquor through his syndicate, so he locked up the market."

"How did Bernie get out from under Joey?"

"Bernie's family always owned the Manor from the time it was a roadhouse and offered rooms to travelers on their way to Tri-City.

When his father died, it passed to him. Bernie saw the Manor as his opportunity to go straight," Mrs. Barry said. "He upgraded the Manor and booked entertainment on the weekends. The Manor was doing well and for the first time became a destination spot for the Tri-City elite."

"It sounds like he was doing a good job. How was Roxie involved?" Charles asked.

"While Bernie was working for Joey at his club, he met Roxie Fenton. She was a singer and unfortunately Joey's girlfriend."

"Let me guess. There was a confrontation between Joey and Bernie over Roxie."

"It was more than Bernie stealing his girl. Joey wanted a piece of the Manor," Mrs. Barry said. "He sought to extend his boot-legging territory. He thought the Manor should be his northern headquarters. Bernie refused. They fought and Joey supposedly went back to Tri-City."

"Do you think Bernie killed Roxie?" Charles asked.

"No, I don't. I believe Joey killed Roxie and Bernie. He disposed of Bernie's body to create the impression Bernie was the killer."

A couple walked over and sat near them. Mrs. Barry stood, greeted them, and asked them if they were enjoying their stay. She mentioned there was fresh coffee available on the table behind them, and placed the pastry tray near the coffee. Then she turned back to Charles and said, "Mr. Faraday, I've those historical records you wanted to see in my office. If you don't mind coming with me, I'll be happy to get them for you."

Charles was sure the comment about the records in the office was to avoid offending the guests with their abrupt departure. Mrs. Barry nodded and smiled at the guests as they left the sitting area.

28

Unlike the first time he and Carrie walked through these offices Charles noticed today they were eerily quiet. There was no sign of Albert or any other workers. Charles saw police tape stretched across the closed door of Ken's office.

Once they were in the 'owners' den,' Mrs. Barry went to a bookshelf in the corner. Even though she was tall, she used a small wooden step stool to reach the top shelf. She carefully lifted an album from the shelf and carried it to the conference table.

"We'll be more comfortable if we sit at the table while we look at this. I found this family scrapbook after my parents passed."

She handed the album to Charles, and he carefully opened it.

"You can skip those first couple of pages and read them later. They're the newspaper announcements of the Manor's grand reopening after my parents officially took over," Mrs. Barry said.

Charles turned those pages and started looking at photos and additional news clippings surrounding the murder of Roxie and Bernie's disappearance. As he read, Mrs. Barry went to the fireplace and poked at the wood that was slowly burning. The faint smell of smoke drifted across to where Charles sat.

"With all this adverse publicity, trying to keep the business operating couldn't have been easy for your parents," Charles said.

"It wasn't, but there were other challenges. As I mentioned, mother and father continued running the place for seven years, without knowing what their future would be," Mrs. Barry said.

After several more pages, Charles stopped at a single shot of a very handsome man who looked like a combination of Ryan and Tom. There was a definite family resemblance. Charles then saw a photo of the same man and a woman.

"I assume this is Bernie. Is this Roxie with him?" Charles asked pointing to the photo.

"That's Bernie and his sister Barbara. You can't tell from the black and white photo, but they both have the red hair that runs in the family. Roxie was a blonde."

"You mentioned Bernie had a sister. Why didn't the Manor pass to her?" Charles asked.

"It could have. But his sister fell in love with a soldier. They assigned her husband to a military base out west," Mrs. Barry said. "Then she had a daughter and was concentrating on raising her and supporting her husband's career. Bernie knew they wouldn't be interested in running the business. That's why he left the Manor to Dad and Roxie."

"You mentioned there was a stipulation in his will, that his sister receive a portion of the profits annually. Was she given a set amount?"

"No, the will left the dollar amount up to my parents based on how the business was doing. But I assure you my parents were always generous with what they paid," Mrs. Barry said.

"Did your family keep in touch with Barbara?"

"An occasional letter or a Christmas card with a brief note."

"Did you ever meet her or her daughter?" Charles asked.

"When her husband left the military, he took a job with a company in London. They educated their daughter over there and remained in Europe." Mrs. Barry said. "We never traveled overseas and to my knowledge they never returned to the states."

She returned to the table and sat next to Charles. "Then we received a letter from her husband informing us Barbara passed away. That was the only letter we received from him. Barbara's will bequeathed all future payments from the Manor to her daughter. Then her daughter had a daughter. We continue to send them to Barbara's granddaughter through a bank account in New York."

Charles stared at the woman who was Bernie's sister. Charles thought this woman also looked like someone from Mrs. Barry's side of the family. Perhaps it was Maddy or Marge. He flipped the page and saw a professional shot of a blonde woman. At the bottom of the picture typed in blocks letters was Roxie Fenton.

"So, this is Roxie." Charles said looking at the woman who was staring at the camera with gentle eyes. "She's beautiful."

"Yes, she is. I've often thought about her and Bernie. The Manor might have been a different place if they were in charge," Mrs. Barry said. "I believe they would have relied more on entertainment like those resorts in upstate New York. And who knows if it would have survived beyond the sixties?"

"Personally, Carrie and I are glad your family is in charge. Even though we're here on a special assignment, we've put the Manor on our top list of vacation sites. I assure you we'll be back many times when all this is over."

"I hope the Manor will continue to be here for you," Mrs. Barry said.

Charles for the first time heard a sense of exasperation in Mrs. Barry's voice. He knew the various incidents and especially Ken Harvey's murder were taking a toll on her. Murder was well beyond the pranks they previously experienced.

"Don't worry. Carrie and I will figure this out. The Manor will continue to be the best resort in the region," Charles assured her.

"I hope so."

"Before we end our meeting, I wanted to share something else with you. When Carrie interviewed Ken, he made a point to mention Bernie as the apparition everyone was seeing," Charles said. "It seems to us he was helping to focus people's attention on Bernie and the history from the past. That's another reason I wanted to know more about Bernie."

"Did he now! You know, I'm deeply sorry about Ken's... death." Charles noticed Mrs. Barry avoided the word murder.

Then she added, "I can't help but wonder if Ken was involved in some of the other incidents we've experienced."

"We don't have an answer for that yet, but it seems likely. Had Ken been with you long?" Charles asked.

"Almost six years. He came to us from a smaller conference center up north with high recommendations," Mrs. Barry said. She placed her hands together as if she were trying to remember his credentials. "We had no reason to question his work or his loyalty until recently."

"And what made you change your mind?"

"I noticed he seemed almost pleased when he reported declining sales numbers or when he discovered people were checking out," she said. "Then he became overly concerned about the location of the conference center. He's the one who first suggested we change the direction of the new building."

"Carrie and I found it interesting that you included Ken in the construction meeting, until you explained."

"Most people assume that the family decides everything in a vacuum. But on bigger projects we include staff members to get their expertise. Ken knew how a conference center should operate and what made participants happy with a location. We valued his knowledge and input."

"Aside from the proposed construction changes, Ken also shared with Carrie stories about guests who checked out because of noises they heard," Charles said. "I wanted to ask a few questions about those stories."

"Ask away," Mrs. Barry said.

Charles thought Mrs. Barry seemed more relaxed now that the conversation shifted away from members of her family to Ken.

"Ken said there was an incident where guests awoke in the middle of the night to the sounds of machinery running. They also heard muffled voices."

"I remember the incident. It was the first event where we lost guests and really the start of the problems," she said. "Three couples reported being disturbed. We offered everyone upgraded rooms in another location on the property, along with extras like dinner in the Williamsburg Room. Two couples accepted our offer, but the third couple checked out."

"Was that the only time the noises were reported in those rooms?"

"Yes, but there's another reason for no additional reports. Because we're not fully booked, we've not used those rooms. They're located the furthest from all of our amenities," Mrs. Barry said. "Although after the incident we had Ryan and Tom sleep in those rooms."

"And..." Charles prodded.

"Nothing happened. The boys slept soundly the entire time," Mrs. Barry said. "You may not be aware, but the highway is just beyond the woods on that side of the property. We thought maybe a semi-truck broke down. What the guests heard was the winch on one of those big diesel tow trucks and the voices were those of the men doing the repair."

"You would think the woods would block the sounds," Charles said.

"Normally it would. But given the right atmosphere sounds can travel."

"Interesting," Charles said. "Too bad we don't have more history with those rooms."

"Maybe we'll have new incidents to report. Ryan moved his team to those rooms to get them away from all the activity around Ken's office."

He closed the album and leaned back in his chair. "Could the construction have caused the sounds?" Charles asked.

"No, all construction stops around four in the afternoon. These incidents all occurred in the early morning hours."

"Where's the new conference center construction site in relation to these rooms that Ryan is using?"

"Originally we planned the new conference center on the same side as the utility complex overlooking the gardens. The conference center would add a gym, a pool, but would be isolated from the rest of the hotel."

"You said originally. Did last night's meeting cause you to change your mind?" Charles asked.

"Mr. Toberson and others believe it would save money to build the conference building up the hill and attach it to the existing east wing. The land designated in our original plan takes a steep slope. We would have to spend more money to reinforce the building," Mrs. Barry said.

"Tom mentioned that changing the direction of the building would cause delays and delays cost money. I would have thought Toberson would have suggested a major change like this sooner," Charles suggested.

"There was always going to be a small delay between finishing the new restaurant, the theatre and the utility complex and starting the conference center. But you're right. It would have been better if Toberson alerted us sooner to the possible change."

"Did he say why he delayed in suggesting an alternative?"

"Three reasons. He claims when they started surveying for the new building, he was more aware of the sloping landscape. Second, he realized the utility complex when in use might provide unwanted noise for the nearby sleeping rooms. Last, with the current site there isn't sufficient room for an entrance off the road that runs behind the Manor. And having the conference center with its own entrance is a positive"

"Will you make the change?"

Charles waited as Mrs. Barry hesitated before answering. He thought she might be thinking through what her decision would be.

"I've called a meeting of the board. Lizzie is on her way back from her buying trip abroad. Marge and Maddy and my son, Martin, will all come up from Tri-City. We'll decide as a family what to do."

"I hope we have time to see Marge and Maddy. Carrie and I are fond of those ladies and we would also love to meet Lizzie."

"And Lizzie wants to meet both of you. I feel better having this opportunity to talk with you. Is there anything else I can tell you?"

"Well, there's one item before I leave. I've another idea to help us solve the case," Charles said. "For it to work, I'll need your help."

29

nother day passed, and Carrie spent her morning talking with staff members about their duties at the Manor. Every person said their goal was to make the guests comfortable and satisfied with their stay so they would come back.

She knew management picked the staff members she was interviewing. But she felt even if she randomly selected workers, they would have said the same thing. From talking with these folks, she realized the Manor included lots of family histories. Many of the workers were second, third and even fourth generations working for the Millford family.

This was a good thing for the Manor, but she felt it would be harder for her and Charles to expose the culprit. No one stood out as discontented with their job.

After typing her notes, Carrie picked up the brochure from the two sisters. She turned it over and saw a small map. It reminded her of the maps she saw in Ken's office. After a quick call to Albert and a trip to his office, Carrie secured copies of the Manor maps from the past to present day. She was on her way back to the suite when she met Charles in the hallway coming back from his swim.

"Did you get what you wanted from your morning interviews?" Charles asked.

"Nothing new from the interviews. More happy workers. But this may prove interesting," Carrie said holding up the rolls of paper.

"Looks like maps. Are they the ones from Ken's office?" Charles asked.

"Yes. Get this. Millicent was asking about borrowing the maps for her research. Albert retrieved them from Ken right after my interview."

"That solves the mystery of how they were in Ken's office and then disappeared," Charles said as he unlocked the door to their suite. "I wonder what Ken was doing with them?"

"He told Albert he wanted to check positioning of the proposed construction change before the meeting with the family and the Tobersons," Carrie said. She started to spread the maps out on the dining room table.

"It seems everyone wants to look at these maps. Could the maps have anything to do with Ken's death?" Charles said.

"I've four maps of the Manor property. One from the late eighteen-hundreds when it was a roadhouse, one from the twenties, one from the fifties when Bernie Millford was in charge and finally the most current."

"Good job! Let me look," Charles said.

Carrie finished laying the maps on the table. She put the oldest map on the bottom and then layered the other maps with the current map on top. Carrie used the original Manor building to line up each of the maps.

"Does anything immediately jump out at you?" Carrie asked once she aligned the maps.

She watched as Charles flipped the maps between the top and bottom copies.

"The one thing is the amount of construction the family members developed through the years. If you look at the original map, it's very much like the picture on the brochure Maddy and Marge gave us."

"On the first map you can see it was basically a farmhouse on the southbound stagecoach route," Carrie said. "Then if you look on the 1920 map, we see the results of the first major construction. They added a new wing, and the Manor looks more like a small hotel."

Carrie moved closer to Charles so she could see the maps more clearly. They continued flipping back and forth between the original drawing and the second map.

"Millicent was correct, Bernie really made major additions to the property in the fifties. With this much construction Bernie would have needed major investment dollars. Maybe money played a role in his death," Carrie suggested.

"Then, you think he's dead?" Charles asked.

"I do. Especially now that I've seen the maps. A man who invested this much energy and money into renovating his property wouldn't just disappear," Carrie said. "Wait. Go back to the original map. What are those lines going from the Manor into the woods?"

"Are these on all the maps?" Charles said as he leaned in for a closer look. "They don't appear on the first map but they're on the second map. Meaning it was something that was added. Although it doesn't appear to be linked to a structure."

"Charles, look. Those lines don't appear on the most recent map. Could the new construction have eliminated them?" Carrie asked.

"I don't know about that. They don't just remove something because it's a newer map," Charles said. "I think these lines look like they might be underground."

"You mean like sewer or water pipes?"

"Possibly, but they don't show water and sewer pipes anywhere else on the map," Charles said. Then he added, "Is it possible..."

"Come on, share. What are you thinking?"

"These type of lines might indicate a railroad," Charles said.

"A railroad!" Carrie looked again at the map. "There's nothing showing it's a railroad. The nearest train station is way over here and it's marked," Carrie said pointing to the location "I've another question. We see where the lines come into the Manor, but where do they come out on the other end?"

"I'm afraid I can't answer that question right now," Charles said. "Besides, I'm hungry. Let's get something to eat and we'll work on this later. I want to discuss something else with you."

"I hope you want to discuss a miraculous breakthrough you've had about this case."

30

Carrie and Charles were at a corner window table in the Old Mill Restaurant. They were early for lunch and there were few people in the establishment.

When another group arrived, it seemed unusual they sat at the table right next to the couple when so many empty tables were available. Then she realized it was Benson, the executive chef, along with chefs Harold and Kathy. Carrie noticed Harold quickly grabbed the chair that put his back to the couple.

"Well, it's nice to see the chefs eat in one of their restaurants for lunch," Charles said laughing.

"We like our food, but we have another reason for eating in this restaurant," Benson said. "A new server is joining the staff today. We like to provide a friendly table to get the new employee started."

"I assume you'll also give him some friendly pointers if needed," Carrie added.

"We do, but we would welcome your comments, too. He'll be serving you and your husband."

"We'd be happy to share our experience," Carrie said. She turned back to Charles and lowering her voice asked, "What did you want to tell me? Have you discovered something new?"

"Not discovered something, just decided something. We need some additional help with this case, so I asked..." Charles stopped mid-sentence.

Carrie first thought Charles stopped talking because of listening to something the chefs next to them said. Then she saw he was watching the approaching waiter.

"Good afternoon. I'm Christopher, and I'll be your server. Let me tell you about today's specials. Then I'll get your drinks while you think about what you want to order."

Carrie barely heard the lunch specials. She was in shock as she stared at Charles's nephew.

"Now what can I get you folks to drink?" Christopher asked.

They ordered iced teas and Christopher scurried off to get their drinks.

"When did you decide to bring Christopher here and why didn't you tell me?" Carrie whispered turning her head so the chefs next to them couldn't hear her. She hated being kept in the dark and really wanted to yell her question at Charles.

"I was going to tell you. I mean this minute. That's why I suggested lunch," Charles said stumbling through his answers. "I didn't know Christopher already started working."

"Do you think it's safe to have him here?" Carrie asked.

Carrie didn't get an answer from Charles, as Christopher returned with their drinks. Christopher took their food order and then introduced himself to the chef's table and took their drink order.

"He'll be fine. He's only here to listen and watch," Charles said once Christopher walked away. "You agree that we need some fresh eyes on the case."

"There's a murderer out there," Carrie said. She realized in answering Charles she had raised her voice. She saw Harold lean his head back as if he was trying to hear what they were discussing. Why was Harold interested in their discussion?

Charles spotted Harold's motion, lowered his voice, and said, "Carrie we need to discuss this later."

The restaurant was filling, and they ate their lunch quickly. They gave Christopher a nice tip and Carrie told the chefs their waiter was pleasant and provided good service.

* * *

The couple was walking off their lunch with a leisurely stroll around the gardens. The day was lovely with a fresh breeze from the surrounding mountains enhancing the fragrance of the new spring blossoms. Although Carrie was enjoying the walk, she looked continually at her watch.

"Do you think we can go back to the restaurant when it slows down and talk with Christopher?" Carrie asked.

"I don't think that's a good idea. It would show we had a connection to Christopher and focus attention on him. Remember, only a few people know we're related to him, besides...." Charles reached into his pocket and pulled out a small piece of paper. "Christopher slipped me this note when he gave us our bill. He'll come to our suite at five after his shift is over."

"Something else you didn't mention. That reminds me, I'm still mad at you for not telling me your nephew was working here."

"Might I point out that my nephew is also your nephew. When you married me all my relatives conveniently became your relatives," Charles said. "And I should add, most of them prefer you, over me, as a relation."

Charles always made her laugh, but she still felt obligated to hold him accountable. "That's because they know I won't keep secrets from them."

"Let's sit down for a few minutes and I'll tell you everything and try to redeem myself," Charles said.

Carrie plunked down on an empty bench near the entrance to the Azalea Garden.

"When I approached Mrs. Barry about needing some ears and eyes working with the employees, she agreed with my suggestion to bring Christopher on board."

"And knowing our nephew, he jumped at the chance to work on solving a mystery," Carrie said.

"Good, I'm glad you're calling him our nephew again," Charles said. "And you're right, he couldn't wait to come."

"Although I'd the impression you didn't expect Christopher to appear as our waiter," Carrie said.

"You're correct. I thought Ryan scheduled Christopher to start work tomorrow. He's supposed to work in the evenings serving banquets," Charles said. "I thought I'd plenty of time to discuss his arrival with you. When we see him, I'll have to ask why he was working a day shift."

"I almost blurted out 'What are you doing here?' but fortunately I couldn't find my voice."

Carrie thought for a moment and then added. "Obviously, he's using his first name Christopher, but what's his last name?" Carrie said.

"He's using James, so he's Christopher James."

Carrie felt a little twinge when she heard the name. James or Jamie was Christopher's father's name. Carrie knew and loved Jamie when they attended college, and it was his unexpected drowning that brought her back to Tri-City. Working with Charles to solve his brother's murder brought them together. She felt Charles take her hand, and she left her memories behind.

"Another thing. Only Mrs. Barry and Ryan know the relationship between Christopher and us. She told Ryan so Christopher has someone younger to go to if he has questions or spots something to report and she's not around," Charles said. "The fewer people who know he's related to us, the safer it is for him."

"That's what concerned me when I saw him. We've placed him the middle of something we haven't figured out," Carrie said.

"I had a long phone conversation with Christopher. He understands he's only to observe. He's not to get involved in any situations."

"That sounds better," Carrie said still hesitating.

"We need Christopher. No matter where we go behind the scenes or who we interview we'll never infiltrate the social environment of those who work here," Charles said.

Carrie didn't respond as a group of a dozen ladies arrived on the garden path near the bench where they were sitting. A Manor staff member was explaining the naming of the gardens, the types of plants on display, and how the gardens were maintained throughout the year.

"As you can see this is a great place to come and relax on a pleasant afternoon," the guide said smiling at the couple.

Carrie returned the smile and nodded as the tour group moved past. Once the group was out of hearing distance, Carries said, "I guess you're forgiven, but I'm still concerned. I want to make sure Christopher understands there's danger, a real danger in this assignment."

"We'll make this clear when we talk with him at five," Charles assured her.

"It's lovely here. Should we sit here and wait until it's time to meet Christopher or do you have something else in mind?"

"Actually, I have something for us to do," Charles said. "I would like to see if we can find out more about those Manor maps. I believe they may hold some secrets to help us."

31

Charles wanted to discuss the maps with Albert, but learned he was out of the office. He decided to go and find Ryan. "Mrs. Barry told me Ryan is in the same rooms where the guests reported hearing the strange sounds of machinery running and the unexplained voices," Charles said.

"We should line the rooms up on the construction maps and see what the possibilities are for something causing those sounds," Carrie said.

The couple had just stepped off the elevator, when Charles saw Ryan coming down the hallway of this unoccupied floor in the Manor.

"Hi, Mr. and Mrs. Faraday. How goes it?"

"Working on a little background information for the brochure," Carrie said loudly for anyone listening.

Even though Charles knew Albert wasn't available he said, "We're looking for your Dad."

"Dad went into the village to talk with suppliers. He won't be back for several hours, but I can probably help you," Ryan said. "Come down to my temporary office."

The couple followed Ryan down the hallway to the last suite on the floor. Ryan checked the hallway to make sure no one was around and then closed the door. Stacked against one wall was the bed frame and mattress. Ryan's desk and file cabinets filled the center of the room.

"I see you have paper maps of the Manor," Ryan said. "I believe those are the same maps I have on my computer."

"The paper maps are on the computer?" Carrie asked.

"Yes, two years ago I had them professionally scanned. This year I added the new construction map. This preserves the history of the changes in case anything happens to the paper maps. Plus, I can do a lot more with the computer version in terms of overlaying or focusing on a smaller section of the property.

"That's interesting," Charles said.

"Why do you say that? It's the best way to make sure there's a permanent record," Ryan said.

"No, I didn't mean that. Carrie saw a set of maps in Ken's office when she interviewed him," Charles said. "The night of the murder the maps were not in Ken's office and you discovered someone tried to get into your computer."

"You think the murderer was looking for these maps?" Ryan asked.

"Don't know. But it's an interesting coincidence," Charles said.

"Yes, it is," Ryan said. "Since you brought the paper maps let's spread them out on the table. They'll be easier for the three of us to see."

Charles helped Ryan unroll the maps and spread them out on a table in a corner near the kitchen. When the maps were unrolled and fastened to the table, Charles and the others gathered around them.

"This is the section I'm not sure about," Charles said pointing to an area of the map he viewed earlier with Carrie. "It looks almost like a miniature railroad track. But it makes little sense since the railroad depot is on the other side of the covered bridge almost two miles away. Was this a railroad siding?"

"You're correct. It's a track, but it's not a siding and it never belonged to the railroad," Ryan said. "Let me explain. When you arrived, you drove through the village and easily navigated the hills leading to our front door."

"That's the best way to get to the Manor, isn't it?" Charles asked.

"It is now. During our early history getting up those hills was a challenge, especially for the horse-drawn wagons bringing in supplies. The back side of the property is flatter, but there was no access."

"It looks like the tracks end before reaching the back of the hotel," Carrie said.

"That's correct. You see this mark here? That's a tunnel," Ryan said.

"A tunnel! You mean like a mining tunnel?" Carrie asked.

"Originally, yes. Below this large hill was a silver mine," Ryan said pointing to the map. "The family bought that piece of property after the mine closed in the early years. We kept the mine tracks and extended them over to the railroad depot."

"I guess in the early days the supplies came mostly by train," Carrie said.

"Correct. They used a small engine that ran on steam and pulled several flat-bed cars to bring supplies from the train depot," Ryan said. "The tracks made a very gradual climb through the tunnel up the hill to a depot at the Manor where the supplies were unloaded. This method saved time and money."

"On the map it looks like the tunnel is under some of the new construction at the back of the Island Grill Cafe."

"The map makes it appear closer than it is." Ryan stared at the map as if he was seeing something for the first time. "I need to check the latest blueprints but I'm sure we're not building near the original tunnel."

"Would it be a problem if the construction was over the tunnel? I assume the mine's been sealed," Charles said.

"The mine is still under the hill. But the county pulled up the tracks to the depot, and we sealed the entrance to the tunnel many years ago."

"I remember Ken said one reason for moving the new construction was because it increased your costs to build it on a hill. Was he also thinking of the tunnel?" Carrie asked.

"I don't know if Ken specifically knew about the supply tunnel or was repeating what the Toberson's said about the costs of building on a hill," Ryan said. "Although he may have heard about the Manor's interesting history."

"Now you've got my attention. What history?" Carrie asked.

"Before I tell you that. Could I get you folks something to drink? I've a single-cup coffee maker and a refrigerator full of soda, water and juices."

"Maybe something cold. Do you have a cranberry juice?" Carrie asked.

"Sure do, that's one of my favorite drinks," Ryan said.

Charles nodded in agreement and Ryan grabbed three bottles of cranberry juice and returned to the table.

"The Manor was part of the Underground Railroad system to help free slaves during the Civil War," Ryan said. "We had many free-born blacks working for us, so it was very easy to hide the escaped slaves within our staffing ranks."

"I didn't know that was part of your history. I hope Millicent captures this information in her book," Carrie said. "You were saying you helped slaves to escape."

"According to historic documents, when bounty hunters arrived looking for escaped slaves, we hid them in the tunnel," Ryan said.

"When it was safe for the escaped slaves to continue their journey to Canada, we used our supply tracks to secretly transport them to the main railroad depot. This is one of the few occasions where the underground railroad used an actual train."

"When did you stop using the tunnel for receiving supplies?" Charles asked.

"We used it a lot longer than you might think. Most of our deliveries came in by rail until World War II. When the war effort needed the railroads for transporting war materials and troops, we switched to bringing all supplies in by trucks," Ryan said. "It was also when we started to buy as much as possible from the local shops in the village to cut down on shipments."

Charles and the others were so engrossed talking about the railroad tracks they didn't hear Millicent enter the office. It was only when she approached the table, Charles spotted her.

"Oh, Millicent, where did you come... I mean hello," Charles said. He moved slightly to block Millicent as she maneuvered to see what was on the table.

"Can I help you, Millicent?" Ryan asked coolly.

"I was looking for your father. I wanted him to review a draft of material I've written about the Manor." Millicent said holding up a folder.

"Dad went to the village. Should be back around four," Ryan said.

Millicent didn't leave but inched even closer. "Are those old maps of the Manor? I asked your dad for a copy."

Neither Charles nor anyone else responded to her question, so she added, "The old maps could add to the history I'm writing."

"I'll email you a digital copy of the maps," Ryan said.

Charles couldn't help noticing Ryan's short answers as an effort to encourage her to leave. Perhaps he didn't care for the attention she was paying his father, or the attention his father was paying to her.

"We were just talking about the maps and the part the Manor played with the underground railroad. It would be perfect for your piece," Carrie said.

Charles knew Carrie was trying to break the coldness between Ryan and Millicent.

Millicent turned and faced Carrie. "Thank you for thinking of me when you came across something you knew I could use in my research."

Carrie was about to say something when Charles interrupted. "What's that noise? It sounds like a machine running."

"I don't hear anything," Millicent said.

"I do," said Carrie. "It sounds like it's beneath us, but it's very faint."

They continued to listen and then the sound abruptly stopped.

"We're near the new utility complex. Maybe they were doing a test on some of the equipment," Ryan said.

They all waited to see if the sound repeated, but everything was silent.

"I better get back to work. Ryan, I'll leave your father a voice-mail that I was looking for him," Millicent said.

Charles noticed that although Millicent originally wanted to stay, she now seemed anxious to leave the trio. He watched as she left the room and Ryan went over and checked the hallway to be sure she was gone.

"You know there's something about her that doesn't ring true," Ryan said. "I know what you're thinking. It's not because my Dad seems interested in her. I'm glad there's someone who can offer him an alternative to being on call twenty-four-seven for the Manor."

"It's interesting you say something doesn't ring true," Charles said, "We've the same feelings about Millicent Ford."

"Was Millicent selected as part of the writers' program? Is that what brought her here?" Carrie asked.

"I assumed so, but now that you mention it, I'm not sure," Ryan said. "Dad introduced her to everyone as a writer and said during her stay she would be in one of the cottages."

"Your father said nothing about her previous writing credentials?" Carrie asked.

"He said she was a great researcher known for her articles about historic buildings and towns. She wanted to focus on the Manor for her next assignment."

"Ryan, did she arrive before or after the first incidents occurred?" Charles asked.

"Let me think. About the same time as the first incident."

32

Carrie was standing next to the door of their suite at five. When she heard the knock, she opened the door in a flash and pulled Christopher into their room. She grabbed Christopher in a bear hug then pushed him back to arm's length and looked at him.

"Charles, this boy has grown another couple of inches. He'll soon be taller than you."

Charles came over and shook hands with his nephew and patted him on the back. "Thanks for coming to the Manor on such short notice."

"Hey, not a problem. I had nothing lined up for spring break. I must admit this place isn't bad. Besides a decent wage I get free room and board. And they are generous with the amount of food we're allowed to eat for free," Christopher said. "It's just like when I lived with you two. I'm part of the Manor's family."

"I'm glad this job is working out for your food needs. But I want to remind how serious this situation is," Charles said.

"Remember, only Mrs. Barry and Ryan know you're related to us and have a purpose other than serving guests. If you see or hear something and can't find us, go to one of them."

"If you need to talk to Mrs. Barry or Ryan, make sure you're in a secure area where no one can see you or overhear your discussions," Carrie said. "I worry about you, and I want you to be very careful."

"Don't worry. I'm sure you noticed I didn't acknowledge you at the restaurant. Which reminds me, thanks for the nice tip," Christopher said. "And I'm being careful. For this visit, I used the steps so no one would know what floor I visited."

"What are you telling people about how you got hired?" Charles asked.

"I tell them I'm from Florida, not Tri-City. Ryan and I fabricated a bit of a story. I got hired because my brother knew Tom in college."

"Christopher, come and sit down," Carrie said. "We don't need to talk standing by the door."

Christopher spread out on the sofa while Carrie and Charles took the two chairs facing him.

Charles asked, "Has anyone questioned your story?"

"The HR person who interviewed me when I was filling out my paperwork. And the floor manager and wine guy for the Williamsburg Room asked the same question when I arrived for my shift. They all seemed to accept my answer."

"Anyone else?" Charles asked.

"The guy in the Manor Pub, Tim," Christopher said.

"What were you doing in the pub? I thought you had to be twenty-one to work there," Carrie said.

"I can serve food, but you're correct you have to be twenty-one to serve the booze. But in this case, it didn't matter," Christopher said. "I wasn't working in the pub. Harold, one of the chefs, asked me to run a tray of sandwiches over to Tim."

Carrie exchanged a glance with Charles. Was Harold an innocent participant in a non-event or did he deliberately send Christopher to the pub so Tim could meet him? They needed to do more research on Harold. Carrie returned to the conversation.

"Hey, did you two know ghosts haunt this place?" Christopher asked. "I was talking with some of the servers and they told me all kinds of stories, everything from ghost sightings to other strange happenings."

"We know. The reports of all this ghost activity is the reason why we took this case," Carrie said.

Christopher looked confused, so Charles jumped in. "You see your aunt was buying several books about ghost sightings at the local bookstore in Tri-City. You remember Marge and Maddy who own the bookstore."

"Yeah, they're nice ladies. They're always willing to help."

"They're cousins of Mrs. Barry, and also sit on the board that runs the Manor," Charles said.

"They told us about the problems here at the Manor being blamed on the paranormal, and asked for our help. I may have bought a book about spirits, but your uncle and I believe these activities are of the human variety and not ghostly," Carrie said.

"That's why we wanted someone on the inside who could listen to what the staff is saying and separate the spirits from some human pranks that are occurring," Charles said. "I wouldn't worry if people are blaming the ghosts."

"I'm not worried. I'm hoping to see Roxie and her boyfriend wandering the halls. That would be awesome," Christopher said. He stood up, stretched, and walked over to the French doors. "This is a cool view. Lots of green to look at."

Carrie laughed out loud at Christopher's youthful exuberance. "What staff members are telling you ghost stories?" Carrie asked.

"I heard most of the stories from the guys who share the room next to mine. Paul who is a bartender for the pub and Jason who is a server like me. Although everyone on staff seems to have a ghost tale."

"You said the guys in the room next to yours and who is your roommate?" Charles asked.

"I've a single room. But don't get too excited by that. My room is very, very, very tiny. It's about one third the size of the room that Paul and Jason share," Christopher said. "I've a mini balcony which the bigger rooms don't have. Although when I say mini it's small. It holds one chair and the only way I fit is to dangle my legs over the ledge. But I've a feeling after working a full shift, a breath of fresh air might be a better deal than having a larger room."

"I hope that between eating and getting some fresh air you're able to find some clues. You only just arrived, but do you have anything to report?" Charles asked.

"Actually, I've been here for two days," Christopher said looking guilty. "I know, I know I should have told you I was here. I was going to after I met with Mrs. Barry and Ryan, but I had to move my stuff in," Christopher said rattling his sentences off quickly. "Jason and Paul didn't have to work last night. They invited me to go to a fast-food joint in town to get something to eat. When I got back, I found out I got assigned to the lunch shift at the Old Mill. And there you were, my first customers."

"It's fine, Christopher. You made the right choice. We don't want you running up here every minute and blowing your cover," Charles said. "Keep in touch, but only when it makes sense."

"Did you learn anything from your outing with Jason and Paul?" Carrie asked. "Do they think ghosts are causing the problems?

"Even though everyone is telling ghost stories, they think it's something else," Christopher said. "Paul didn't go into details but based on a conversation he had with Ryan, he thinks there's something funny going on with the liquor stock."

"No further details?" Charles asked.

"No. And at this point I didn't want to be too inquisitive. They also find it hard to believe it's a disgruntled employee." Christopher returned from the French doors and sat on the arm of one of the living room chairs.

"Why do they say that?" Charles asked.

"They like their jobs and everyone they work with feels the same way. I learned management recently held a meeting where they asked the staff to be alert to any activities that might disturb the guests but didn't go into any details. That's as much as I've learned for now," Christopher said.

"You've done well for two days on the job. But listen, Christopher, I don't want you taking any chances. You're just here to observe and keep us informed. If you face anything more serious, don't get involved," Charles said.

"That includes if you see any ghosts," added Carrie.

"Okay, I hear you," he said laughing. "Hey what's with the camera and the digital recorder, Auntie Carrie? If you don't think it's ghosts, what are you doing with all this ghost hunting equipment?"

"It's true I have a camera and a digital recorder which capture ghosts, but it also captures humans doing ghostly activities," Carrie said in a serious tone.

"I'll let you off this time, but if you capture a ghost voice, I want to hear it," Christopher said. "Well, I better head back. I'm serving a small banquet tonight."

Christopher opened the door slowly and then poked his head out to make sure no one was around. Carrie waved goodbye as Christopher closed the door.

After Christopher left, Carrie asked, "What do you think about Paul's comment concerning the liquor?"

"Don't know. Did someone hope to hide a discrepancy in the liquor inventory by trashing the storage room?" Charles asked. "By trashing the room, they should have known it would trigger a more detailed count."

"There's something else we should investigate," Carrie said.

Charles said one word. "Harold."

"Yes, Harold," Carrie said.

33

That night after much anticipation, the Manor's new Island Grill was ready to open. Charles thought management might have waited because of Ken's murder and also the lack of guests. Then again, he admired owners who wouldn't change their long-range plans because of events they couldn't control. Manor management felt it was important to give the sense of normalcy through these difficult times.

Current Manor guests learned of the opening through the internal television channel and the posters displayed in various locations throughout the property. Charles found out the grill would have a 'soft' opening for two weeks. This meant management wouldn't advertise the Island Grill to the general public to give the serving staff and chefs the opportunity to work out any minor issues with limited patrons.

The couple arrived for their reservation and sat at a table near the movable glass wall with a magnificent view of the gardens and water fountains. It was a cool night and the wall was closed to the outside patio, but the Tiki torches were lit creating lovely reflections on the fountains' waters.

"This is pleasant. Different from the other Manor restaurants, but a nice addition," Carrie said. "And once the weather gets a little warmer, it will be nice to have a meal out on the patio."

Charles was admiring the outside view when their waitress brought them a printed paper menu with tonight's specials. Charles recognized their waitress as the same wispy haired young lady that waited on them for breakfast their first day at the Manor.

"Welcome to the Island Grill. My name is Taffy and I'll be your waitress tonight," Taffy said and then she recognized the couple. "Oh, hello again. You may not remember me, but I waited on you when you first arrived and met with Mrs. Barry."

"Taffy, we remember you and the fine service we received. Have you switched from the Old Mill to the new grill or are you just helping with the opening?" Carrie asked.

"I was taking college classes at night and working during the day in the Old Mill. I got a scholarship from the Manor so now I can go to college during the day and finish sooner," she said. "Mr. Albert let me switch to the new grill where I can work two nights and one weekend day to earn some money."

"That's wonderful. We wish you lots of luck with your studies," Carrie said.

"Thank you. Let me tell you about our specials. We have a limited menu but some great entrées for you to enjoy," Taffy said. "We have a fresh salmon filet, New York strip steak, chicken teriyaki, lamb chops and a vegetarian dish. Each entrée is served with fresh grilled vegetables and roasted potatoes. Did you need a few minutes to decide?"

Charles looked at Carrie and knew what they both wanted. "We'll have the lamb chops, grilled medium well. And is there some wine available?"

"Excellent choice. I'll get your order started and send the wine steward over with the list," Taffy said.

After a leisurely dining experience Charles could once again say that he and Carrie enjoyed another wonderful meal. The Island Grill might be doing a limited opening, but the food and the service were perfect. Charles left Taffy a nice tip and he and Carrie wandered out to the gardens for a leisurely walk.

"The Manor has another winner with that restaurant," Charles said. "It's not as fancy as the Williamsburg Room and offers a lighter fare, but I think the patrons will like the alternative."

"I know I liked it. I don't feel stuffed, but a nice walk will still be good for our calorie intake. And it will hopefully help to clear our heads."

"Does your head need clearing?" Charles asked.

"You know what I mean. I feel we're still going around in circles with this case."

"Why don't we walk up to my favorite bench and do some thinking together?" Charles suggested.

Within a few minutes they were sitting on the bench near the Japanese gardens.

"I see why you come here to read. This is a great spot," Carrie said. "And the nighttime view with the lighted fountains from the Island Grill is stunning."

"It's a great spot for reading, but it also lets me keep my eye on anything happening on the grounds."

"That's the problem with this case. I don't know what's happening," Carrie said. "Everyone I've interviewed loves the place. So why all the pranks and why a murder?"

"That's what makes the situation challenging. The pranks were basically harmless except for affecting business. Then Ken's murder took it to a whole different level."

"Charles, that's it. We've been concentrating on finding reasons for each incident and at the same time being misdirected by Roxie sightings, rattling glasses, the lady writers, machine noises and the other various incidents," Carrie said. "We already know the answer. It's about the money or as you just said it's about the business."

"The real question is who stands to gain from the Manor going under?" Charles asked.

The couple sat quietly for a moment each with their own thoughts until Charles broke the silence. "Is that a light I'm seeing over by the construction area?"

"It looks like someone is moving through the area with a flashlight." Carrie said.

"Look, I see another light trailing behind the first. I should check this out," Charles said.

"We should check this out. Christopher is on the premises."

Before Charles could stop her, Carrie was up and running across the grass towards the light. Fortunately, she stopped as she needed to regain her bearings on the direction of the light.

"Hey, slow down. We don't know who we're running towards," Charles said, "I'm not sure who has the light but I'm sure that's Ryan with someone else trailing behind him."

Charles followed where Carrie was pointing. "That's definitely Ryan and…. Come on, let's go."

This time Charles led the charge towards the movement. They reached the area near the construction.

Charles called out using a voice slightly louder than a whisper, "Ryan, where are you? It's Charles and Carrie."

There was silence and then he heard footsteps coming towards them. Charles instinctively stepped in front of Carrie.

"Here, I am," Ryan answered.

"Me too," said Christopher.

"Christopher! What are you doing out here?" Carrie asked.

"Ryan and I were in his office working on the computer program. I looked out the window and saw someone with a flashlight moving around the grounds. We came to investigate," Christopher said nonchalantly.

"You two realize a murder occurred on these premises. Why would you come to investigate on your own?" Carrie admonished.

"We didn't come alone. I called security," Ryan said. "But you're right we should have waited for the guards. I'm sorry I put Christopher in danger."

Charles appreciated Ryan's apology but felt that it was still foolish for them to be wandering around the grounds. He needed to have another conversation with Christopher about limiting his activities concerning the case. Before he could say anything, he heard the sounds of footsteps approaching from two different directions. The beam from Ryan's light picked up two security guards approaching them.

"Did you guys see anyone?" Ryan asked.

"No one. Everything is quiet. We even searched under the tarps at the utility complex," the one guard responded.

"I'll be glad when the new doors arrive and we can lock this building down," Ryan said. "Thanks, guys, for your quick response. If you could pay special attention to this area when you do your rounds the rest of tonight."

"No problem. We'll monitor the area," said the second guard. "Maybe it was a guest leaving the Island Grill and took a wrong turn trying to get back to the main building."

"And the light?" Christopher asked.

"We all have lights on our phones. Maybe they were using it to find their way to a path," the guard added.

"Whoever was out here seems to have found their way and perhaps returned to one of the buildings. Thanks again," Ryan said.

Charles watched as the guards headed down the path that went behind the construction area. He agreed with them that whoever was wandering about left the area. Although he seriously doubted it was a lost guest from the Island Grill.

"I heard Christopher say you guys were working on the computer program when you saw the light. Ryan, how are you doing with your scheduling program?" Charles asked.

"I'm ready to share what I've discovered so far. How about meeting Tom, Christopher, and me for coffee in the morning?"

"I'll be there," Charles said. "Christopher, no more following any lights or any other adventures tonight."

"Christopher, I want your promise you'll do what Charles asked," Carrie said.

"I promise," Christopher said.

Charles took Carrie's hand. He watched for any movement in the shadows as they walked to the Manor entrance closest to their room. He felt Carrie stop.

"What's the matter?" Charles said.

"Look at the glass entrance door. Do you see someone standing there?"

"Yes, there's a woman looking out."

"Charles, that's Roxie. Look at her lower body. It's transparent."

Now he was seeing what Carrie saw with his own eyes. It was only seconds before the image of the woman faded away. When they reached the door, Charles looked for signs of how someone could have created the image.

"What are you thinking?" Carrie asked.

"Could someone have projected the image onto the glass?"

"That's a possibility with a glass door, but how did they project Roxie in our room?"

"I honestly don't know," Charles said.

When Carrie first told him about the apparition of Roxie, he wasn't sure what to believe. After having his own experience, he still wasn't sure what to believe. The one thing he did know. They both had another reason for finding a solution to what was going on at the Manor.

34

The next morning Charles and Carrie didn't discuss the vision they witnessed of Roxie. In Charles's mind there was nothing to discuss until they could make a more thorough investigation of the glass door to see if the image was mechanically generated.

For the moment, Charles was more interested in seeing the results of Ryan's programing efforts. He asked Carrie to join him for coffee with the guys, but she opted for more sleep.

As Charles headed to the lobby, he worried about meeting Christopher in such a public spot like the coffee shop. Would other staff members wonder why Ryan and Tom invited a new staff member to a meeting? Would the meeting blow his cover? Now that Christopher was working so closely with Ryan, was he in additional danger? Perhaps it was time for him to reevaluate Christopher's involvement.

Mornings at the Manor were all about coffee. The wonderful smell of the brewing beverage drifted towards Charles and he felt a sense of wellbeing. Carafes of various coffees from strong brews to the delicate flavor of a mild blend sat on the serving tables.

Flavored coffees were available for folks who wanted to start their day with the taste of blueberry, toasted coconut, French vanilla or some other fanciful flavor. A staff member was also standing by to prepare specialty drinks like espressos and lattes. And for the non-coffee drinker there was an assortment of teas, hot chocolate, and fruit juices.

Charles spotted trays of mini Danish, doughnuts and muffins waiting to satisfy the need to start the day with something sweet. He could hear Carrie's voice reminding him about his consumption of too many sweets. He fixed his coffee and passed by the trays of pastries.

The morning coffee shop was in the same room where the Manor held their afternoon tea. Since most people took their coffee to go, the staff roped off the largest section of the room leaving a smaller seating area. Ryan was already in the room seated at a table away from the self-serve area where most people congregated. Those folks who stayed to drink their coffee wanted tables near the window with a view of the grounds.

As Charles approached Ryan's table, he said loudly so anyone nearby could hear, "Hello, Ryan, do you mind if I join you?"

Ryan caught on and said, "Oh, good morning, Mr. Faraday. I'm just catching up on a little paperwork, but I'd rather chat with you." Ryan shut the lid on his computer.

Before Ryan and Charles said anything more, Christopher arrived. Christopher wasn't much of a coffee drinker. Instead, he ordered a cup of hot chocolate with a huge mound of whipped cream on the top. Right behind Christopher was Tom, who grabbed a coffee and loaded a plate with every sweet available for the men to enjoy. Charles decided a few small pastry items wouldn't hurt his diet.

"I see you like a little hot chocolate with your whip cream," Ryan said smiling.

"Give him a break, Ryan. You're just envious because you didn't select hot chocolate for your drink," Tom said.

They all laughed. Charles found he didn't have to worry about eating too many sweets because the guys quickly emptied the plate. Then Charles said lowering his voice, "Before we get started, I want to talk about Christopher's involvement with our investigation. Christopher I may have been foolish in bringing you into this."

"Uncle Charles, I've been observing and listening like you advised. Last night I was with Ryan because we were working on his program," Christopher said. "And I think we made progress."

"Mr. Faraday, Christopher has really been a great help and last night's excursion was poor judgement on my part, not his," Ryan offered.

"He's quite good at observing people," Tom added.

Charles looked at both Tom and Ryan and then saw the pleading look on Christopher's face. "Then I guess we better get started looking at your program?"

"The program has limits, but I'm beginning to see some trends," Ryan said.

"I can't believe you designed a program with limits, Cuz," said Tom.

"Thanks, Tom. But as they say it's not the program but what gets entered. I had some trouble getting the schedules and names of people from the outside contractors."

"Did you finally get everything you wanted?" Tom asked.

"I'm not sure," Ryan said.

"We're saying, we don't know what we don't have," Christopher piped in.

"Exactly. I've a fair amount of information but I could still be missing data from someone who may be involved," Ryan said.

"And what have you discovered?" Charles asked. He appreciated Ryan's explanation, but he wanted to hear names.

"From our staff four names keep coming up. Although none of these people are a one hundred percent match for every incident. The names I'm about to give you cross reference at least three times." Ryan said. "As you might suspect Ken Harvey is on the list. Then there's Harold, one of our chefs, Tim the evening host for the pub and Geoff the wine sommelier for the Williamsburg Room."

"Interesting, these folks would all have access to schedules and would probably have a line on where management was within the building," Tom said.

"I would also be remiss if I didn't mention both of our resident writers came to stay with us just prior to the first incident. And there's something else I'm seeing," Ryan said and then paused.

"Don't leave us hanging. What is it?" Tom asked.

Charles realized perhaps without meaning to, Ryan was building a sense of suspense.

"You may not like this, Tom. I'm seeing two outside companies with people on site at the Manor during key moments. One is Mr. and Mrs. Toberson along with several of his construction workers," Ryan said looking at Tom.

"In some ways that isn't surprising. Toberson is teaching seminars and his construction guys are still finishing projects like the utility complex," Tom said.

"I waited on the Toberson's for lunch yesterday. Every time I approached their table they stopped talking," Christopher said. "With my other customers I usually have to wait until they finish their conversation, before they even notice I'm there."

"Did you hear any of their conversations?' Charles asked.

"Only once when they didn't see me approaching. Mrs. Toberson said, "don't worry, just a little while longer. We're almost finished.""

"It could mean the seminar they're running is almost over or the change in plans for the new construction is almost decided, or the utility complex is almost complete," Charles said. Charles saw the deflated look on Christopher's face so he added quickly, "or it could mean the incidents around the Manor are coming to an end."

"Ryan, you said I may not like what you had to say. Surely if the Tobersons are behind this, I'm all for exposing them," Tom said.

"I said there were two groups. Your father and two of his drivers were tagged by the program. Even though we have limited camera surveillance, I spotted the drivers on video footage during many of the incidents."

Tom remained quiet but Christopher asked, "What's the connection between your father's liquor company and the Manor?"

"We purchase most of the wine and liquor we serve through his father's company," Ryan answered. "To the casual observer it would seem perfectly normal for these men and the delivery trucks to be on the premises."

Charles was thinking back to the conversation he and Carrie overheard in the pub. They were sure the one voice they heard was Ken Harvey. Was Bill Toberson or Tom's father, Doug, the other voice?

"To summarize, you've identified a handful of staff members, the writers, the Tobersons and Tom's father as our chief suspects," Charles said.

"It's true, Dad is always at the Manor and his company makes deliveries all the time during the day. But why would two of his delivery men be here when some of the incidents occurred at night?" Tom said as if he was thinking out loud.

The others sat quietly not knowing what to say to Tom. Then, suddenly, Tom jumped up and said, "Wow, she's early. She wasn't due for a few more hours."

35

Charles watched as Tom approached a tall woman with reddish blonde hair creating a great deal of activity in the lobby. The staff scurried around as if she were royalty.

Joseph was making a fuss over her as the bellmen brought multiple pieces of luggage into the lobby.

"Who's that?" Christopher asked.

"That's Tom's mom and that also makes her my Aunt Lizzie," Ryan said. "She must have caught an earlier flight, because Tom thought he was picking her up at the airport later this afternoon."

Lizzie was not as tall as Mrs. Barry and while Charles would describe Mrs. Barry as striking, he would say Lizzie was stylish. She wore a stunning dark burgundy pants suit with a floral scarf draped over her shoulders.

Charles watched as Lizzie smiled at Joseph and spoke with the staff for a few minutes before Tom pried her away and guided her to their table. Charles stood as she approached and Christopher followed his lead, but Ryan remained seated working on his computer.

"Mom, this is Charles Faraday and Christopher James. My mother, Elizabeth Millford."

"Please, please sit down. No need for such formality gentlemen. And call me Lizzie, everyone does except for the staff who feel they're taking sufficient liberties by calling me Elizabeth," Lizzie said as she smiled.

Charles noticed that her smile was warm and friendly just like Albert's.

"Hi, Aunt Lizzie," Ryan said looking up from his computer for a second.

"Hello, Ryan. What are you working on with so much intensity?"

"Mom, sit down and we'll fill you in on what's been happening."

"Don't tell me there's been more incidents," Lizzie said.

Ryan looked up. "Aren't you aware of the latest news?"

"If you're talking about local Millford news, no. I flew in from London in the early hours and haven't seen the Millford paper or even the Tri-City news," Lizzie said. "But before you tell me what's going on, I don't believe I've met Mr. Faraday or this young man before. I believe you said Christopher."

Tom checked to make sure there were no unwanted ears nearby and then answered his mother, "Mr. Faraday and his wife are the folks we brought in to discover the reason for the incidents. We told staff members Mrs. Faraday was writing a new marketing brochure."

"I see. Is the cover story holding or are there rumors about what they're really doing?" Lizzie asked.

"Not that we've heard," Tom said. "They probably accepted the story because our marketing materials need a big-time makeover."

"I can't deny that awful brochure needs help," Lizzie said smiling at Charles. "I thought one day when I had some free time, I would take a stab at updating it."

"Mrs. Faraday provides marketing services to companies for a living, so if anyone checks her story, she's genuine," Tom said as he excused himself and went over to the coffee bar. He returned with a cup of coffee and several mini muffins for his mother.

"Thank you, Darling. I really need this coffee. The reason I came directly here and not to my home is I knew I had nothing in the refrigerator."

Lizzie took several sips of coffee and downed the first muffin in two bites.

"Christopher, how are you related to all of this?" Lizzie asked.

"Christopher is Mr. Faraday's nephew. Since we suspect employee involvement, he's working as a waiter and staying in the employee dorm," Tom said.

"He's also helping me in gathering information and creating my computer program," Ryan added continuing to click away at the keyboard.

Charles ears perked up. He wasn't aware Christopher was actually helping Ryan create the program even though he knew his nephew was good with computers.

"I see. But you said additional incidents. What's happened?" Lizzie asked.

Before anyone could respond, Joseph approached the table. "Sorry to interrupt, Elizabeth, but I wanted you to know that your luggage is in the Western Suite," Joseph said as he handed her the key card.

Charles noticed, as Lizzie indicated, Joseph called her Elizabeth. He also knew that no one on staff would think of calling Mrs. Barry, Beatrice.

"Perfect. Thank you, Joseph," Lizzie said flashing another smile.

Joseph smiled back and stood there for several minutes until he realized the group was waiting for him to leave. "I guess I better get back to the desk."

While Joseph was talking Charles took note of Lizzie's jewelry. She wore several strands of a gold necklace, matching heavy gold earrings and several rings on her fingers that looked antique and expensive. The only thing missing was a wedding band.

"Now, as I was saying, what's happened?" Lizzie asked again.

The guys looked to Charles for an explanation. "I guess it's my turn," Charles said. "I'm afraid there's been a murder."

"What do you mean a murder? Whose murder?" Lizzie said in obvious shock.

"As part of my wife's cover, she was gathering information about the various events at the Manor," Charles said. "The morning after my wife interviewed Ken Harvey. Ryan found him murdered in his office."

"Ken Harvey Oh, my heavens. How awful. There's no doubt it was murder?" she asked.

The men all shook their heads, no, and Ryan said, "Someone shot him in the head at point blank range."

"Why would anyone kill Ken? He was a decent event manager and basically harmless," Lizzie said.

Charles thought the phrase 'basically harmless' was an interesting way to describe Ken. But the more he thought about Lizzie's comment the more he thought it was an accurate assessment. He may have been harmless but that didn't stop someone from murdering Ken.

"Is that why you're meeting to discuss the murder?" Lizzie asked.

"No. We're discussing the program your nephew designed to match people's work schedules with the incidents occurring at the Manor," Charles said.

"Aren't you the clever one," Lizzie said. "What have you discovered? Do you have names to share?"

No one at the table said anything. Instead, Ryan turned his computer screen towards his aunt. They all watched her eyes as she read down the list.

"I see," she said. She sat quietly for a moment and then said, "What are our next steps?"

"We don't know. Perhaps monitor these folks. We really have no hard evidence against any of them," Ryan said.

"Mom, if you didn't know about Ken's murder, what brought you back early from your buying trip?" Tom asked.

"Albert texted me saying there was more negative activity. He and Bea wanted to announce our community project to have something positive happening. He never mentioned the murder," Lizzie said.

"Dad probably didn't want to worry you since there was nothing you could do from overseas," Ryan said.

"I'm sure that's the reason. He always watches out for me," Lizzie said. "Anyway, I came back for the bridge announcement."

"You mean the Old Mill Covered Bridge you pass when entering the town of Millford?" Charles asked.

"Yes, before I left, I was working on a project with the town leaders to renovate the covered bridge. I figured he wanted me back to help launch this project," Lizzie said. "I believe Albert scheduled the announcement for tomorrow."

Charles understood the cousins tried to keep the Manor running normally, supporting their employees and being a good partner for the village. He wasn't sure that a bridge renovation would offset the negative publicity from Ken's murder, but he knew he wanted to be at the announcement.

36

Charles and Carrie ate a filling breakfast at the Old Mill Restaurant. After breakfast they moved to seats in the lobby where they were relaxing before the big covered bridge announcement.

"Charles, look at that poster," Carrie said pointing to an easel by the front door. Charles reached into his pocket for his glasses.

"Don't bother, Darling. I'll read it to you," Carrie said.

"I don't remember that poster being there yesterday," Carrie said.

"When I had coffee with the guys and Lizzie yesterday, I can guarantee you it wasn't there," Charles said.

Carrie discovered their seats were perfect for watching the guests arriving. Car after car was pulling up to the front of the hotel and the staff was racing to get all the cars parked.

"Seems like short notice for something as big as a renovation announcement," Carrie said.

"Lizzie said they wanted to do something positive to offset all the negativity," Charles said. "And they are also taking advantage of Lizzie's return. It was obvious to me the way the staff treated her she is well liked."

"You know what's interesting? The sign is so vague," Carrie said. "It says nothing about a covered bridge. They could use this poster to announce anything."

"Lizzie said it's about the covered bridge," Charles said. "Maybe they want it to be a surprise."

"An awful lot of people are showing up for a surprise," Carrie said. "But this probably also says something about the Manor. When they have an announcement, regardless of any negative events, the village turns out."

Carrie recognized Meagan who checked them in on the first day at the Manor as today's official greeter. She wore the Manor blazer but had a multicolored ribbon holding back her hair which made the uniform look more festive. Carrie wondered how she could keep her balance in her stiletto heels that also dressed up her outfit. Carrie long ago gave up wearing heels that high.

"Looks like the whole village of Millford is turning out. I recognize the manager from the ice cream store," Carrie said.

"And here's Greg who sold us the digital equipment," Charles said as he nodded a greeting to him.

Next to arrive was the shuttle bus filled with what appeared to be the government officials from the town. Riding with them were Tom and Ryan.

"And here come the cousins," Charles said.

Carrie watched Albert, Mrs. Barry, and another woman whom she assumed was Lizzie enter the lobby. Carrie waved at Albert.

"Hello, you two. Are you coming to our announcement?" Albert asked.

Charles diplomatically said, "Wouldn't miss it. We'll be right in."

"Excellent," Albert said and started greeting folks as he entered the room.

"I assume the rather striking strawberry blonde in the designer outfit is Lizzie?" Carrie asked.

"That's her. For the few minutes I spent with her yesterday, she seems genuinely nice," Charles said.

"You said Lizzie showed no emotion when she saw her husband's name on the list of suspects," Carrie said.

"None. All she said was, 'I see,' almost as if she expected his name to be on the list," Charles said.

Carrie and Charles stood ready to follow the crowd into the tearoom when Carrie saw Christopher coming down the hallway carrying a tray loaded with fluted glasses of different fruit juices. She pulled on Charles's sleeve and nodded towards her nephew.

"Are you joining the family for their announcement? Would you like a glass of juice?" Christopher asked formally.

"Yes, we're going in," Carrie said as she reached over the tray and took a glass of orange juice. Then under her breath said, "I assume you're working this event?"

"Yup, I volunteered. Figured it was a great way to see all the suspects," Christopher said. "Better go."

Carrie said quietly to Christopher, "Be careful and remember, don't get involved. Just report."

"Got it," Christopher said and went into the room.

Carrie arrived at the entrance to the room, at the same time as Bill and Leslie Toberson.

"Hello, you two," Leslie said. "Any idea what the announcement is about?"

Leslie and Bill wore sweaters, slacks, and scuffed walking shoes as if they had been hiking. Carrie thought their dress was rather causal compared to the townsfolk and staff arriving for the event.

Before Carrie could answer Leslie's question, Bill jumped in "I hope they're announcing a change in the plans for the new wing."

"Would they invite the whole town and all these officials to announce they changed the direction of a building?" Carrie asked.

"No, you're probably right," Bill said.

"Then I guess we better find out what's happening," Leslie said.

"Maybe it will mean the opportunity to bid on a new contract for you, Bill."

When the couple entered the room, Carrie watched as Bill and Leslie immediately went to the bar to grab two Mimosas rather than the plain fruit juice Christopher was serving. Carrie spotted Millicent in one of the front row seats but saw no sign of Mrs. Kent. Carrie guided Charles towards seats at the back of the room. From these seats she could watch all the players.

Albert introduced the Millford Village mayor, the president of the Chamber of Commerce and several other town officials. Then Albert introduced Lizzie for the big announcement. Carrie could feel a real sense of excitement in the room with the overwhelming applause that erupted from the audience.

"Thank you all for coming. For those of you who don't know me, I'm Elizabeth Millford."

The muffled laughter in the room implied to Carrie everyone knew who Lizzie was. She smiled and continued, "It has always been part of the Manor's mission to be a good employer but also a good partner for community projects for the Millford area," Lizzie said in a voice Carrie thought sounded a little like Lauren Bacall.

"Our latest community project is the restoration of the Old Mill Covered Bridge. The bridge will close while we reinforce the braces, replace the flooring and add a fresh coat of paint."

Carrie thought the audience seemed a little restless at the announcement of the road closing even if it was for a good cause.

"We'll rebuild the top of the bridge off-site to limit the time the bridge remains out of commission. We expect to need only six weeks to complete the entire project."

The room erupted in thunderous applause. Lizzie held up her hand to quiet the audience. "The Old Mill bridge has been part of our heritage for over one hundred fifty years, and it's important we maintain this historical site for our town."

Lizzie left the podium and walked to a covered easel. Both Albert and Lizzie lifted the drape to reveal the proposed renovation. Once again there was thunderous applause from the guests.

"Please enjoy the refreshments and look at the proposed renovations. Family members are here to answer questions," Lizzie said.

More applause. Carrie gently nudged Charles and nodded towards the Tobersons. "Leslie and Bill don't look so happy."

"Maybe Bill's construction company doesn't renovate covered bridges," Charles answered.

"I have the feeling it's something else," Carrie said.

37

"Why do you keep looking over your shoulder?" Charles asked Carrie as they walked down the long path towards the writers' cottages.

"I'm worried about breaking into the cottage in broad daylight. What if someone sees us? Carrie said. "What if she returns?"

"If we broke into the cottage at night, the odds of someone working inside or returning to the cottage would be higher," Charles said. "At this hour, we know both ladies are with Albert."

"Are we sure Mrs. Kent is with them?"

"Yes, Albert called me from the lobby when they were leaving. Mrs. Kent didn't attend the covered bridge announcement because she apparently was at a critical point in her writing but made time for today's outing with Albert."

"What if she gives an excuse and comes back early to do more writing?" Carrie asked as they reached the paths that led to the various gardens.

"That won't be a problem. Albert took them to the village using the Manor's shuttle, so we know we have at least an hour before the shuttle returns from the village," Charles said. "They're visiting Tom at the bookstore and then Albert is taking them to lunch to keep them in town longer."

Charles took Carrie's hand knowing she was nervous. He also knew holding hands helped their cover for anyone watching them. They were a couple enjoying a casual afternoon walk in the gardens and under other circumstances this would be true.

"Albert will text me when they are on their way back. Stop worrying," Charles added.

"You're sure Albert is okay with what we're doing?" Carrie asked.

"He seemed supportive of our snooping because he's hoping we'll find information that will help solve the case."

"Don't you find it interesting that he wouldn't protect Millicent?"

"I still haven't figured out that relationship. Maybe he's not as infatuated with Millicent as we first thought," Charles said.

"In that case, let's get on with our break-in," Carrie said.

Charles stopped Carrie as she turned towards the path leading directly to the cottages. "Whoa, wait a minute, my fellow cat burglar," Charles said. "Even though we know where the ladies are, you're correct about the possibility of someone else seeing us. Let's enter the cottage from the back."

Charles spotted a few visitors heading down the path to the Azalea Garden. The good news was that once these visitors reached the Azalea Garden, the writers' cottages were hidden.

Charles and Carrie reached the lily pond and walked around to the far side which placed them closer to the cottages. Charles waited until he was sure no one was around. Then he made his move.

Charles and Carrie darted behind the shrubbery that protected the pond. Within moments they emerged from the trees behind the writers' cottages. They quickly walked to the patio of Millicent's cottage. Charles tried the sliding door as he continued to survey the area for the signs of any people.

"Were you expecting it would be unlocked?" Carrie asked.

"Not really. Millicent seems very buttoned-up, so I'm interested to see what her cottage looks like on the inside," Charles said.

"What now, Sherlock? How are you planning on getting in?"

"We use the key." Charles reached into his pocket, extracted a key, and held it up for Carrie to see.

"Where did you get that key? Did you pick someone's pocket?"

"I didn't have to use my pick-pocketing skills. Albert lent me his master key for the cottages," Charles said.

Charles checked again to make sure no one else was around and unlocked the door. He slid the door back and waited for Carrie to enter. Once inside, as he expected, everything was in order. No dirty dishes stacked in the sink. Nothing on the kitchen table, and the living room was neat and tidy. Charles realized Carrie hadn't moved and stood looking around the room.

"What's the matter? Getting cold feet?" Charles asked.

"No, we're in now. I was thinking with Millicent having everything in such perfect order, we need to be extra careful. We can't leave anything out of place to tip her off we were here."

"Good point," Charles said. "Since you're the writer, why don't you search the desk. I'll check the bedroom."

"I would bet Millicent has most of her writing on her computer which is probably password protected, but there are stacks of papers on the desk. I'll start with that," Carrie said.

Charles headed to the bedroom, while Carrie sat at the desk and started looking through piles and piles of the research Millicent assembled about the Manor. After a significant period, Charles returned from the bedroom.

"Did you find anything interesting?" Carrie asked looking up from the latest paper she was reading.

"Two things," Charles said holding up an item in each hand.

"Ah, tell me more."

"The first item is a package of women's hair dye," he said holding up his right hand. "There are more packages in a drawer in the bedroom. Our friend Millicent isn't a natural blond."

"Many women color their hair, but I get the impression from your comment you think she's using the color as a disguise."

"Yes, I do. And my second item is even more interesting," Charles said as he turned a picture frame around to reveal the photo inside. "It's a picture of Bernie."

"Bernie Millford! Are you sure?" Carrie asked.

"Positive. This is the same picture of Bernie that was in Mrs. Barry's family scrapbook."

"Now that's a clue. Although I guess she could have come across the photo in her research," Carrie said.

"Except, this is an expensive frame for a photo you discovered while doing research. Have you found anything interesting?"

"Millicent has a huge amount of research on the Manor."

"Is that unusual considering she's writing a book about this place?"

"Possibly, but my question is how long has she been working on this topic. There's too much material for someone who just started this project a few weeks ago when she arrived at the Manor," Carrie said. "And one more thing, in relation to the picture you found. There's a lot of research about Bernie."

"We need to look for a connection between Bernie and Millicent," Charles said as he left the room to return the photo and the hair dye package.

When Charles returned to the room Carrie said, "Since we're not checking her computer, I think we're finished here."

Charles checked over the desk where Carrie was working to make sure everything appeared orderly. As he looked up, he spotted something out the window.

"Will you look at this," Charles said. "What's the matter?" Carrie asked.

"Guess who's coming this way? Harold our mysterious chef and Geoff the wine steward from the Williamsburg Room."

"Are they coming to the writers' cottages?"

"I don't know. Be ready. We might have to leave quickly if they come to the front door," Charles said.

Charles carefully watched from a slit in the blind while Carrie waited in the kitchen.

"We're okay. They're following the path leading away from the cottages," Charles said. "Where could they be going?"

"More importantly, why are they together?" Carrie asked.

"They were both on Ryan's suspect list."

38

It was a beautiful morning the day after the couple searched Millicent's cottage. Carrie was doing research on her computer. Since there was nothing Charles could do to help her, he took his book and headed for the gardens. He needed to think about the various suspects and what he knew about each of them. Soon he was sitting in his favorite spot next to the Japanese gardens. He could read his book, but he also had a clear view of the Island Grill and the back of the Manor.

He felt there was something about the new construction and specifically the utility complex that was not quite right. He agreed with the observation Millicent shared with Carrie. *Why at this late date would Toberson suggest a change in the location of the new building? Was he saving the Manor money or was there another reason?* Charles decided when he met Carrie in the pub for lunch, he would get her take on the construction and the Tobersons.

Charles was reading the final chapters of his thriller when something caught his attention near the utility complex tarp.

He pulled a small pair of binoculars from his jacket pocket and focused the lens. He saw Millicent Ford emerge from the plastic tarp that was still covering the entrance to the utility complex near the new café. Charles watched as she glanced around to be sure no one was in the area. Then she spent a few moments brushing dust from her clothes.

Why was she visiting the construction area? What was she doing that made her clothes so dusty?

"This is a lovely spot for birdwatching."

Charles jumped at the sound of a voice. He turned to see Lizzie Millford standing next to him.

"Yes, it's a lovely spot, but it wasn't a bird that caught my attention." Charles handed his binoculars to Lizzie.

She focused and said, "Is that Millicent? Seems a funny spot to take a walk."

"She emerged from the construction tarp," Charles said.

Lizzie handed the binoculars back. "Is she one of your suspects?" Lizzie asked. "Or is everyone a suspect at this point?"

"Not everyone," Charles said. "Millicent's intense interest in the Manor's history drew our attention to her. Please, join me." Charles said pointing to the open spot on the bench next to him.

Lizzie sat next to Charles and gazed out across the grounds. "Not to mention Millicent's interest in my brother," Lizzie said.

Lizzie impressed Charles. Like her siblings she seemed to have a complete grasp of everything happening at the Manor past and present.

"As I remember, Millicent wasn't high on Ryan's list, but my ex-husband was."

Charles looked at Lizzie. Her face showed no emotion. "Ryan mentioned that both writers arrived before the first incident, but there was no way to track their movements. I sensed seeing your husband's name on the list of suspects didn't surprise you."

"There were two reasons my husband and I divorced after twenty-plus years of marriage."

Lizzie hesitated as if she was thinking through her response. "First, Tom finished college and took the job of managing my cousins' bookstore here in Millford. He loves his job, and I felt between the bookstore and his responsibilities at the Manor, his future was secure," Lizzie said. "Second, I tired of Doug's constant lies and get rich quick schemes."

Charles caught himself from jumping in to ask more questions about Doug. He waited and gave Lizzie time to gather her thoughts. Instead he said, "This truly is a lovely spot. I've read most of my book sitting on this bench."

"You've found a wonderful spot for reading and thinking. I've sat in this same spot to make most of the major decisions in my life," Lizzie said. "I made my decision to divorce Doug, sitting here."

"You said Doug was always looking to get rich."

"Yes, he resented that my family had money. He was always looking for the one business venture that would give him a financial footing equal to mine."

"Did he find it with his liquor distribution business?" Charles asked.

"To some extent. The money he received in the divorce settlement gave him the start-up money for his business," Lizzie said. Then she quickly added, "I don't mean to imply I'm involved with his liquor business. I'm not. It's his operation and it has nothing to do with the Manor other than having our current liquor contract."

"You know, your husband could have made Ryan's list because he's on the premises so often making deliveries. Carrie and I have also seen him eating his meals and visiting with other members of the staff," Charles said. He avoided mentioning that Carrie saw him with Ken the day of the murder.

"Perhaps. Are there others on your list?"

Charles thought about sharing information with Lizzie. Her ex-husband might be a suspect, but he liked Lizzie and felt he could trust her. Besides, she wasn't on site during most of the activity.

"I mentioned the two writers. You know, Albert gave us permission to search Millicent's cottage."

"Did he now? Perhaps he hasn't lost his head over her as much as people think."

"There's something else. We found lots of materials on Bernie Millford during our search," Charles said.

"Bernie? Now that's interesting. He seems to be number one for creating mischief from the ghost suspect list," Lizzie said. "Who else is on your list?"

"Harold, one of your chefs and Geoff, the wine steward are recent additions to the list."

"I don't know much about Geoff. I remember we advertised an opening for a sommelier and HR thought he was the best candidate. But I know Harold. Why do you suspect him?" Lizzie asked.

"He avoided Carrie's camera when we took Albert's tour on our first day. He was on the premises during several of the incidents. And yesterday we saw him walking with Geoff down the path near the writers' cottages."

"Anyone else?" Lizzie asked.

"The Tobersons were on Ryan's list, but their names aren't really a surprise."

"I agree. In addition to managing the current construction, they give several seminars a month here on security," Lizzie said. "You, your wife and Ryan have an interesting list with some overlapping names."

"Perhaps, but there are problems with the list. One of our initial suspects was Ken Harvey."

"You think someone murdered him because of his involvement in these incidents?"

Charles could tell her question revealed her concern.

"Yes, we do, even though we don't know the reason for his murder, yet. You saw Ryan's list. Everyone on that list had some interaction with Ken from your husband, the wine steward, the chef, the serving staff and even the Tobersons because of the conference center construction," Charles said.

Charles waited hoping Lizzie would provide more comments about the different suspects.

Instead she said, "Looks like your work is cut out for you as you narrow your suspect list." She stood. "After spending time with you, I've complete faith you'll find a solution to this mess."

Charles stood. "Thanks for being so honest about Doug."

"There may be another way I can help. I'll let you know," Lizzie said.

Charles watched as Lizzie headed back to the Manor. He could not help wondering if she came to this spot today to make another major decision like the change in the construction site. And what did she mean about there might be another way she could help?

39

Carrie was glad when Charles returned. She had lots to share with him and was surprised when he said he had news to share with her.

"Before we share the latest news with each other I need a cup of coffee. Do you want one?" Charles asked.

"Yes, please. I've earned a coffee break," Carrie said.

Carrie watched Charles prepare the coffee. She always thought Charles was a good-looking guy, but all the fresh air and exercise restored a certain vitality in him. It was obvious their time at the Manor was good for him, even though they were dealing with difficult problems.

"Why have you earned a break?" Charles asked.

"I finished the brochure layout. I've a mock-up ready to show the cousins. If I say so myself, my version is a huge improvement over what they currently have," Carrie said. "I can't wait to show it to them to see what they think."

"I'm sure you've gone above and beyond anything the cousins had in mind."

"What have you been doing? You said you have news, but I thought you were reading your book. And you're returning later than usual from your walk," Carrie said.

"That's because I've been sitting in the Manor Pub waiting for a certain beautiful lady who promised to join me for lunch."

"Did I promise that? I did, didn't I? Charles, I'm sorry. Why didn't you call me?"

"The one and only conference at the Manor let out early and the pub was standing room only. I decided it was not the best place to eat. I came to find you before you made the trip downstairs."

"Good, then it worked out." Carrie gave Charles a big hug. "I lost track of time when I started some new research."

"I thought you said you finished the brochure."

"I did. But I decided to check some of our suspects," Carrie said. "Here's what I found. The Tobersons have been in business for over twenty years. They had a rough spot about five years ago when they invested in a large property and then had to sell it at a loss."

"Did your research show what kind of a property?" Charles asked.

"From what I could tell it looked like about 110 acres and was zoned for commercial development. Maybe they wanted to develop it as a hotel, but the market took a downward swing before they could get the financing and start the project."

"That's interesting information. Who's next?"

"Geoff has a background in wines. His ex-wife's family has a huge vineyard in the western part of the state, and he was part of their business. I guess after the divorce he needed a new job."

"Even though he's a sommelier at the Manor, I'm sure it doesn't provide him the financial freedom he enjoyed in his previous lifestyle. Money seems to be the number one reason to break the law,"

Charles said. "Were you able to find anything on our camera-shy chef, Harold?"

"You of little faith. It took a lot of searching, but I found him," Carrie said. "He has a prison record. While serving his term for car theft, he learned how to cook."

"How did you find that out?" Charles asked.

"I thought about why someone would want to avoid having a picture taken. I decided to look for information on prison chefs and cooking," Carrie said. "I found a magazine article that featured Harold along with several other prisoners on how training and education in the prisons was changing lives."

"And last but not least, our mysterious Millicent?" Charles asked.

"Mysterious Millicent is a good way to describe her because I've found absolutely nothing on her. I've searched the internet high and low for Millicent Ford," Carrie said sounding frustrated. "She told me she wrote many articles about old inns and villages for years. Albert introduced Millicent to us as a published writer, so why can't I find her?"

"Maybe she uses a pseudonym," Charles suggested.

"I thought of that, but how can I find the name she writes under without asking her?"

Carrie was trying to think of other options when Charles suggested, "I've got an idea. About two years ago we ran a series of articles on old taverns, roadhouses, and inns in the Tri-County area for the magazine. The article even included Perkins Tavern. You remember, the tavern where several of the Barrington's hung out."

"Don't remind me. Being accused of killing Todd Barrington during our second case was an experience I would just as soon forget. But how would those articles help?"

"I thought we could look up the articles and contact one or two of the writers. Maybe they've heard of Millicent since they're writing about the same subject."

"You know that's not a bad idea. That's why I keep you around for those occasional gems of wisdom." Carrie gave Charles a kiss on the cheek. "You said about two years ago?"

"Yes, and it would have been one of the spring issues. We were giving readers ideas for summer road trips."

Carrie quickly accessed the website for the Tri-County Magazine and started searching the archives for articles. She checked the spring issues from two years ago and found nothing.

"Nothing here. Could it have been last year?"

"I'm pretty sure it wasn't last year. Try three years back. You know how time flies when you're having fun and getting older."

"You're not getting older. Should I add, you're just getting better," Carrie said laughing.

"I don't know. Sometimes I feel like the file drawers in my brain are crammed with too much stuff."

"That's an easy fix. Just throw out everything you've stored before you met me," Carrie said.

"As always, you've a perfect plan," Charles said.

While they were talking, Carrie continued flipping through the listing of the articles from old issues of the magazine. Suddenly she stopped her search.

"I found it," she said. Carrie pulled up the first page of the article. "Will you look at this?"

"What, what did you find?" Charles pulled a chair over and sat next to her.

"I found the article and the author who wrote it. Look at the name of the writer and the accompanying picture."

Carrie watched Charles as he processed the information.

"Bernadette Millicent Sprawls. Well, I'll be. She's our Millicent Bernadette Ford with red hair," Charles said.

"I thought we knew the names of all the Millfords," Carrie said.

"We know all the names of the players from Mrs. Barry's side of the family. Remember, Mrs. Barry also told me that Bernie had a sister who had a daughter," Charles said.

"You think Bernadette Sprawls is that child?" Carrie asked.

"No, Millicent or Bernadette is closer to Ryan's age. She would be the granddaughter of Bernie's sister."

"This revelation also answers another question. When we first met Millicent, or I should say Bernadette she was staring at you. I thought it was your good looks."

"And now you're taking my good looks away."

"No, my Darling, they'll always be a part of you," Carrie said. "Thinking back to that initial meeting, I think Millicent was waiting to see if you recognized her."

"I guess she didn't know I rely on my editors to handle the articles from the writers. Should we assume Bernadette is responsible for all the disruption at the Manor?" Charles asked.

"No, I don't think so. When I spoke with her, she was annoyed Bernie was being blamed for the pranks," Carrie said. "She wants Bernie remembered for the good things he did for the Manor."

"I agree. She would have no purpose in bringing down the Manor. According to Mrs. Barry, the Manor still pays her a percentage of the profits."

"Yes, but why wouldn't she reveal herself if she were fully supporting the Manor. And what about Albert?" Carrie asked. "He seems to genuinely care for her."

"I'm rethinking the Albert situation. Maybe we've misunderstood his fondness for Bernadette as something else."

Carrie paused for a moment as she thought over what Charles said. "You may be right. If Albert was in love with Bernadette, he wouldn't want us searching her cottage. He would want to protect her."

"Instead, he gives us a key to her cottage, knowing we might discover something about her."

"But back to the real question. Why is she here and what do we do next? Do we confront her?" Carrie asked.

At that moment, the phone rang and there was no chance for Charles to answer Carrie's questions.

40

harles answered the phone.

"Mr. Faraday?"

"Yes, this is Charles Faraday."

"This is Harold. I'm a chef here at the Manor. I met you during your tour with Mr. Albert."

Charles motioned for Carrie to come over. He tilted the phone so Carrie could hear.

"Yes, Harold, I know who you are." Charles emphasized the words 'who you are.'

"I thought you might. Would you be willing to talk with me? I need tell what I know to someone I can trust."

"All right, Harold. I'll meet with you. Do you want to come up to our room?"

"No, no, I can't do that! Eyes everywhere," he said sounding nervous. "Look, I rent a cottage down the lane from the Manor. I walk home along the path by the gardens and pass the writers' cottages. No one would think anything if they saw me walking home."

Carrie shook her head, "Too dangerous," she mouthed.

"What happens if someone sees us meeting?" Charles asked.

"No one will see us. Several feet pass the last cottage is a bench. It's not visible from the Manor and no one is currently living in the last cottage," Harold said. "We won't be disturbed."

"What time?" Charles asked watching Carrie who was frowning.

"I get off at six. By the time I change clothes and leave the building I should be there by six-thirty. And Mr. Faraday, please come alone. If I see anyone else approaching with you, I'll leave."

"Fine. I'll meet you at six-thirty on the bench near the last writer's cottage," Charles said and hung up the phone.

"Well, I can tell you right now you're not going alone. That's an isolated path and you're meeting with one of our suspects," Carrie said. Then continued, "There's already been one murder and we don't know Harold's role in all this. It might be a trap."

"Harold isn't dangerous, he's scared. I need to meet him alone," Charles said. He then told Carrie about his conversation with Lizzie. "Why don't you take a few more pictures around the Manor? Then I'll meet you in the pub for dinner and tell you everything Harold says."

Carrie hesitated as she thought over Charles's offer. "I guess you're right. We don't want to spook Harold."

"Nice phrasing, adding the word 'spook' to your sentence," Charles said.

"Thank you, Dear. I try to keep it light."

* * *

Charles was surprised when Carrie left with her camera an hour before his meeting with Harold. He expected her to try again to come with him.

Charles waited until after six before he started down the path towards the writers' cottages. He took his book as he usually did when he went to read in the gardens. Anyone watching would think this was his normal behavior. He saw no one as he wandered down the path. He glanced at the bench where he sat with Lizzie earlier. It was empty.

Charles passed the first cottage. He saw no signs of Harold, but he understood why Harold picked this location. From the writers' cottages, you could see anyone coming from the Manor, exiting the gardens, or entering the property from the outside lane.

As he approached the last cottage, he noticed the front window was open. He made a mental note to call Albert and let him know.

Beyond the cottages was a small clearing. Harold was sitting on the bench. "Hello, Harold," Charles said.

"Mr. Faraday, thank you for agreeing to talk with me."

Charles sat down on the bench next to Harold. "I'm willing to talk to anyone who can shed light on the problems here at the Manor. I assume you know my wife and I are looking into the activity," Charles said as Harold nodded his head. "I take it you know something that will help us."

"I'm not sure, but it's time I tell someone what I know."

"I have to wonder why you didn't confide in someone before now. The owners all believe in helping their workers." Charles noticed that Harold's sleeve was caught on part of the bench revealing markings on his wrist.

"Management gave me a chance by giving me a job, and I believe in them," Harold said.

"Do they know about the time you spent in jail?" Charles watched Harold's surprised reaction. "I saw your prison tattoo," Charles said pointing to Harold's wrist.

"Something else I did for self-preservation. Getting this tattoo made the other prisoners leave me alone. To answer your questions, one member of management knows about me. She suggested I talk to you," Harold said.

Charles knew he was referring to Lizzie. He remembered when Lizzie left the bench her parting words were there might be another way she could help.

"I assume it was Lizzie who suggested you talk with me," Charles said, and Harold nodded. "What do you know?"

"Not much. I only know firsthand about one incident. I didn't want to do it, but I had no choice."

"The incident in the kitchen. The one with the open freezer doors, and the food thrown around?" Charles asked.

"Yes, but I did my best to minimize the damage. I threw around leftover food scraps that I saved from the previous night. I also lowered the temperature in the freezer to protect the food inside even with the doors open."

"Harold, how did you get your job? Did Lizzie help you?"

"Yes. The Manor management team does a great deal of charitable work. I learned my chef skills through a program at the prison, and I was doing a temporary work release program at a fancy restaurant in Tri-City."

Charles said nothing and waited as Harold stared at the ground and gathered his thoughts.

"When it was time for my release, the prison manager who ran the work program knew Elizabeth. He called her and asked if she could use another chef. She said she would give me a try."

"Why did you get involved with sabotaging the kitchen after everything the family and particularly Lizzie did for you?"

"I'm only two months away from not having to report to a parole officer. I can't let anything happen to keep me from achieving this," Harold said. "I felt trapped."

"Harold, who got you involved with doing this stunt?"

"Doug, Elizabeth's ex-husband and Geoff, the Manor's wine steward, are the people who threatened me. They said if I didn't help them, they would tell my parole officer I was stealing liquor and food and reselling it."

"And throwing food in the kitchen would keep them quiet?"

"I foolishly thought so. They told me they wanted to stir up the ghost stories to get Elizabeth and management to make some changes of how the Manor operated. They assured me my only involvement would be this onetime prank." Harold said. He took out a handkerchief and wiped the sweat from his face. "But after Ken's murder, I knew this was more than a onetime prank. I knew I needed to tell Elizabeth what was happening."

"Did you tell her?" Charles asked.

"I was waiting for her to come home from Europe. I knew she was busy and then she called me. We talked, and she told me to call you."

"Did you tell her what you just told me?"

"I told her about my involvement but not all the details. That's the other reason I wanted to talk with you. I didn't mention Doug," Harold said. "I didn't want to hurt her."

Charles was going to tell Harold that Lizzie knew her husband was a suspect but decided against it. Instead he asked, "What did you tell Lizzie?"

"I told her it was Geoff who threatened to tell my parole officer. I told her I didn't know what to do."

"How did Lizzie respond?" Charles felt this conversation was like pulling teeth. He had to keep prodding Harold to tell him the whole story.

"She apologized for not being here to help me sooner. She told me not to panic, to avoid Geoff and to talk to you."

"Harold, what do you think is going on?"

"I don't know. I mean the ghost thing could have been a prank Doug wanted to play on his wife. And maybe Ken's murder had nothing to do with the ghost stuff, but I don't think so."

Charles wasn't sure if Harold knew anything else, but he felt this conversation was over. "Harold, thanks for talking with me. I don't how this will end, but Carrie and I will do our best to keep you out of it."

"That's what Elizabeth said you would do. I better get home. I'm on the early shift tomorrow."

Charles sat on the bench and waited until Harold was out of sight. Then he headed back to the Manor. As he passed the last cottage he went up to the open window. "Please be sure to lock the window and the door when you leave so I can return Albert's key."

"All right, smarty. Wait for me. I'll be right out," Carrie said.

Charles waited until Carrie came around from the back of the last cottage and they started their walk back to the Manor.

"Did you hear everything?" Charles asked once Carrie joined him.

"Most of it. I heard the part where Lizzie asked him to call you. That Geoff and Doug were the ones pressuring him. I find it hard to believe those two were doing these things to send a message to Lizzie. Especially since she wasn't even on the premises during most of the incidents."

"Good catch. You heard the highlights of the conversation," Charles said. "What you couldn't see was the body language. I believe Harold is generally sorry for the mistake he made."

"I agree. He's not our murderer," Carrie said.

"We've eliminated Harold as a suspect, but Geoff and Doug have moved up on the list," Charles said.

"That's the problem. We have lots of suspects and pieces, but I can't form the puzzle picture."

Charles felt Carrie's frustration. He also knew from their previous cases it took time to see how the pieces fit together. The problems at the Manor centered on the why. Why the pranks? Why the murder? Figuring out the "why" would help them narrow down the list of suspects.

"Don't worry. As with all our cases something will come along," Charles said taking Carrie's hand. "Let's get back to our room and think about what to do next."

When they opened the door of their room, they found an envelope addressed to them on the floor.

41

The next evening after they found the note, the couple was waiting for valet parking to bring their car to the front of the Manor.

"Can we be sure the note is genuine?" Carrie asked.

"Yes, it's real. I received a text this morning from Christopher asking if we received the note Ryan delivered," Charles said.

"What else did Christopher text?"

"Nothing, other than the way he always ends his text messages with he would see us soon."

"I wonder why this meeting is offsite away from the Manor?" Carrie asked out loud knowing Charles didn't have an answer.

Once in the car they drove slowly down the steep hill that led from the Manor into the village of Millford.

"Why do you think Christopher used Ryan to deliver the note?" Carrie asked.

"I'm sure it concerned Christopher someone might see him up on our floor," Charles said. "As a food server he wouldn't have a reason to be on any of the guest floors."

"Makes sense. Ryan can wander anywhere without arousing suspicion." Carrie reached into her bag and pulled out a pair of sunglasses. It was a beautiful evening, but they were driving directly into the piercing setting sun as they travelled towards the village.

"The note says to follow Main Street through the village. Then go two miles to Lancaster Street," Carrie said.

Carrie sat silently until Charles said, "Coming up on two miles."

"There's Lancaster Street. You want to turn right and continue until we reach Bascomb Lane," Carrie said.

Carrie noticed the houses in this part of Millford were much older. Most of the homes had stone fronts making them look like the English cottages described in Agatha Christie-style Golden Age mysteries. Even the grounds surrounding the houses were showcases of lovely gardens. She wondered whose house they were about to visit.

"Here's Bascomb," Charles said. "Now what?"

"Turn left, travel down the street until you see a mailbox with a blue post. Pull into the driveway and park out of sight behind the house," Carrie said.

Bascomb Lane was even narrower than Lancaster and the gardens seemed more expansive encroaching onto the roadway. Carrie sat up straight as she stared at each driveway looking for the blue mailbox post.

"There, Charles. Blue post on the right," Carrie said.

"Got it." Charles said as he turned into the driveway and drove to the back of the house. "This seems like a lot of intrigue for a meeting."

"Hopefully, we'll find out more when we get inside," Carrie said.

They walked up the deck steps and tapped lightly on French doors. Tom Larkin appeared and opened the door.

"Glad you found my home. Come in, come in," Tom said.

Even though Tom's house was in an older neighborhood, Carrie expected the décor inside to be modern reflecting the styles of someone Tom's age. It wasn't. Instead of an open floor plan there was a series of small separate rooms. Tom led them through a kitchen and a dining room, through a living room lined with bookcases, a sunroom, and then into a study with a massive fireplace and more bookcases.

"Welcome to my cousin's hideaway. The den of a young book hoarder who not only collects the books but lives in a home right out of the Victorian era," Ryan said.

"Reminds me of some of the houses in the old murder mysteries that Aunt Carrie lent me," Christopher added laughing.

Carrie smiled as she remembered the same memory of when she got Christopher interested in reading mysteries. She also noticed that Christopher was very relaxed with his new friends from the Manor and they seemed to have accepted him even though he was much younger. Carrie continued surveying the room with its comfortable overstuffed chairs surrounding the fireplace until her eyes met Tom's.

"Yes, I know what you're thinking. My mother is an interior designer, and you would expect something a little less Victorian for me," Tom said. "But she approves of my English cottage and helped me figure out how to get the maximum number of book-shelves installed in the various rooms."

"Tom, Carrie and Charles didn't come here to talk about your home's design," Ryan said.

"Yes, now that we're all here, why are we all here?" Charles asked.

Carrie watched as Tom went to the window and moved the drapes back just enough to look out at the roadway. "You're sure no one followed you?"

"Positive. No one was around when we left the Manor and I checked several times on the way here," Charles responded.

"All right, enough with all this secrecy. What are you guys up to?" Carrie asked.

"Please sit down, and we'll tell you what we have discovered," Tom said. "Can I get you an iced tea, beer or would you prefer something stronger?"

"Iced tea is fine for me," Charles said.

"Me too," Carrie echoed and then instinctively looked to see what Christopher was drinking. He wasn't legally old enough for anything alcoholic, and she was pleased when she saw an iced tea glass in front of him.

Carrie helped Tom with the glasses for her and Charles as he poured the iced teas from a pitcher on the table.

"Okay, Ryan, it's your show," Tom said.

"It all started the day you and Charles came to my office and we reviewed the maps of the Manor," Ryan said. "I found a dis-crepancy between the original maps I digitally copied for the archives and the map Toberson was using for the construction."

"What kind of discrepancy?" Charles asked.

"Our current construction map shows the underground tunnel in a different location," Tom said. "It's about two hundred feet off from the location on the original maps."

"Sounds like it could be a simple mistake," Charles said.

"Is that the ground the Tobersons and Ken Harvey were proposing for the new conference center?" Carrie asked.

"No, what's near this location is our new massive utility complex. Remember you saw the back of it the night we were outside the Island Grill looking for an intruder," Ryan said. "It houses generators, battery operated pumping stations and other electrical circuitry designed to keep the Manor running if there are major storms or other natural disasters."

"Originally, we were attaching the conference center to our new Island Grill restaurant," Tom said. "It would place the conference center on the same side as the utility complex. The Tobersons want the conference center built on the other side of the current west wing away from the utility complex."

Tom's knowledge of the Manor and its projects impressed Carrie. Obviously, he was more involved with Manor activities than just running the cousin's bookstore.

"When I interviewed Ken, he suggested the change would give the conference center a separate entrance which would help with traffic," Carrie said.

"That statement is true. When a large conference opens and ends there's a lot of traffic all at once on the main entrance road to the Manor," Ryan said. "Bill Toberson also pointed out the utility complex when running might be noisy for the guests trying to sleep if the building was on the same side."

"What did the Manor board decide about making this change?" Charles asked.

"We took the Tobersons' suggestion and we're attaching the new construction to the existing west wing," Ryan said.

"I guess I'm missing something. The construction maps the Tobersons used could be a simple mistake. And it sounds like this mistake led to a better decision for the next construction phase." Carrie said. "Why do you think something is wrong?"

"We're not sure why, but something doesn't seem right," Ryan said.

"And there's another thing," Tom said, and then he hesitated, looking at Carrie. "We didn't ask him to do this, but Christopher took some pictures of the new utility building from all angles."

Before Carrie could say anything, Christopher jumped in. "Earlier today I went back and took lots of pictures of the Island Grill and the utility building and especially the section with the tarps."

"They're installing the doors tomorrow morning on the utility complex, so the tarps will be gone," Ryan interrupted.

"I was taking a few more photos when this guy appears and starts yelling. He wanted to know what I was doing."

"Christopher, this isn't good. There are bad things happening here that we haven't solved," Carrie said. She looked at Charles as if to say I told you he could be in danger.

"Nothing happened, Aunt Carrie. I told him I was a new worker at the Manor, and I was exploring," Christopher said. "He told me the area was under construction, and I could get hurt. I thanked him and left."

"There's one more thing Christopher noticed. The guy who came out of the building was wearing a polo shirt with the logo from my dad's liquor company," Tom said.

No one spoke and the only sound Carrie heard was the ticking of the clock on the mantle.

"Tom, just because one guy was wearing a shirt with your father's company logo doesn't mean your dad is involved," Charles said. "It might be an ex-employee or..."

Tom interrupted, "I appreciate the support, but at this point whatever is going on involves my dad."

Ryan looked at his cousin and continued, "Charles, you remember the cork you found in the liquor storage the morning they trashed it?"

Both Carrie and Charles nodded their heads.

"That cork was not from wines we serve. I found this same cork in some of our most expensive wines," Ryan said. "I opened a few of these bottles. I'm not a wine expert, but I think it was a fairly cheap variety in the bottles."

"Did you check with Geoff your wine steward?" Charles asked.

"No, because he's on my list of possible suspects, and could be tampering with the wine," Ryan said.

"But I dropped the bottles off to a friend of mine whose dad owns a vineyard. I'm waiting to hear what he thinks we're serving in these bottles," Tom said.

Again, there was silence until Carrie asked, "Christopher, can I see the pictures of the complex?"

Carrie spread the pictures out on the coffee table.

"This is a large complex with a very large parking lot," Charles said peering over Carrie's shoulder to look at the photographs.

"We deliberately made the parking lot large to accommodate big utility trucks if they responded to a problem," Ryan said.

"Where does this road go?" Carrie asked pointing to part of a road captured in the pictures.

"It goes out the back of the property. You can turn right and go over to Route 24 to Hanley or turn left and take another road into the village. Both routes avoid the main road at the front of the Manor," Ryan said. "This is the road we would link the new conference center too.

"We have a utility complex at the back of the Manor with its own access road that accommodates large trucks," Carrie said.

"We have wine bottles we don't think contain what the labels indicate," Ryan said.

"A new complex that seems to be guarded by men from my father's company," Tom said.

"The real question is, what is the relationship among all these people and solving the puzzle?" Carrie asked.

42

Carrie tossed and turned most of the night replaying the information she heard from the guys. Most of it was circumstantial evidence. They had suspects but still had nothing solid. Now that she was awake, she continued to review in her mind all the information she and Charles discovered.

Harold identified Doug and Geoff as the guys who pressured him. Ryan's program showed Doug on the premises during most of the incidents. It appeared the clues were pointing to Lizzie's ex-husband. But why? What was the motive? Why would he damage a business that was his biggest client and his son's relatives?

What about the Tobersons? Were they manipulating the construction plans for a reason? What had Ken's role been in these incidents? And then there was Millicent or Bernadette. What were her motives? Carrie's brain needed a rest, and the opportunity presented itself when Charles walked into the room.

"Look at you dressed for the day, bringing me coffee and a lovely plate of pastries," Carrie said as she stretched her arms over her head before taking the cup of coffee from Charles and a cheese pastry from the plate. She took her first bite of the breakfast treat and asked, "Where did you get the pastries?"

"I made a trip downstairs to the Manor's continental coffee bar.

I wanted to see if anyone was around."

"And...?" Carrie said licking her fingers after she popped the last piece of the pastry in her mouth.

"The only person sitting in the room, and not getting items to go was Leslie Toberson." Charles sat on the bed next to his wife and selected a pastry.

"No signs of Mr. Toberson?"

"I didn't see him. The Mrs. was sitting at a corner table working on the computer. I waved but didn't stop to chat," Charles said.

"Maybe she was using the time to prepare for a security seminar. When we passed the event board last night, I noticed a seminar listed for today," Carrie said.

"Or maybe she was reviewing construction maps of the Manor," Charles suggested.

"That's also a possibility. Should we return to the breakfast bar and have a chat with her?"

"Not sure it would do much good. Just because Ryan and Tom think the construction mistake was unusual, we have no real evidence. And if it wasn't a mistake, like I believe, we don't want to tip our hand," Charles said. "It's the lack of evidence that keeps rearing its ugly head and we need to go and find some proof."

"Okay. What do you suggest we do next? Where can we find more evidence?" Carrie said. "Or maybe we should take a long walk around the Manor and work off some of these pastry calories. Thank heavens there's no scale in this room. Not sure I could take the shock."

Charles wasn't responding to Carrie's suggestions for exercise. "Or we could do something other than exercise," Carrie said. "Do you have a suggestion for how to spend the morning?"

"I was thinking we should go for a drive."

Carrie was about to protest. She couldn't imagine why Charles would want to be in a car driving around on such a beautiful day. She also knew that Charles usually had a plan to go with his suggestions. "Where do you want to go?"

"I thought you might want to get some shots of the covered bridge before they close it down," Charles said.

"The covered bridge!" She thought for a minute and then quickly responded, "Actually that's not a bad idea. Covered bridges make good photos and I can work one into the Manor's brochure," Carries said.

"And I would like to see where that road goes on the other side of the bridge. Ever since we saw Ken Harvey on our first day here, I've wondered about it."

"I thought we concluded he was coming to work or maybe he was off-roading and was running late," Carrie said.

"Except Albert told us Ken moved into a new condo in Millford Village. When I checked the maps, there's nothing out that way except woods. There are no areas for off-roading," Charles said. "Based on the maps we know the Manor's property line runs along that road."

"You know we didn't question this before, but Harvey had both a new jeep and a new condo. Now, I'm wondering about the source of his money."

"Good point. For today let's check out the source of that road," Charles said. "I'll clean up the breakfast while you get dressed."

As Carrie was getting dressed, she had another thought. Maybe Ken was checking something out at the back of the Manor property. Charles's suggestion for a drive to the covered bridge was a good next step.

* * *

"Let me see if I understand your premise. You're connecting the different events at the Manor with the covered bridge," Carrie said as they drove down the long hill from the Manor and through the village of Millford.

"Not the actual covered bridge, but the road that goes over the bridge. As I said, that road runs along the back of the Manor's property line," Charles said. "And there's one more thing. According to the old Manor maps, I believe part of the old underground tunnel ends just beyond the covered bridge."

"Those old tunnels keep popping up," Carrie said and then stopped as she thought her statement through. "Wait, since the old tunnels run under the Manor in this direction, you believe there's another entrance into the Manor from a tunnel."

"You got it," Charles said. "I'm wondering if a second entrance to the Manor is the real reason Toberson wanted to change the direction of the conference center?"

They came to the fork in the road with the bridge on their left, but Carrie watched as Charles didn't turn toward the bridge. He stayed on the main road until he found a place where he could safely pull the car onto the shoulder.

"Why are you parking way down here?" Carrie asked.

"You wanted shots of the bridge, and I can't stop the car on the bridge. Also, our car is out of the way and hidden if any other vehicles come along."

"Always thinking, my fellow sleuth." Carrie pulled out her camera and placed her handbag under the car seat. While Charles watched for traffic, Carrie stood in the middle of the road and took multiple photos of the bridge from different angles.

"I'm glad they placed that sign about no trucks of a certain weight at the edge of the road. If it was any closer to the bridge, it would be in every shot and ruin the ambience."

"Do you think you have enough shots?" Charles asked.

"Almost, I never know what shot or which angle will work the best in a brochure until I get to the layout phase. Are you getting impatient?"

"No, but when you're done with your shots, I would like to look underneath the bridge at the construction," Charles said.

Carrie finished her photo session with a few more shots from inside the bridge looking out towards the countryside. Then she and Charles carefully climbed down the embankment next to the bridge and stood looking at the trickle of water running under it.

"I'll use the rocks in the creek bed to get under the bridge for a closer look. Do you want to wait here?" Charles asked.

"No, I'm happy to go with you if you promise to hold my hand," Carrie said.

"It would be a pleasure to hold your hand."

Carrie always enjoyed holding her husband's hand whether it was in a romantic moment or when he was protecting her like now. They hopped from stone to stone until they were dead center under the bridge.

"Look at this," Charles said.

"What is it?" Carrie looked where Charles was pointing.

"Someone has reinforced this bridge with metal braces."

"Where?" Carrie asked. "I don't see any metal."

"Look closer," Charles pointed to a section in the bridge's corner. "They've painted the braces a dark brown to blend in with the wood."

"Maybe the town reinforced the bridge until they could start the renovations."

"This is more than temporary reinforcement," Charles said.

"If it wasn't the town, who would do this type of repair?"

"Maybe someone in the construction business?"

"You mean Toberson. Maybe, that's why he didn't look happy when Lizzie announced the plans for the renovations. He knew this work would be discovered," Carrie said. "I've another question. Why would he reinforce this bridge?"

"The obvious answer is to allow those heavier trucks the sign warns against to use this road."

Charles no sooner finished his comment when Carrie said, "Charles, listen. What's that noise?"

"Sounds like a vehicle approaching. Carrie, come closer to me."

Carrie huddled with Charles as they crouched under the bridge.

The boards of the bridge rumbled and shook but held steady as flakes of dust fell on them.

The truck barely reached the end of the bridge when Charles proclaimed, "Come on, Watson, the game is afoot."

43

Charles guided Carrie as they retraced their steps over the stones in the creek and raced back to the car. Within minutes they were chasing after the truck.

"Do you see it?" Charles asked as he navigated the twists and turns of the lane.

"Not yet, but you need to slow down," Carrie suggested.

"I don't want to lose them. They have a good head start on us, not to mention the speed they were traveling."

Charles felt Carrie fall against his side as he took a turn at a speed greater than posted.

"Darling, I understand you don't want to lose them. But remember, I have to look across your body to scan the property on the same side as the Manor," Carrie said. "At this speed, I'm having trouble spotting clearings and lanes where the truck could turn in."

Charles heeded Carrie's advice and slowed down. "By my calculations we can't go too much farther, or we'll be beyond the Manor property line."

"There, in that clearing." Carrie blurted out.

Charles brought their car to a halt in the middle of the road. "Did you see the white truck?" Charles asked.

"Not the truck, but I saw a big cloud of dust. What else could cause that except a vehicle?"

Charles backed up along the road. He saw the same cloud of dust Carrie spotted. Then he moved the car forward.

"Now where are you going? Shouldn't we follow the truck?" Carrie asked.

"I can't take a chance turning into the lane and having them spot us. We need to find a place to hide the car."

About one hundred feet from the lane Charles found a small clearing. He backed the car into the opening which descended downhill. Charles and Carrie left the car and walked across the road to the other side. When Charles looked back the dip in the clearing hid the car from any vehicle passing on the roadway.

They walked single file down the lane in search of the white truck. After a few minutes Charles stopped as Carrie walked ahead of him.

"What's the matter? Why have you stopped?" Carrie asked.

"Listen." Charles ran forward, grabbed Carrie's arm, and pulled her behind a huge tree just in time. Another truck rumbled down the lane kicking up a plume of dust as it sped past them.

"Did you see the markings on the truck?" Charles asked.

"Sure did. It had the Larkin Liquor Distribution logo," Carrie said. "It's not looking good for Doug."

"Come on, let's see what else we can discover," Charles said.

Charles held onto Carrie's hand to help steady her. They needed to walk along the rough edge by the woods and not in the lane in case another truck approached. This slowed their progress. Finally, they reached an opening which revealed a large parking area.

Backed against a wall of hedges and overgrown bushes was the truck they followed from the bridge. The second truck that passed them on the lane was parking on the far side of the lot.

Charles waited with Carrie using the trees for cover until the man driving the second truck entered the tunnel. Then he tightened his grip on Carrie's hand.

"Quick, let's go. We need to get behind those hedges," Charles said.

Once they were hidden behind the hedges Charles peered out and saw a small gap between the truck and the opening to the tunnel. He watched as two men unloaded boxes using a portable roller conveyor attached to the back of the truck. Charles waited.

After several more minutes Charles saw the two guys detach the roller from the truck. One man got into the truck and then addressed the second man.

"Blake, get your truck unloaded and keep those guys in the back working," he said. "Doug wants to get as much of the liquor converted, before as he said, 'his do-good ex-wife shuts the covered bridge down.' We only have a few days left before that happens." he said.

Charles exchanged a glance with Carrie at the mention of Doug's name.

"Don't worry. Today is payday and the boss won't hand out the checks until the men finish the job," Blake said.

"You're right, I forgot about that. Anyway, I've got to get on my route and start making deliveries or all this work will be for nothing."

Charles watched as Blake waited for the first truck to pull away and then he ran over to the other truck. It was obvious he was moving the second truck into position for unloading.

"Time to go," Charles said.

Charles held Carrie's hand one more time as they slipped into the tunnel.

At the entrance, Charles stopped for a moment to make sure no one was around. When he was sure it was all clear, the couple entered the Manor's old underground railroad tunnel.

"Should we call the authorities for backup?" Carrie suggested.

"And tell them what? Doug is using an old tunnel to store liquor?" Charles said. "Let's do a little more snooping and see what else we can find."

Once inside, Charles discovered the tunnel was quite wide. Then he remembered that besides hiding slaves it was also used to bring supplies over from the train station to the Manor. The tunnel needed to be wide enough to handle flatbed cars attached to a small train engine.

Charles moved down the length of a long stretch of the tunnel passing stacks of cartons of wine and liquor along each wall.

"Check out these cartons of liquor," Charles whispered. "Half the cartons are a top shelf liquor or wine and the other half is the cheapest variety on the market."

"Wouldn't a distributor carry both?" Carrie asked.

"A distributor would carry all varieties. Not just the most and least expensive," Charles answered.

Charles looked back to the entrance and saw the truck was not yet in position.

"Where are the rest of the workers Blake mentioned?" Carrie asked. "We need to be careful."

"Maybe there are more workers down by the machinery I hear running," Charles said as they continued walking towards a light coming from a room on the far left.

"Do you think this could be the noise some guests heard?" Carrie asked "Remember, they reported hearing machinery running in the middle of the night. It's very loud."

When they got nearer the light, Charles saw there was a huge open area. This room had rows and rows of liquor cartons stacked several feet high.

Charles steered Carrie behind a row of cartons as they moved closer to the machinery. Charles found a spot where they could look between a break in the stacked boxes. They saw three men operating two machines.

One machine was pulling corks from the wine bottles and the operator was dumping the wine into a huge vat. He passed it to a second man who refilled the bottle from a supply of the cheaper wine. They passed the refilled bottle to the third man who placed the bottle in a position to have a new cork seal the bottle.

"You know what they're doing?" Charles whispered to Carrie.

"Yeah, putting cheap wine in an expensive bottle."

Charles heard several blasts from a truck horn. The men shut down the machinery and moved out of the room. Charles was unable to stop Carrie as she ran to the machines and grabbed several corks and labels from the work area.

Before Carrie got back to where Charles was hiding, a man jumped out from a row of boxes on the other side of the room and grabbed her arm.

"What's going on, Blake?" Doug Larkin asked as he entered the room.

"Hey. Boss. Good thing I stopped to tie my shoe, or I might have missed our little sneak thief," Blake answered.

"Ah, our amateur ghost hunter or should I say detective," Doug said. "Charles, you might as well come out. I know you two travel as a team."

"You can let go of Carrie's wrist," Charles said as he joined the group. "Obviously, we're not going anywhere."

Doug nodded to Blake, and he released Carrie's wrist. Charles rubbed her wrist to help release the tension. He wished she had waited a few more moments before running out to grab evidence. But it was too late now. He heard the whirring of another machine.

Within seconds an electric vehicle pulling a flatbed car stopped at the entrance to the storage room and two men started unloading cartons. When they entered the room, they stopped and looked at Carrie and Charles.

"Come on in. These two won't hurt you," Doug said. "You guys keep working while we deal with our ghost hunters."

"You won't get away with this," Carrie said.

"Thanks for that vote of encouragement, but I'm doing just fine," Doug said laughing. "Blake will lock you in another of the tunnel rooms until I figure out what to do with you."

Charles squeezed Carrie's hand and then added, "We're not the only ones who know what you're doing. Doug. I want you to think about the fact that your son knows what you're doing."

44

"Oh Charles, I'm so sorry I got you into this. I should have waited until I was sure no one was around before leaving our hiding spot," Carrie said. "We could have been back at the Manor by now and deciding on a place for dinner, instead of trying to escape from a locked room."

"Don't be ridiculous. We're in this together." Charles said.

Charles was trying to sound braver than he felt as he bent down and kissed his wife on her forehead. "Besides what a great adventure, locked in a room in a tunnel with the woman I love. Let's take a closer look at this room," Charles said producing a small flashlight from his pocket.

"What are we going to do? Yelling won't help. No one will hear us since we're below ground, and the machinery will drown out our cries." Carrie pulled out her phone from her pants pocket. "No signal, so no calling the help squad. That's probably why Doug didn't take our phones."

"We'll have to find our way without calling your 'help squad.' Don't worry," Charles said.

Charles's flashlight only provided a narrow beam. He slowly shifted the light around the room. The heavily reinforced walls would prevent cave-ins and escapes but did nothing to eliminate the dampness.

"One thing I do know, if we're stuck here, you'll have to keep me warm. I'm freezing," Carrie said.

Charles put his arm around her and pulled her close.

"I guess the good news is we were looking for evidence and we certainly found it," Carrie said. "After seeing how the covered bridge was reinforced, I was convinced Bill Toberson was the one trying to bring down the Manor."

"And now?" Charles asked.

"There's no denying Doug is tampering with the Manor's supply of wine which means he's making a larger profit. And Harold verified Doug along with Geoff was behind the prank in the kitchen," Carrie said. "But I can't see Doug murdering Ken."

"What about our third suspect, Millicent?" Charles asked. "I still can't figure Millicent."

Charles felt Carrie pull away from him. "Charles, what's that mist?" She asked.

In the darkness Charles could see a white mist swirling in the far corner of the room. He pointed his light directly at it and watched as Carrie moved toward the anomaly. When she got close it started to fade.

"It's probably some condensation from all this dampness," Charles offered.

"You're probably right except...."

"Except what?" Charles asked.

"That condensation sure looked like a human form. I thought I saw arms and legs. Don't tell me you didn't see the same thing."

"Well, I guess it's like when we look at clouds. Our minds create images we recognize."

Charles continued flashing his light around the area, but no other mists appeared. The room was made smaller by multiple wooden shelves. Pushed against the wall in the far corner was a desk.

"It appears this room is an office," Charles said. "There's a desk and several old file cabinets."

"Yes, an office, but not one currently in use. This wood is old and even with the dampness there's lots of dirt and dust," Carrie said. "It doesn't appear Doug is using this room for anything other than holding prisoners."

"I agree. It's definitely not being used by our current bootleggers."

"Charles, shine your light in this section," Carrie said. "This wall panel is loose."

Charles moved over to where Carrie was standing. "Hold the flashlight for me."

Charles reached into his pocket and took out a penknife.

"First a flashlight and now a penknife," Carrie said.

"I knew we were coming to what I thought was an abandoned tunnel and thought I might need these." Charles used his knife to edge around the loose panel. He tried to pull the panel with his fingers but couldn't get the leverage. "See if you can find something thin that we can use to wedge this panel open."

Charles flashed his light around the room to aid Carrie in her search. "Try the desk. Maybe there's something in one of the drawers," Charles suggested.

"See if this will work," she said handing him a metal ruler she found in the desk.

Charles jammed the ruler into the opening to pry at the panel. As the panel loosened Carrie and Charles worked together to pull it away from the wall. The panel gave way and the splitting wood made a loud cracking sound.

"Stop for a moment," Charles said as he scooted over to the door.

"What's the matter?"

"With all the noise we're making I want to make sure we haven't alerted the men." Charles listened. "Nothing. Hopefully, the sound from the machinery covered the noise we were making."

"Charles, something is hidden in the wall. Shine your light in here," as she pulled back more of the panel.

Charles cast the light into the opening of the exposed wall.

Carrie stepped back. "Do you see what I'm seeing?"

"It's shaped like a body, but maybe it's the way the tarp was stuffed in there," Charles said. "Let's try to remove it."

Several nails held the material in place. Charles pulled on the tarp, the nails popped out, and the panel gave way. The contents dropped to the floor in front of him. Now there was no doubt in Charles's mind it was a body wrapped in the tarp. The skeletal hand that pushed through the material was definitely human.

Charles carefully pulled away more of the tarp. He noticed the human remains were bone, but the suit covering the body was in remarkably good condition. It appeared to be an outfit from the fifties. Carrie bent down and carefully opened the suit jacket.

"What are you doing?" Charles asked amazed at his wife's bravery.

"I'm looking for identification. I think this body might be someone from the Manor's past?"

"We should leave this to the police." Charles said. "Unfortunately, there doesn't seem to be a policeman around."

Carrie extracted a leather wallet from the inside jacket pocket. Like the clothing, the wallet was in good shape. When she opened it, a letter dropped to the floor. Charles picked the letter up while Carrie checked the rest of the contents in the wallet.

"Well, will you look at this." Carrie turned the license towards Charles. "Just who I thought it might be."

"Let me guess, Bernie Millford," Charles said. "That solves one mystery. What else is in his pocket?" Charles no sooner bent down next to his wife when Carrie stopped her search.

"Shh, I heard something," she whispered.

"Quick, put the wallet back in his pocket." Charles said. "We need to take cover."

Charles slipped the letter in his pocket. He grabbed Carrie and moved her behind him next to the door. Charles turned off his flashlight. He waited as he heard the doorknob slowly turn.

Charles was ready to attack whoever entered the room. He figured it might be their only chance to escape. As the door slowly opened light entered the room from the tunnel. He saw a small hand on the edge of the door frame. It wasn't the hand from one of the brawny men operating the equipment. Then the face of Millicent Ford peered around the edge of the door frame.

"Millicent," Charles said surprised. He wondered for just a second if Millicent was working with Doug.

"Millicent, not that I'm not glad to see you, but what are you doing down in the tunnels?" Carrie asked.

Millicent looked up and down the hallway and then came into the room while holding the door slightly ajar.

"I discovered the entrance to the tunnels a few weeks ago while exploring the construction site. Then I discovered Doug's operation," Millicent said.

"Why didn't you alert the authorities or a member of management?" Carrie asked.

"No proof. When I discovered the workroom with the corking machine, I figured they were tampering with the liquor," she said. "On my return trips, I've been taking photos and gathering small bits of evidence."

"Return trips. Why would you keep returning? Weren't you afraid someone would discover what you were doing?" Carrie asked.

"I had to keep searching..."

Before Millicent could continue Charles interrupted, "I believe Millicent was looking for something other than evidence of what Doug was doing. Perhaps evidence for a crime committed long ago."

"Bernadette, you've been looking for your Great Uncle Bernie," Carrie said.

Charles noticed Bernadette showed no reaction to Carrie's revelation of her correct name.

"I'm not surprised you know who I am. I know you searched my cottage," Bernadette said.

"How did you know we searched it?" Charles asked. He wanted to store this information for any future searches he and Carrie might do.

"Something simple. A hair wedged in the sliding door in the kitchen and another hair on the piles of research on my desk. They were both missing," she said. Then a huge smile engulfed her face, and she added, "And the sound sensitive recorder I hid behind the books on the shelf picked up most of your conversation."

"Well done, Bernadette. I assume you would prefer we call you Bernadette?" Charles said.

"Bernadette is fine, although Millicent is my middle name," she answered carefully opening the door and peering down the tunnel. "The men are loading the truck, but they'll be back in a few minutes. While they're doing that we should get out of here."

"Bernadette, before we go..." Carrie hesitated. "We found your great uncle."

"What? Where? Are you sure it's Bernie?" Bernadette asked. Her eyes darted around the room, but without more light she couldn't see the body on the floor.

"We pulled off a wall panel and found the body," Charles said. "Carrie found identification."

They heard a truck door slamming. Charles blocked Bernadette from moving forward.

"We need to go," Charles said seeing the disappointment on her face.

"You're right. Uncle Bernie was missing for decades. I guess he can wait a little longer before we tell everyone we found him," Bernadette said. "Let's go."

45

Charles and Carrie left the room and waited while Bernadette slid the bolts back in place.

"Just in case someone checks," Bernadette said. "With the bolts still in place, hopefully they won't open the door and look inside. Let's hurry. The boys might need our help."

Carrie wasn't sure what Bernadette meant by the boys needing help, but this wasn't the time to ask. They needed to get out of the tunnel before the men discovered they were missing.

It was difficult walking along the rough edges next to the tunnel wall. Carrie knew they could move faster walking in the smooth center lane, but they needed the additional cover the wall provided. Bernadette suddenly flattened herself against the wall and following her lead Carrie and Charles did the same. Carrie looked over her shoulder and saw the light from the transport vehicle. It was a single bright light like on a train engine and it lit the entire area in front of the vehicle. They waited to see if any of the men spotted them.

"Can't we keep moving?" Carrie whispered. She was feeling anxious about what Bernadette said and needed to ask her who needed help.

"Wait another minute until we're sure it's safe. It won't help if we get captured again along with our rescuer," Charles said.

After a few more seconds, Carrie saw the headlight on the vehicle go out.

"Okay let's go," Bernadette said. "In another few feet the tunnel takes a turn and we won't have to worry about being seen."

When they arrived at the turn in the tunnel and were out of sight of the men Carrie said to Bernadette, "Before we go on, what did you mean when you said the boys might need help?"

"I overheard Ryan, Tom and that new server, what's his name..."

"Christopher?" Carrie suggested.

"Yeah that's him. Anyway, they said they wanted to search the utility complex," Bernadette said.

"Charles, we need to get out of this tunnel. Christopher could be in danger," Carrie said.

Carrie saw the confusion on Bernadette's face and added, "Christopher is our nephew."

"The boys may run into Doug, but I'm sure Doug wouldn't harm his son," Charles said. "But you think more than Doug is involved. You think it's the Tobersons who are the dangerous ones, don't you?"

"You're right, it's the Tobersons I'm worried about. I don't think either of them has much regard for human life, only money," Bernadette replied.

"What's their game?" Charles asked.

Carrie remembered the large piece of property they purchased and then lost. Had they plans for building a competing hotel?

"I'm not one hundred percent sure. All these delays about changing the direction of the new wing and building the utility complex over the old tunnel entrance," Bernadette said. "I think it's more than helping Doug. I think they have bigger plans, but I don't have any real proof what they might be."

"Our research provided us with three suspects. Doug, the Tobersons and…" Carrie stopped.

"It's alright, I know I was on your list. And what were your conclusions?" Bernadette asked.

"We concluded you care about the Manor. You want it to survive to preserve all the work your Uncle Bernie started. And Doug is only interested in a get rich quick scheme. That left the Tobersons as having a more sinister motive," Carrie said.

"Like you, we don't have any proof, but I think one of the Tobersons killed Ken. I believe Ken wanted a bigger payout for helping them," Charles said and then added, "perhaps he threatened to tell management what was happening if they didn't comply. They complied by eliminating him."

"What made you think it was the Tobersons?" Carrie asked.

"Their name kept coming up in the bits and pieces of conversations I overheard while wandering around the Manor including the men working here in the tunnel. When I was with Ken, he talked about how smart they were and understood how to run a hotel the right way," Bernadette said. "But without a confession from the Tobersons what I overheard won't hold up in court, especially my conversation with a dead man," Bernadette said.

"Bernadette, we need to get to the end of this tunnel as fast as we can," Carrie said as she tried to calculate the distance from the Manor to their current position. She figured they were nearly at the end. The center lane made it easier to walk, but for the last several minutes Carrie was aware their climb was going uphill.

"Where are we?" Charles asked.

"We're working our way up to the utility complex. We need to be careful to make sure anyone in the complex doesn't hear our approach," Bernadette whispered.

In a few minutes they arrived in front of an elevator. Carrie saw one of the electric carts Doug was using to transport the liquor parked to the side. The group climbed over the cart to get to the steps and then quietly edged their way up the steps towards the utility complex.

"Wait," Bernadette said. "I hear voices."

Carrie stopped and listened. "That's Ryan talking."

"You're behind all the negative activity on the property. But why, Bill?" Ryan asked. "We awarded you a valuable contract for our latest expansion."

"It's simple. I want the Manor," Bill said. "My wife and I can run this enterprise in a way where we can realize huge profits. Not the way you run the business by sharing your profits with employees and the village businesses."

"And how are you going to get the Manor?" Tom asked.

"I've bought the financial papers from the local banks that hold the Manor's loans including all the new construction loans. That's what happens when you deal with smaller banks. They package the loans for sale," Bill Toberson said. "If people aren't booking, you're not generating income. As soon as you miss a payment, I'll call in your loans."

Carrie, Charles, and Bernadette reached the top of the steps and moved behind one of the large generators for cover. Carrie was trying to see if Christopher was in the group, but Charles's arm restrained her movement. "Stay back," he whispered. We don't want Toberson to know we're here."

Carrie stayed behind Charles but maneuvered so she could see Christopher standing just beyond Ryan.

"Do you think our family would allow an outsider to take over the Manor?" Ryan said forcefully. "The nice thing about using local banks is they alerted us that someone was buying up our loans."

"You must think we're stupid," Tom said. "My Aunt Beatrice suspected what was going on. She just didn't know who was doing it."

"She's smart, so what," Bill said smugly.

"She contacted an old school chum who runs a New York financial firm. She arranged through him to have all our loans covered in case they were called in," Ryan said.

"You're making that up," Bill snarled. "There's no way she could know what was happening."

"You seemed to have forgotten the Manor's reputation. It's the largest employer in the area and we have lots of friends. We only needed one person to alert Aunt Beatrice our loans were being purchased," Ryan said.

Carrie could hear the anger rising in Bill Toberson's voice as he realized his grandiose plans for the Manor were slipping away. He seemed paralyzed for a moment until his wife broke the silence.

This was the first time Carrie realized Leslie was in the room. And as Leslie moved forward, Carrie also saw Doug Larkin.

"Let's get this moving. We can't stand here all day," Leslie said with no emotion in her voice.

"Leslie let's not make a mistake," Doug said. "We have everything in place to take over the Manor's operations. There's no need to do anything other than let events play out the way we planned."

"You heard what they said. They have their loans covered," Leslie snapped.

Carrie saw Bernadette turn to the wall to block the light from her phone as she sent several text messages.

"Bill, are you going to kill us the way you killed Ken?" Ryan asked.

Good for you, Ryan, Carrie thought. Get him to admit to the murder. Carrie took out her phone and set it to record.

"You killed Ken?" Doug asked genuinely surprised by Ryan's question. "You said his death was because of his gambling debts."

"Don't be a fool, Doug. Ken's a perfect example of what happens when you interfere with our plans," Leslie said. "Come on, Bill, we need to end this."

"What are you going to do? You can't shoot all three of us," Tom said.

"Actually, you can't shoot all four of us," Bernadette said as she appeared from the curve in the wall that was hiding her position.

"Actually, there's six of us," Carrie said. She wanted to follow Bernadette out from their hiding place, but Charles moved in front of her and blocked Carrie from being in a direct line for Bill's gun.

"I should have known better than to leave you two alone or did you have help escaping?" Doug asked looking at Bernadette.

Carrie noticed as he spoke Doug edged closer to his son, Tom.

"This escapade is over. Let's have the gun," Ryan said. walking towards Bill.

Tom joined his cousin and moved forward. Doug shifted his position to align with his son.

"Give me that gun," Leslie said to her husband.

Carrie couldn't believe how quickly the next series of events occurred. Leslie tried to grab the gun from her husband, but as Bill struggled with her several shots fired. Doug pushed his son out of the way and took a direct hit to his chest. Simultaneously, Ryan moved to protect Christopher and took a shot to the head. Charles leaped taking Christopher to the ground and then covered him. Bernadette charged Bill Toberson and knocked the gun to the ground and then kicked the gun towards Carrie.

Carrie picked up the gun and fired a shot into the ceiling of the complex to end the melee. "That's enough. It's over," Carrie said.

As everyone turned to look at Carrie, Lizzie arrived with two security guards who had guns drawn. They quickly took Bill and Leslie Toberson into custody. The Millford police were next to arrive and Carrie handed over the gun she fired.

Tom was holding his father in his arms. When Lizzie reached her son, he said, "Dad is dead. He died saving my life."

Lizzie knelt on the floor next to her son and put her arms around his shoulders.

Bernadette was with Ryan and when she saw his condition she yelled, "We need the paramedics, now."

"They're on their way," Albert said racing into the room. Then he saw his son.

46

Albert ran to his son, dropped to the floor, and cradled Ryan in his arms. In seconds, Ryan's blood was seeping onto Albert's clothing as tears were streaming down his face.

"Come on Ryan, it's Dad. I've got you now. Can you open your eyes for me?" Albert asked in a choked voice.

Carrie watched Albert holding his son. She was sure she saw Ryan's eyes twitch, so she knew he was alive.

Albert must have seen the same movement because he said, "That's my boy, you keep fighting, hang in there."

Carrie could feel the tears welling up in her own eyes as she clung to Charles's arm and held Christopher's hand. She wondered where the help was for Ryan when Mrs. Barry and three paramedics hurried through the door.

The first medic immediately knelt next to Albert and said, "Oh my, Mr. Millford, when I got the call, I didn't know it was Ryan who needed our help," he said.

Albert looked up and recognized the young man from the Millford Fire Department. "I'm glad you got the call, Jim."

The next two paramedics guided a gurney into the room which also carried their case of medical supplies.

When the patient transfer board was in position, Jim said, "Okay, Mr. Millford, let us take over."

Albert clung to his son, "No, I need to stay with my boy." And with that Albert pulled Ryan closer to him.

Carrie knelt next to Albert and put her hand on his shoulder.

He looked at her and said, "They shot Ryan."

"Yes, Albert, I understand. But now you have to let the paramedics take over." He didn't answer but kept his grip on his son. "Albert, saving his life will depend on Ryan getting quick medical attention. Please let these folks help him." Carrie said.

Carrie watched as he slowly released his son. Carrie helped Albert to his feet.

It took only seconds for the paramedics to take over from Albert. They bandaged Ryan's head to curtail the bleeding and secured a neck brace. They lifted him onto the board and then onto the stretcher. They attached fluids. One of the medics was on the phone with the hospital describing the wound and giving Ryan's vital statistics. This team worked quickly and within minutes they wheeled Ryan out to the waiting ambulance.

"Where are you taking Ryan? What hospital?" Charles asked the last medic to depart.

"Shock trauma in Tri-City," he responded as he continued moving the patient out the door. "Our local hospital doesn't have the surgery skills to handle a gunshot wound to the head."

"Do you think he'll survive the long ambulance ride?"

"We're only getting him to the Manor parking lot. We have a medivac helicopter coming."

Carrie heard a commotion and turned to see Albert arguing with the paramedics.

"Mr. Millford, you can't go with us in the ambulance. I'm sure these folks will help you get to the hospital."

During everything that was happening, Carrie was surprised when she saw Charles pull out his phone. He dialed a number, spent only a few minutes on the phone and then turned to Albert. "I've called Dr. John Jenkins, a friend of mine and the head of surgery at the Tri-City General Hospital. Fortunately for us he was home and will meet the helicopter. He'll have a team ready to get Ryan immediately into surgery," Charles said.

"See, everyone is looking out for Ryan. Now we need to help you. The hospital won't let you see Ryan until they evaluate his condition," Beatrice said. "While you change your clothes and pack a bag, I'll make arrangements to get you to the hospital."

47

It was late evening on the day of the shootings and from the chaos in the Utility complex, order began to prevail. Mrs. Barry arranged with a local pilot at the Millford airport to use his plane to fly Albert to Tri-City. She called her cousins Madge and Marge so they could meet Albert at the airport and get him to the hospital.

The local police had the Tobersons in custody and were processing them at the Millford village station. They also rounded up the men working in the tunnels.

The state police were in charge of the crime scene investigations and interviews. They sequestered Carrie, Charles, Christopher, Tom, and Bernadette in one of the Manor's meeting rooms. They stationed a policeman in the room to make sure they didn't talk with each other about any details of the event.

After several more hours the interviews were over. Lizzie appeared to take Tom home. They invited Bernadette to join them, but she opted to return to her cottage. Charles, Carrie, and

Christopher returned to the couple's suite. At last they could have a conversation with Christopher and find out what happened before the couple arrived for the final confrontation.

"How did you guys end up at the complex confronting the bad guys?" Charles asked.

"We held another meeting at Tom's house because we wanted to inspect three things. The original and current construction maps for the Manor, Ryan's program of who was on the premises during the incidents, and the photos I took of the utility complex," Christopher said.

"And what did you guys determine?" Carrie prodded.

"Simple. Everything seemed to center around the construction of the new utility complex. You know wanting to move the conference center, the place being guarded by Doug's employees, and incidents like that. And the Tobersons were in charge of the construction," Christopher said. "You got anything to eat? I'm hungry."

Carrie looked at Christopher in disbelief that he wasn't focused on the case. But he was still a teenager, and teenage boys are constantly hungry. Whenever Christopher stayed with them their food bills doubled. Carrie handed Christopher the room service menu. "Here you go," she said. "As long we're ordering I could eat a hamburger and a big pile of fries."

While Charles took care of ordering food for everyone Carrie made coffee for her and Charles and found a soft drink in the mini-fridge for Christopher.

"While we're waiting for the food let's talk about the discoveries you guys made," Charles said. "You said everything centered around the utility complex and Toberson."

"Ryan calculated they built the utility complex in the same spot as the old supply depot. That meant it was right over the entrance to the old tunnel connected to the Manor," Christopher said. "And Ryan concluded there was no way Toberson didn't know this."

"Your aunt and I came to the same conclusion about Toberson, and while you three were in the utility complex we also found out what Doug was doing," Charles said.

"Let's get back to you. You decided to investigate," Carrie said. "This was even after we reminded you to only observe and not become an active participant."

"I was observing. I tagged along with Ryan and Tom to observe if they found the entrance to the old tunnel," Christopher defended. "And remember, we did this in daylight while the Manor was fully operating. It's not like we were skulking around at night."

"Okay, enough, you two. We can't go back and change the fact they were in the complex," Charles said as he poured cream in his coffee. "What happened before your aunt and I arrived?"

"We were in the complex literally using a tape measure figuring out where the tunnel opening might be, when we heard a whirring sound," Christopher said. "At first, Tom and I thought it might be a generator kicking in, but Ryan said they weren't functioning yet."

"And what was the noise?" Carrie asked. Carrie thought it might be noise from the bottling machinery in the tunnel.

"It was an elevator coming from below the complex. It was hidden behind the generators. And when the doors opened Tom's father, Doug, was standing there."

"I assume Tom was surprised to see his Dad," Charles said.

"That's an understatement. His father tried to say that he was checking out the lower level of the complex, but he was pushing a cart loaded with liquor." Christopher stopped while he gulped some of his soda. "Then Doug said he worked with Toberson to design a quicker way to get supplies to the Manor," Christopher said.

"Was Bill Toberson with him?" Carrie asked.

"No, Mr. Toberson entered the building from the parking lot while Tom was yelling at his father for being selfish and hurting the Manor. It was only a few more minutes before you two and Bernadette showed up and we all know what happened next."

There was nothing more to add to Christopher's story. Their room service order arrived, and Carrie suddenly realized how hungry she was. Carrie avoided talking about the shooting while they ate and instead got Christopher to tell about his experiences working at the Manor.

"You know I wouldn't mind having a job here during the summer," Christopher said. "The cousins, as they call themselves, are good people to work for, not to mention earning some money."

Carrie noticed in the short time Christopher was an employee at the Manor he was like the rest of the staff and had nothing but praise for the folks who ran the resort.

When they finished their meal, Carrie realized they all needed sleep. She insisted Christopher stay in the suite with them and got him settled on the sleep sofa in the living room. After his adventure and with a full stomach he was asleep in minutes. She kissed him on the forehead and then joined Charles in the bedroom where he was finishing a phone call.

"Were you calling about Ryan?" Carrie asked.

"Yes. I was able to talk with John because he was out of the surgery."

"And... I hope the news is good," Carrie said.

"Well, he gave me the standard response. Ryan is doing as well as expected and came through the surgery fine."

"Surely he could share more than the typical hospital phrase," Carrie said.

"He was hesitant since I'm not family, but he said they got the bullet out, and the next forty-eight hours are critical. But so far so good."

"Well, at least the news is positive," Carrie said. "And now we need to get some sleep. We have some decisions to make in the morning."

48

All of the events exhausted Carrie, but unlike her husband and nephew she found it difficult to fall asleep. Her mind kept reviewing everything that had happened. She worried she had missed a clue that would have helped them solve the case sooner. She knew they couldn't have prevented Ken Harvey's death. His murder happened too soon after their arrival. In recent days, the clues were pointing to the Tobersons. Could they have saved Doug if they revealed his liquor operation sooner? Could they have prevented Ryan from being shot?

Ryan was standing between Bill Toberson and Christopher. She hadn't thought about it before, but the stray bullet could have hit Christopher instead of Ryan. Christopher was her nephew, but he was also the son she and Charles never had. All the possibilities continued to haunt her until sheer exhaustion engulfed her and she fell asleep.

Carrie wasn't sure how long she slept before something changed in the room. She knew Charles was sleeping soundly next to her and she was safe, but she felt cold. She gathered the covers closer to her body. It was as she gazed around the room, she saw it.

There was a white mist developing in the room. As her eyes adjusted to the various shades of white and gray, she saw the image of Roxie beginning to form. Roxie raised her hand slightly and gave Carrie a demur wave. Carrie said nothing but nodded at Roxie.

Carrie didn't experience the same fear she had during their first encounter, but she could feel her adrenaline rushing. Roxie wasn't moving and Carrie wondered what she was doing, but then she saw a second form taking shape.

This time the form was a handsome young man a little taller than Roxie. His physical characteristics reminded Carrie of Ryan. Dressed in a double-breasted suit with wide lapels and a multi-colored tie Carrie felt his outfit was probably high fashion for men from the fifties. Carrie watched as Roxie pointed to him and mouthed the words 'Bernie.' Carrie smiled at Bernie as he leaned over and placed a kiss on Roxie's cheek.

Carrie hadn't time to think about it earlier but finding Bernie's skeleton in the wall proved that Bernie didn't kill Roxie. For the first time in over sixty years, he was free from the stigma of being a murderer. Carrie wondered if Bernie haunted the Manor all these years just waiting for someone to uncover his remains and prove his innocence.

She barely finished her thought when the mist in the room began to dissipate. Bernie and Roxie were still holding hands as their forms disappeared. The last thing she saw was Roxie mouthing "thank you" and then as quickly as they appeared, they left.

Carrie thought about waking Charles, but there was nothing to say that couldn't wait until morning. There was no rational explanation for her experiences with Roxie, but she felt differently about accepting the existence of paranormal activity. After seeing Roxie for what she knew was the last time, Carrie felt a sense of peace and happiness that she was part of resolving the Manor's mystery. She rolled over and went back to sleep.

* * *

"Darling, I can't help but think it was a dream. By your own admission you were in a deep sleep from exhaustion," Charles said.

"I know you're still looking for a logical explanation even after the experience we shared of seeing Roxie's image on the glass door," Carrie said.

"You're right. I'm stumped for an explanation, but like Mrs. Barry I keep searching for the answer that's not paranormal," Charles said.

Carrie didn't respond to what Charles said, and he continued, "I'm only suggesting that what you visualized wasn't a paranormal experience but the result of an intelligent mind realizing what yesterday's events meant in solving Bernie's death."

"Nicely done, darling. I can't explain Roxie's appearances either and your explanation makes sense. I'll let you off the hook for the moment, at least until we get home."

"Speaking of home. The Manor is a wonderful vacation spot. I would love to come back sometime. But for now, I'm thinking its time for us to take Christopher and head home," Charles suggested.

"I agree. I'm looking forward to doing nothing more exciting than convincing Baxter to curl up with me while I read a good book. And not a book about ghosts," Carrie said.

49

As expected, the morning after the shooting, Mrs. Barry took charge. She was making sure the Manor continued to run flawlessly for their guests during all the turmoil and swirling gossip. When Charles entered the executive offices, people were quietly going about their tasks.

"Mr. Faraday, good morning. Did you, Carrie and Christopher get any sleep last night?"

"Yes, we did, but what about your family?"

"Lizzie and Tom are grieving over the death of Doug. We all knew Doug's flaws, but it was still a shock when we discovered he was helping the Tobersons in their plot to take over the Manor. That's the part that's hard to comprehend."

"Did you suspect the Tobersons were part of the plot?"

"Not initially. It wasn't until I knew our loans were being purchased that I looked at who had access to the information. That's when I suspected the Tobersons," she said. "I was waiting for a report from a friend of mine who was trying to track down the loan purchases."

Charles remembered during the confrontation with the Tobersons, Ryan said his aunt had a friend from school who was standing behind their loans. He wondered if he was the same person preparing the report. Before they could continue their discussion, a staff member approached them.

"Sorry to bother you, Mrs. Barry, but I need a signature for this week's payroll and with Mr. Albert...."

"It's all right. I'll sign for you. Even with all the turmoil we need to make sure everyone gets paid as usual."

Charles waited as Mrs. Barry checked the numbers on the sheet, signed and handed it back. The staff member thanked her and then headed down the hallway.

"Looks like the staff is coping with the situation," Charles said.

"The staff that's still here is doing fine."

Charles said nothing but gave Mrs. Barry a questioning look.

"Geoff emailed with his resignation this morning," she said. "We have no proof, but we think Geoff was involved with the wine switching. If he thought the customer knew wines, they received the proper bottle."

"And if they didn't, they received the cheap stuff," Charles said.

"Exactly. I shudder to think how many events paid for a higher-priced product, but received the lesser quality."

"Ryan did an excellent job creating his list of suspects, including identifying Geoff. Speaking of Ryan, any updates this morning?"

"It's all good. He came through the surgery and is making progress. Something else we have to thank you for. We know Dr.

Jenkins doing the surgery made a difference," she said as she patted Charles's hand. "There're no signs of any infection and for a brief moment this morning he seemed to recognize Albert."

"That's wonderful. Ryan has youth on his side and I'm sure he'll make a full recovery." There was a pause. Then Charles added, "There's another reason for finding you this morning. It's time for Carrie and me to return home."

"Oh, no you can't do that!" Mrs. Barry said and then stopped herself. "I mean we could use your help at least for a few more days."

"If you need us, we'll be glad to help anyway we can."

"I didn't mean to make a demand but both Lizzie and Bernadette have asked for your help."

* * *

When Charles returned to their suite Carrie was on the phone.

"Yes, I'll be happy to go with you. I'll meet you in the lobby in ten minutes," Carrie said as she hung up the phone. "Charles, I'm afraid our departure will have to wait a little longer. Bernadette asked me to go with her while they remove her great uncle's body from the tunnel."

"No problem. Mrs. Barry also asked us to stay a little longer."

"Really. I would have thought with the case being solved she would be glad to get things back to normal which includes not having us around," Carrie said as she brushed her curly brown hair and applied some lipstick.

"I don't know. I think with Albert focusing on Ryan in Tri-City and Lizzie and Tom planning Doug's funeral, she would be glad to have our support. And there's one more thing," Charles said. "She said that Lizzie and Bernadette may also need our help. And obviously Bernadette just called you."

"I see what you mean. Mrs. Barry knows about Bernadette. When I see Bernadette, I'll ask a few more questions about when she revealed her true identity to Mrs. Barry."

"I'm sure you'll also want to give Bernadette this," Charles said handing Carrie the letter they removed from Uncle Bernie's wallet.

* * *

The police activity was not visible to most of the Manor guests. Only the utility complex where the shootings occurred, and the tunnel operation were off limits. This helped to eliminate additional gossip with the guests.

The medical examiner verified the body Charles and Carrie found in the tunnel office was decades old and not part of the current murder investigation. The body would be transferred to the morgue where a more extensive examination would be conducted to determine the cause of death.

Carrie waited with Bernadette outside the room where she and Charles were held captive. It was only yesterday but seemed a lifetime away after all that happened. Bernadette was granted the opportunity to spend a few moments with her great uncle before the medical examiner removed the body. Within minutes the morgue team came out and nodded to the ladies to enter.

"I guess we can go in," Bernadette said.

"No, you go in without me," Carrie said. "You need time alone with Bernie. I'll wait for you here."

When Bernadette emerged from the room she said, "I can't tell you how much it means to me that you discovered Great

Uncle Bernie's body. After all these decades it brings closure for my side of the family," she said as she wiped a tear from her eye.

"I'm glad there's something good coming from all this mayhem," Carrie said as she gave her a hug. "I've something else for you." Carrie handed Bernadette the letter. She explained how she found it in Bernie's wallet when they were trying to determine the identity of the body.

Bernadette opened the envelope, unfolded the letter, and read it silently. Carrie saw the letter was only one page with writing on one side. When Bernadette finished, she handed the letter to Carrie to read.

My Dearest Roxie,

I'm writing this note because I'm concerned something may happen to me. Joey Molanaro is trying to muscle in on what I'm creating here at the Manor to secure our future. I hope I can convince him that the Manor makes little sense for his bootlegging operation, but as you know he's hot-headed and unpredictable. If anything happens to me take this letter to my cousin, Edward. He'll know what to do.

I've also left the Manor to you and Edward. I know you like him and with his help the Manor will be a special place and provide for you for the rest of your life.

My darling, I hope you never receive this letter. Regardless, know that we'll always be together forever.

Love always,

Your Bernie

When Carrie finished reading the letter, she took a tissue from her pocket and wiped her eyes. It wasn't just what she read in the letter, but what she remembered from her dream. Roxie may not have received the letter, but she knew the love Bernie and Roxie shared was forever.

"I guess that explains their murders. Joey caught up with both of them. Roxie died before she knew Bernie left her a share in the Manor," Bernadette said.

They stood back as the assistants from the morgue wheeled the body out on a gurney.

Bernadette asked, "What made you look behind the wall?"

"There was a loose panel, and we were looking for a way out," Carrie answered. "We hoped by removing the panel we'd have access to another room."

"Amazing. If you and Charles weren't locked in that room Bernie could have remained hidden for many more decades," Bernadette said.

Without mentioning the mist that she and Charles saw in the room she said, "Yes, it seems as if some outside force guided us to the discovery."

Carrie put her arm around Bernadette as they started their walk out of the tunnel to Bernadette's car. They drove to the tunnel entrance since the utility complex entrance was blocked by the police investigation.

"I assume the cousins knew your true identity," Carrie said.

Bernadette stopped and looked at Carrie and then smiled. "You assumed I was undercover the entire time."

"Weren't you?" Carrie asked.

"No, Albert knew my real identity from the beginning but no one else. He was helping me find information about Bernie."

"Albert knew you were a family member!" Carrie said.

Carrie was shocked but Bernadette broke into a hearty laugh. Carrie noticed the police team working in the liquor room stopped and looked at the women. She was sure their forensic work rarely generated laughter. Carrie moved quickly past the men as she headed for the tunnel opening.

"Albert comes across as this loveable brother of his two dynamo sisters, but he's very smart. When I first met him for an interview to discuss my writing an article about the Manor, it was only a few minutes before he suspected I had a deeper connection to the Manor," Bernadette said. "As you now know I'm a redhead," Bernadette said. "I guess between my red hair and my in-depth knowledge about the Manor, it wasn't long before Albert was asking me about my background."

"He figured out who you were?" Carrie asked.

Bernadette unlocked her car and Carrie got in. Once inside, they sat for a few moments.

"At the end of the interview Albert stared at me. Then he said based on my looks I could be a member of his family and he waited," Bernadette said. "He impressed me with his sincerity and his love for the Manor. I confessed and told Albert who I was, and I wanted to find out what happened to my great uncle."

Carrie listened to what Bernadette revealed and then said. "When Albert first introduced you to Charles and me, we saw Albert's fondness for you."

Bernadette laughed again. "No, you didn't, be honest. You thought Albert was romantically interested in me."

This time Carrie laughed. "You're right we did. Was that part of your plan?"

"Yes. I needed to be in constant contact with Albert and one way to facilitate that was to let everyone think he was interested in me," Bernadette said. "He also suggested the blonde hair. He said if he recognized me other members of the family could reach the same conclusion."

Bernadette started the car and headed back towards the Manor. Neither woman spoke for several minutes as Carrie digested what Bernadette said.

"And Albert didn't reveal your identity to his sisters or his son?" Carrie asked.

"No. The running of the Manor is such a joint effort. I believe he was enjoying doing something that only he knew about and was completely in charge of handling," Bernadette said and then she added, "Although he told me if I uncovered any facts about Bernie's death or any information about the other events happening here at the Manor, we both would go to his sisters and tell them."

"But you didn't tell Albert about Doug's liquor operation," Carrie said.

"As I told you, I needed just a little more proof. I found a couple of invoices for the bottling equipment in the processing room with Bill Toberson's signature. I was on my way to find Albert when I saw you and Charles enter the tunnel. Fortunately, I stayed around and could rescue you."

"There was no time to discuss this with Albert, so how did Mrs. Barry find out?" Carrie asked.

"Remember when we were in the tunnels and I sent a text to Albert to get help and meet us there? I also added I had proof on both Toberson and Doug," Bernadette said. "Even with everything going Albert told his sister about me when she drove him to the airport. She called me early this morning and invited me for breakfast."

"And..." Carrie prompted.

Bernadette pulled into the entrance of the Manor. "She was lovely. She told me how glad she was to meet the other half of her family," Bernadette said. "She wanted me to know I could stay and be a part of the Manor family if I wanted."

"Do you want to do that?" Carrie asked.

"You bet I want to. I haven't been this happy in a long time." Bernadette pulled over and stopped the car. Carrie handed her a tissue so she could wipe the tears from her eyes.

* * *

While Carrie was with Bernadette, Charles accompanied Lizzie and Tom as they made final arrangements for Doug. They would bury Doug in his family's plot along with his parents and next to a brother who died serving in Afghanistan.

When Charles returned to their suite Carrie still wasn't back. After the morning events he wanted some quiet time to reflect. He left Carrie a note saying he was sitting on the bench at the Japanese gardens.

Charles had only a few pages left to read in his thriller, and he was hoping to finish it. When he arrived, Lizzie was sitting on the bench gazing absently across the lawn to the Manor. Charles turned to leave but Lizzie saw him.

"Charles, don't leave. I would appreciate the company," Lizzie said.

Lizzie slid over to make room. "Thank you for going with Tom and me this morning. It was nice to have your support."

"It was an honor to be asked. Are you on our favorite bench to make some decisions?" Charles asked.

"No, this time I'm looking for answers. Trying to understand all the craziness. Was there more we could have done to prevent what happened? Were there signs that we missed?"

"You're talking about Doug's activities?"

"Doug I can explain. With him it was all about the money. He wanted money, and it didn't matter if the method was illegal. That was a major flaw in his character," Lizzie said.

"There was one flaw he didn't have, and that was how he felt about Tom. In the final moments of his life, he stepped up and did the right thing. He saved Tom," Charles said.

"Was it a fluke?"

"No, Lizzie. I saw him deliberately move several times to make sure he was between Tom and Bill's line of fire. It was a selfless act."

"That's what Tom and I will have to remember. Not his illegal activity but his final act of bravery and goodness."

Charles saw Lizzie fold one hand over the other and breathe a sigh. He hoped she found some peace.

"And what about the Tobersons?" Charles asked.

"They came with such high recommendations. For them to think they could manipulate our loans to the point of taking over the operation is unbelievable. They didn't know the strength of Beatrice, Albert and Ryan in managing this place."

"And you," Charles said. "Don't sell yourself short. You're a good person and good for the Manor."

"Speaking of goodness. Isn't it wonderful we now have Bernadette in our lives?"

"Yes, she seems to genuinely love the Manor and certainly has a complete knowledge of its history," Charles said. "She's also a good writer. One of my magazines published one of her pieces. I think she would enjoy finishing Carrie's work on a new brochure."

"What a great idea. Between the brochure and the history piece she is writing on the Manor, looks like she has some projects to get her started in her new role here."

"If she wants to prepare an article on the Manor, I'll be glad to publish it in the Tri-County Monthly magazine."

"I appreciate that. I'll pass it along to her. Some positive publicity for the Manor would help at this time."

Charles looked at his watch. "I guess I better head back. Carrie accompanied Bernadette while the authorities removed Bernie's body from the tunnel. She should be back by now."

"I'm sorry you didn't get to finish your book," Lizzie said.

"Just between you and me, I'm afraid this thriller can't match real life," Charles answered.

50

Another week passed since the events in the utility complex. Charles and Carrie attended the funeral for Doug. There were no public announcements and only the family including Bernadette, was present for the service.

Then they attended the funeral for Bernie. The family buried Bernie in the Millford plot next to his cousin, Edward.

The Manor continued to operate normally, but the staff, the vendors and even the guests checked with management for the latest updates on Ryan's condition. The news continued to be positive. Ryan regained consciousness and while he would face a recovery period, the doctors believed he would have no long-term physical issues. What psychological issues he might experience no one knew. But Ryan was young with a supportive family.

Charles and Carrie were finally ready to return to Tri-City. They would stop by the lobby to say goodbye to the family.

"Hey there. How are my favorite aunt and uncle? Ready to leave?" Christopher asked, as he arrived at their suite.

"As we keep reminding you. We're the only aunt and uncle you have. And as soon as I zip this bag, we're ready to go," Carrie said.

"The fact you're the only ones I have doesn't mean you're not my favorite," Christopher said as he loaded their bags onto the luggage cart.

"That's a nice compliment Christopher," Charles said gazing around the room. "I guess we're ready."

"Does that book on the coffee table belong to you?" asked Christopher.

"Ah yes, the new thriller I planned on reading while I was here."

"And how did that work out for you, Darling?" Carrie asked.

"I didn't do too bad. I finished it last night."

Charles leaned over and gave Carrie a kiss as Christopher pushed the luggage cart through the door.

While they were walking down the hallway Christopher said, "I talked to Mrs. Barry and Bernadette and they offered me a job for the summer."

Charles knew Christopher was waiting to see if they raised any objections. Instead Charles said, "Good, having a real job for the summer is a fine idea. And you can't ask for a better place to get work experience than the Manor."

Charles was secure in knowing the Millfords would watch out for his nephew. It would also provide him and Carrie a reason to return for a real vacation during the summer.

"Good. I mean, I feel I owe it to Ryan and his family to help. After all Ryan saved my life," Christopher said. Then he added, "Don't worry, I'll save the last two weeks of summer to visit with you before I return to school."

"Well that will give us something to look forward to," Charles said laughing. "I'm just kidding, we're always glad to have you with us."

"Didn't I hear you talking with Bernadette at Bernie's funeral about helping her with some research?" Carrie asked. "I gave Bernadette the work I prepared for the new brochure. She promised to finish it."

"I would like to help Bernadette with the history she's writing. It's fascinating, especially with finding Bernie's remains," Christopher said. "I also want to learn more about the forensics used in identifying his body and the cause of death."

"Maybe you would also enjoy working with Bernadette?" Carrie asked.

"I'm not interested in Bernadette. She's too old for me. I mean...," Christopher stumbled.

"Gosh, Charles we must be ancient if Bernadette is too old for this young man," Carrie said.

"That's not what I meant. I just want to understand all the other mysteries that are part of the Manor's history. You know, some of the other ghost stories," Christopher said. "Who knows, maybe I'll write a mystery book about ghosts and publish my book before you publish your book, Aunt Carrie?"

They reached the lobby. When the doors opened Charles saw Lizzie, Beatrice, Albert, and Bernadette. Off to the right were also Maddy and Marge all waiting to greet them.

"Wow, a farewell committee. This wasn't necessary." Charles said as he shook Albert's hand.

Charles saw Albert's entire face light up as Carrie gave him a big hug and said, "Albert, it's so good to see you. We've missed you."

"You don't think that after all you did for us, we would let you go without a formal goodbye?" Albert said. "Ryan gave me the day off, but only if I agreed to come here and thank the two of you."

"One of our reasons for wanting to get home is so we can visit Ryan. And Albert, if you want a change of pace from staying with Maddy and Marge, you're welcome to come and stay with us at our farmhouse," Carrie said winking at the two sisters.

"What a fortunate day for us when our Maddy and Marge introduced us to the two of you. You saved our Manor from criminal activities and brought a long-lost member of our family home to us."

Charles saw an unusual show of affection from Mrs. Barry, as she placed her arm around Bernadette's shoulder.

"Marge and I knew when we asked you to help us you had, what do the kids say, "no skin in the game" but that didn't stop you from helping," Maddy said.

"Maddy, Marge, you're our neighbors and our friends. Whenever you need us, we're here for you." Charles was sure he saw Marge quickly wipe a tear away. Then he added, "and because of you two we now have many more friends."

"There's no way I can thank you," Bernadette said. "Our family, my entire family, is finally free of the stigma surrounding Roxie's death and Bernie's disappearance. Perhaps now they are at peace."

"Please, no more ghost talk. I assume because we've uncovered a human solution to the Manor's mayhem, it will put the talk about all the negative paranormal activity to rest?" Lizzie said.

"I think you can assure your guests the ghosts are satisfied with the outcome," Carrie said. "That's not to say there may still be the periodic sightings as in the past."

Charles raised an eyebrow and looked at Carrie. He thought he detected a certain longing in her voice. He knew she thought it would be great if Bernie and Roxie continued to call the Manor home.

"I'm sure if there are some sightings it's because, like your other guests, they enjoy being here with all of you," Charles said as he put his arm around his wife. "And now, my dear, Carrie, on to our next adventure."

BIO

Millie Mack is a pseudonym for the author who writes the Faraday Murder Series. She enjoys everything mysterious—stories, books, and videos. Even her cats can be very mysterious.

Aside from writing the Faraday Murder Series featuring amateur sleuths Carrie and Charles Faraday, Millie is working on a new culinary mystery series.

In addition to her mystery books, Millie also writes a blog all about mysteries at www.darkandstormynights.com. The blog features mystery authors, detectives, and techniques. And to challenge the reader's mystery knowledge, there is an assortment of word search and crossword puzzles.

Dear reader,

If you enjoyed this book, please consider placing a review on Amazon.com or Goodreads.com.

Thank You,
Millie